# LITTLE
# BABY
# LOST

# LITTLE BABY LOST

From the Editors
Of *True Story* And
*True Confessions*

Published by True Renditions, LLC


True Renditions, LLC
105 E. 34th Street, Suite 141
New York, NY 10016

ISBN: 978-1-938877-91-9

Visit us on the web at www.truerenditionsllc.com.

# Contents

# BABY ON MY DOORSTEP
## Who could the mother be?

There was another loud party next door. I could hear a set of drums being abused, along with a stereo system. My neighbor's daughters were entertaining their boyfriends again. I shrugged my shoulders and picked up my paper. If it was this loud at ten o'clock on a Saturday morning, things didn't look good for the rest of the day.

One of these days, one of those girls was going to get in trouble. I was just happy that they weren't my kids, weren't my problem.

As I sipped my morning coffee at the kitchen table, I had to admit that my sister and I had led a charmed life. Mom and Dad had been great to us, and we always felt we could go to them when we were in trouble. All that seemed so long ago now. My sister moved out of town years ago to pursue her career. My father had passed away ten years ago. Now it was just Mom and me in the same old town.

Even though I'd bought my own house, Mom and I were close. She would pop in every other day with an armful of fresh vegetables from her garden, and I would talk to her often on the phone. Every time she came over and saw the neighbor kids, she would just shake her head and ask no one in particular what was the matter with kids today.

I worked as a loan officer in a bank, and I was dating a nice man I'd met during the course of business. He owned his own computer store, and one day he'd come in to arrange a loan to expand his business.

Bill and I hit it off right away. Mom of course heard wedding bells right from the start, but I had to put the brakes on her hopes. We were just dating, that was all. Right now we were just enjoying each other's company.

My life was going smoothly, just the way I liked it. That is, until the moment someone left a baby on my doorstep.

It was like a moment stopped in time. I'd just finished reading the paper and was on my second cup of coffee when I thought I heard something over the noise the kids were making next door. No, it couldn't be anything. But a strange feeling came over me. I got goose bumps. Something was telling me to go to the front door.

I opened the front door and looked around. I could still hear the noise the teenagers were making in their garage next door, but that was at the back of the house. No, there was something. . . . I looked around the front door, the step, and then the short bushes that grew along the house. I spotted something blue.

It was a laundry basket, one of the cheap plastic kinds, and it was well-hidden in the shrubs. It looked like someone had hidden their laundry in my yard. But as I got closer I heard something. That same sound.

Kittens! Of course, that was it! There were cats in the neighborhood and some little kid was always knocking on the door begging me to adopt one. Of course, that was it. I reached into the basket with new confidence. Some child had gotten tired of taking the kittens door-to-door to find homes for them.

But for kittens, the basket seemed a little heavy. I pulled it out of the shrubs and began opening up the layers of flannelette. Something inside was fighting me. That was one strong kitten!

Then the creature inside the basket let out a howl, as though he had been catching his breath. I jumped back as though I'd been bitten.

A baby! I stood there, staring at him, as he bawled.

I looked around. There was no one around, no one lurking in the bushes. This was no practical joke. Someone had actually left a defenseless baby practically on my doorstep.

I brought the basket inside, all the while staring at the infant as though he would vanish into thin air. Things like this just didn't happen to me. My mother teased me that if my life was any more predictable, even she would hardly be interested in it—and she was my mother.

I knew nothing about babies. I'd been the youngest, and I'd never done much baby-sitting, either. My first instinct was to call Mom.

She wasn't in, so I left a message on her answering machine. I didn't know what to do, and the baby's cries were getting louder. I supposed he needed food or a change of diapers or something.

Mom, where are you? my mind screamed.

I should call the police. Yes, that seemed the right thing to do. And yet I was reluctant to do that. I called Bill instead.

"Yeah, right, Amy. A baby on your doorstep. That's a good one!"

"Bill, I'm telling the truth," I told him.

"Listen, sweetie, I know I told you to loosen up a bit, being a banker doesn't exactly make you the queen of comedy, but a baby? You can do better than that!"

"Bill . . ."

"I'll be over tonight, like we talked about, okay? And get rid of that baby before I get there. Ha, ha. People will start to talk."

I looked at the dead phone. He thought it was all a joke!

The baby was screaming now. How I wished it were a joke!

I picked him up, still wrapped in his blankets. He felt quite heavy for a newborn, if that's what he was. He looked quite clean, as much as I could tell from his red, angry face. Except, he was wet. And most likely hungry.

"I can't help you there, pal," I said, holding him and doing that instinctive little bouncing motion that I'd seen mothers do to calm a baby.

Well, maybe I didn't have a spare diaper, but at least I could get rid of the wet one. I laid him on a table and unwrapped him. Yes, it was a him.

"Who are you, little fella? And where is your mommy?"

He stopped crying then, staring at my hair that was hanging down toward him, reaching out for it. He managed to grab a handful, and it hurt!

"Hey! Aren't babies supposed to be gentle and sweet and all that?" I asked.

He laughed. At least, I think he laughed. It might have been gas for all I knew.

This wasn't funny anymore. I didn't know what the kid wanted. I might do some damage. It was time I got help.

I called the police, who took the information as though they got calls about abandoned babies every fifteen minutes. I could tell they didn't believe me, but they said they'd be over.

"Please hurry. I don't want him to starve to death or anything," I said.

In the meantime, I decided to do something about that diaper. I found a small towel and some safety pins and went to work improvising a diaper. He might look a little funny, but at least he would be clean and dry by the time the police came to pick him up.

He really was an adorable baby. Probably all babies were, but there was just something about this kid. My friends had babies, and I'd done my share of goo-goo talk over them. They were cute, after all. And one day, I might even want one myself. But none had raised any maternal instinct in me before.

I began to worry how this little guy would be treated when he left my house. After all, he'd been abandoned once before today. And the mother—or whoever had dropped him off—must've had a reason for dropping him at my house. Did she know me? I didn't know anyone who was pregnant recently. Was it someone who just saw me on a day-to-day basis?

The rock band was still going strong next door. I wondered: Can it be one of my neighbor's kids or their friends?

The baby was now sleeping in my big armchair. I took another look at the basket. The price code tag was still on it, it looked like it had been bought at a large department store. The blankets, too, looked new. I didn't think they would be able to trace those to the person who bought them. After all, how many people bought laundry baskets and flannelette blankets? Probably hundreds. The diaper he had been wearing was a common disposable type.

I didn't think the police would be able to solve this mystery overnight. And I was right.

I felt a little pang of regret when the officers came in to take the baby away. They said he would be fine, there was a special family who worked for social services who took in babies until they could find a more permanent solution.

"What if—what if the mother appears?" I asked anxiously.

"Then of course we have to look into the reasons why the baby was abandoned. It's not always the mother who does, you know. Sometimes it's the boyfriend. He might have taken the baby from her on the pretense of giving her a break."

"Some break," I said, thinking of some poor young mother whose baby was stolen from her.

They asked me questions about my friends who may have been about to have a baby.

"What about your family, Ms. Marshall? Do you have a sister?"

"Yes, but she lives miles from here. I just saw her a month ago—in a bathing suit. She was definitely not pregnant."

I did mention the kids next door, and they dutifully wrote this down in their notebooks. They took the basket, the blankets, and even the soiled diaper with them as possible clues. They checked out the spot where I'd found the baby.

"Please, please let me know if you hear of anything," I asked, walking with them to the police car, craning my neck to get a last look at the little guy.

I went back in the house and closed the door, but it was as if the baby was still there. I wondered if they were feeding him and had that towel diaper I'd made come apart yet? To me, these feelings were new and strange, worrying about a baby. But any new mom could've told me that it was normal to feel this way.

I tried calling Mom again. What a story I had to tell her! Yet there was still no answer. I was beginning to worry.

I decided to go to her house and check up on things.

She had always left the key under a big pottery jar at the back door. It was there, and I let myself in. Nothing seemed out of place. She wasn't home, though. Finally, I looked on the big message board by the fridge and there was a note.

Amy, honey, I had to leave right away. Tried to call you and your phone was busy. It's Aunt Glenda, she's been rushed to the hospital. Her hip needs replacement, remember? I'll call you as soon as I get there.

Love, Mom

Yes, I remembered that Mom had spoken of her sister's hip. Apparently, she should've gone in for surgery months ago, that her

4

hip joint had deteriorated, but without Mom there she'd refused the surgery. Well, it was a relief that she was finally going to have it done.

But still, I missed Mom. I was feeling at a loss with a baby being left on my doorstep. I needed to talk to her.

Bill came over that evening and finally he believed me about the baby. It was an unsettling feeling, knowing that someone had deliberately abandoned a child right on your front lawn. A crime had been committed, a terrible crime against a child, and it had affected me deeply.

Bill, bless him, just held me close on the sofa that night and we pretended to watch TV. He had never spent the entire night at my place yet, and when he offered to stay, I shook my head. Our relationship hadn't progressed that far, as far as I was concerned.

"I'll be all right. I'll see you in the morning," I said, reminding him of the picnic and canoe outing we had planned.

"Try to get some sleep, sweetie," he said, giving me a quick kiss. "If you hear anything more about the baby, give me a call."

I waited until he got in his car and drove away. For a long time I stood at the door, looking at the place where the baby had been left.

A very unwelcome thought came into my head. How much did I really know about Bill? We'd been dating for about two months. I didn't ask about any past girlfriends he may have had. No, he couldn't have had anything to do with an abandoned baby.

That was the trouble when something like this happened. Your mind played tricks on you, beginning to imagine that everyone you were in contact with had something to do with leaving a baby at your doorstep.

News quickly spread in our small city. At work, I was the center of attention with my customers and my coworkers, not to mention members of the general public who just came in to the bank to ask about the baby.

And all the while I was thinking about him. Were they taking good care of him? Was he happy and healthy? In a strange way I felt like I had abandoned him that day when I'd given him to the police. But that was the only thing I could've done!

I got a visit from the woman next door, the one who was mother to three of the teenaged girls I saw on a regular basis next door. She looked nervous standing at my doorstep, looking about her as if someone was following her.

"I want to tell you that none of my girls had anything to do with this baby, Miss Marshall. You tell the police that!"

"Maybe not," I said, trying to keep my voice calm. "But have you asked their friends? It's possible—"

"No, it's not!" she said, and quickly left.

5

I stared after her, even wondering if she might be the mother. Her boyfriend lived with her, on and off. It was possible that she'd become pregnant and couldn't keep the baby.

But it was just another guess on my part. Really, the baby could belong to almost any woman in town. But why had she picked my house?

I called the police for updates, but it seemed they either didn't know any more or didn't want to leak any information they may have had. It was frustrating.

But, finally, I got to talk to Mom about it, if only for a few minutes. When I told her about the baby, she sounded shocked.

"Oh, those young girls next door! I told you they were headed for trouble. Poor, poor baby, poor angel. Amy, dear, I'll try to be home as soon as I can."

"That's all right, Mom. I'm fine now, I guess. I just think of him lots," I told her.

At night I lay awake in bed, staring at the ceiling and going down a list in my head of all the women I was in contact with. Even bank customers, fellow employees. Why did I think it was someone I knew? When I remembered the baby, the way he looked, there was something familiar about him. He looked like someone I knew.

I tried to put this incident behind me, I really did. It was a very busy season at work, and my mind should've been occupied on my loans. But several times a day, I found myself staring out my office window, wondering what the baby was doing right now. Who was looking after him?

I feel like he's my own, somehow, I thought. But I had no right to feel that way. The mother had probably just picked my house at random. Maybe she saw the car in the driveway and figured that someone must be home, so she could leave the baby here.

How many times since it had happened had I tried to put myself in the mother's thoughts? But it was so hard. I didn't have any experience with being a mother.

Bill was sympathetic, but I could tell he was losing patience with me. He tried to get us to do things that would take my mind off the baby. But when he saw that faraway look in my eyes, he knew what I was thinking about.

"Amy, I think maybe we should stop seeing each other for a while."

"What?" I asked, blinking as though I'd just come out of a trance.

"You know, with the baby and all. I just can't seem to get your mind off him. There's nothing I can do to make you feel better, and believe me, I've tried."

I couldn't blame him. It was true, the baby had become something

6

of an obsession with me. I even called the social services agency to find out how he was doing, and the most I got was some general comment like, "He's doing fine." But I didn't want to know just that, I wanted to know when he woke up in the morning, was he greeted by a loving voice? Did someone hold him each time he cried?

I had to keep repeating to myself: He's not yours, he never was, and he never will be.

But my daydreams about him didn't go away, and neither did my unsettling dreams at night. Dreams that he was being abandoned again, by his foster mother this time. And that somehow I was responsible.

You should've known. You should have known all along.

Those words pounded into my brain. But what should I have known?

Then something happened that would almost make me forget about the baby. Almost.

Mom called to tell me that she was coming home. Her sister was recovering fine from the hip operation. Mom missed me, missed our girl dates and our late afternoon walks. And I missed her! She would be able to talk to me about these strange feelings I was having about a baby who was a complete stranger to me.

But I never got the chance. One night, or rather, early morning, the phone woke me and I nearly fell out of bed from the sudden noise. It was a hospital calling, a hospital about a hundred miles away.

"Ms. Marshall, can you get here as soon as possible? There's been an accident."

It was Mom. My mother had wanted to get home so badly that she'd decided to drive through the night. She'd fallen asleep while driving.

"No!" I screamed into the phone, and it took a while for the nurse on the other end to calm me down.

With shaking fingers I punched in my sister's telephone number.

"Cindy, it's me. There's been a terrible accident. . . ."

I don't remember the rest of the conversation, only that my sister agreed to meet me at the hospital as soon as possible. She'd have to get the next flight. I would get there ahead of her, of course.

As I drove into the night, I thought about Mom driving alone. I could have gone to my aunt's, picked her up, and driven her back. Why didn't I? It would be a question that would haunt me the rest of my life.

I didn't recognize the person in the bed as my mother. I saw someone whose head was bandaged, with only one side of her face showing. And that side was so swollen and unrecognizable that it could have been anyone lying in that bed. Her legs were in traction, and her arms in casts. For a wild moment it looked like one of those dramas you see on TV where the patient in the hospital bed is made to look as bad as possible.

But this was not TV. It was real. My family was crumbling in front of my eyes. My mother was our rock, our harbor in any of life's storms.

And now she needed us. If only we were given the chance to help her recover.

"I can't lie to you, Amy," the doctor told me. "If she survives the night, she has a chance. But I don't want to give you false hopes."

No, please give me any kind of hope, I begged silently.

He left, and I was left alone in the room, holding Mom's hand and listening to the mechanical sounds of the machines around her that were keeping her alive. Somewhere toward dawn I felt someone standing beside me. It was Cindy.

We hugged briefly. Then she told me to go for a break.

"I'll watch her," she promised. "If anything happens, I'll come and get you."

I couldn't rest, though. I just paced up and down the hospital corridors. A life without my mother? I couldn't even imagine it. It was like she was always meant to be with us.

But a few moments later Cindy found me. She didn't have to say anything.

We hugged, and then walked together, arms across each other's shoulders, to my mother's room. She'd passed away quietly, only the machines telling the doctor and nurses that she was no longer with us. They tried to restart her heart, but it was too late.

A few short hours ago, we had been a loving family, the three of us. Now there was just my sister and I left.

In a gray haze of grief, Cindy and I stayed in the city to make arrangements for her funeral. A couple of days after Mom's death, I received a call at my hotel room. Cindy was staying in the next room.

"Ms. Marshall, we've done an autopsy on your mother and we'd like to discuss something with you."

"All right," I said. "I'll be right over." What on earth could they tell me now that would hurt me any more?

I stopped at Cindy's door on my way out. I could hear her crying inside, and I decided not to burden her with this news, whatever it was. The two of us could console each other when I returned.

The doctor and a grief counselor for the hospital took me to a quiet room.

"There's no way we can prepare you for something like this. Ms. Marshall, did you know that your mother had recently given birth?"

"What?" I asked, still not taking in what people said to me. Ever since Mom had died, I was in shock.

"A baby. You of course knew about the baby," the doctor said.

I shook my head and sat down. What on earth were they talking about?

They were insistent that she'd had a baby, and I was just as insistent that she hadn't. In the end, the grief counselor saw that I was just getting upset. She gave me her card and said to call her if I wanted to talk about it.

It seems incredible, but it took me a long time to connect what they'd told me with the baby that was left on my doorstep. Grief does crazy things to the mind. It's overwhelming, all you can think about is the loss of your loved one.

And even when I did make the connection, I still couldn't believe it was possible.

I didn't tell Cindy about what the doctor had told me. She was very upset about Mom's death, and I didn't want to distress her further right then. We arranged to have Mom's body brought home, where we buried her in a simple ceremony with some of her close friends in attendance. In a few days, Cindy had to go home for her job.

But the memory of what I'd been told lingered. They were doctors; they knew about these things, right? But if it were true, then who would the father be? And how on earth had Mom hidden a pregnancy from me?

But I knew the answer to that one. Mom had been a large lady, always intending to go on one diet or another. She always wore large, loose clothing to hide a big stomach. Well, that loose clothing could just as easily have hidden a pregnancy!

I tried to think back over the last months. Mom had showed no signs of being pregnant, but then again she always said her two pregnancies had been a breeze, compared to other women's. And she'd had us both very young. She hadn't yet reached menopause, so it was possible.

But who would've been the father? Mom just didn't go on dates. She socialized with a few female friends, and once in a while they would take one of those bus trips to go gambling in a casino. It was all very innocent.

Except she had mentioned that she'd met a handsome man there, and one night he had taken her group of friends out for drinks. It was a long shot, but it was the only man she'd ever mentioned to me.

I spoke with Marilee, one of Mom's friends who had gone on the trip. The timing was certainly right. But had she really slept with that man, a man she'd hardly known?

I didn't want Marilee to suspect what I suspected, so I went to visit her and we just naturally started talking about Mom. Mom's death had been quite a shock to her, as it had been for all of us.

"But one thing I'm glad of, Marilee, is that Mom had a great time in the last year of her life. She often spoke about that trip you all made to that casino."

"Oh, yes, your mother quite enjoyed herself!" Marilee said. "She was the belle of the ball, you know. Your mother could look very beautiful when she dressed up in a long gown and put on some makeup."

Obviously someone else thought so, too, I thought.

"She mentioned dancing with someone that night. What was his name?" I asked.

"Oh, yes. That would've been Howard. He was in his late sixties, but boy, could he dance! His wife was sick that night, so we ladies took pity on him and kept him company. All very innocent, of course. But finally I got tired and we all left your mother and Howard alone to their dancing."

I left her house and walked home deep in thought. I was thinking the same thing that my mother had probably thought. A married man in his late sixties would not be thrilled to know that he'd fathered a love child. And I was convinced it had to be him.

And my mother, who despaired of me ever finding the right man and starting a family, had left my little brother on my doorstep. Had she intended that I raise him, or just trusted me to do the right thing and call social services to come and get him?

But I had felt the bond of family with that baby from the moment I laid eyes on him. He was family, my family, and now that Mom was dead it seemed more important than ever to get him back.

I contacted the authorities with my story. At first it seemed just too incredible a story to be believed. But I kept at it, insisting on tests to prove that we were related.

I dreaded telling Cindy what I knew. I didn't know how she'd take this, so soon after Mom's death. Finally, I decided to go to her and spend a few days so that I could tell her in person.

At first, it seemed disrespectful to even consider such a thing about Mom. But then, we realized that she had been very lonely for years since our father died. Why did we think it was all right for us to date and be with men and not Mom? But somehow she must've thought the same thing if she hid her pregnancy from us. She didn't think that we, her daughters, would understand. And that was the greatest tragedy in all of this. She'd gone through it all alone.

I called Aunt Glenda, who hadn't been able to come to the funeral. I decided to tell her about the baby. She said she noticed that Mom had been in quite a bit of pain but had tried to cover it up. Of course, she'd have just given birth before she left for her sister's. I wondered if that pain had caused the accident. How different things would have turned out if only she had confided in me!

And I would always wonder what would have happened if Mom had made it home that night. Would she have found the words to tell me about the baby? It would have been a privilege to help her raise him. She wouldn't have been alone, she would have had Cindy and me.

I never stopped fighting to get my brother back. A less determined person might have been in awe of the authorities, but nothing was going to stop me. In the end, I think they knew it. There was a hearing, and in the end they decided to give me temporary custody of my brother, whom I named Alan.

The first time that Cindy came to visit to see him, she fell in love.

"Alan," she said, and then looked at me.

"I know, like Papa. I think Mom would've named him that, too," I said.

The baby seemed to look from one to the other of us. He was a happy baby, always curious, always smiling. A real charmer, just how I remembered Papa.

"Amy, I've made a decision. I'm going to move back here," Cindy said.

"But your career! You're doing so well."

"It's just a job. I can find something here. Besides, why should you have all the fun in raising Alan?" she said.

I think Mom would have been proud of her daughters. And I'm sure she was looking down on us, all three of us, and giving us her blessings. I sold my own house and moved into Mom's. Cindy had some loose ends to tie up in the city, but she would be moving in with us, too. In a way, it was like the two of us girls had come full circle.

I never heard from Bill again, and I wasn't surprised. Some men just don't take to kids, and babies in particular. I was just about convinced that I would never marry. After all, it was quite a responsibility to raise a child. What man wanted to raise another man's child?

And then I did meet someone at a playgroup started in the community. Sam was a single dad, struggling to raise a baby girl on his own after his wife had died. Our two babies, Alan and Emma, hit it off immediately. So much so that they each would wail when we tried to separate them to take them home.

"Looks like the kids have decided for us. Would you like to have supper at our place?" Sam asked that first day that we met.

"Do we have a choice?" I said, laughing as the babies cooed at each other, now that we'd given up trying to get them to their separate homes.

So from sharing baby food recipes to college plans, Sam and I

11

hit it off. Whenever we needed a break, Cindy was more than happy to baby-sit both kids. Sam was spending more and more time at our house and less time in his apartment.

It seemed natural the day he asked me to marry him.

On our wedding day, we dressed the babies up as a miniature bridal couple. Cindy was wonderful, organizing everything and, more often than not, taking care of the kids, too. She offered to baby-sit while we went on a honeymoon.

I came back from my honeymoon more in love with Sam than ever. But we'd missed the kids so much! None of us got much sleep the first day back.

And a couple of months later, I discovered I was pregnant. But before I told anyone, even Sam, I got in the car and took a short ride to the cemetery. I got out and walked along the rows of mature trees, until I found Mom's gravestone.

I told her about Sam and Emma, and now, about my own baby who would be the newest addition to our family. I told her about Cindy and how she'd found a job at the library, and had started to date the local sheriff.

"You can rest in peace now, Mom. Everything is as it should be. We love you and miss you. But we'll be all right," I said, not even bothering to hold back the tears.

A strong ray of sunshine peeked out from behind the lazy summer clouds just then, and I knew that she heard me.

THE END

# I HAD TO STEAL A BABY
## I did it save her—and me

I loved Carmella from the moment I first saw her. She was someone else's baby daughter, and she had a different name back then. I first saw her in their house, in her crib, and I wanted her.

It was hot that summer when we finally knew for sure that I wouldn't have children. I was thirty-five, and Brock and I had been married for ten years. We had always planned to have a big family. The nursery upstairs had been decorated for years, waiting for babies that we knew would never come. On the night I first saw Carmella, we'd come home from work and sat down to a supper of duck and vegetable salad and iced tea. We'd had whole meals without conversation in recent weeks, but Brock had something to say that night.

"Mrs. Joseph's home from the hospital with her baby," he said, frowning. "It's a girl. I wish I understood why God would allow that woman to have children."

I sighed. "I wonder if the baby is affected by the alcohol?"

"Who knows? I heard she had to be dried out. That's why they were in the hospital so long. It's disgusting."

"Maybe she'll stay off alcohol, now."

"Fat chance," Brock shot back. "The woman's a drunkard, and her husband's a monster."

There was little to say to that because it was all true—even if Brock had put it so brutally. The Josephs lived in the dilapidated house next door to us. Mr. Joseph didn't work, unless you'd count pushing drugs as work. Cars were in and out of their driveway at least twenty times a day. The police just didn't seem interested. They had better things to do. Susan Joseph was an alcoholic, and she probably took some drugs as well. They had five children, six with the new baby. They were shabbily dressed, ill fed, and they ran wild. Richard Joseph beat his wife regularly, and I'd seen him smack the boys a couple of times. We'd called the police on them regularly, and so the Josephs no longer spoke to us.

"That's another reason we should consider adoption," I said to Brock. "We could give a baby like that a real good home."

Brock's voice was cold, disgusted. "We've been over this. I don't want somebody else's kid. You don't know what you're going to get. Then you wonder why the kid is stealing cars when he's sixteen? Because he came from trash, that's why!"

"But if you gave him a loving home. . . ."

"We aren't going to have kids. It's time to face that."

Brock never said it, but the message was there, anyway. We weren't going to have kids, and it was my fault. I got up to clear the table and to hide my heat-flushed face. I felt like I'd cry any minute.

After dinner, Brock claimed that he had to go back to the office to finish up some work. He'd been doing that a lot, lately. I went up to the nursery and sat in the rocker by the window in the moonlight. Tears coursed down my face.

We'd bought this house in an old neighborhood because it had plenty of room for a growing family. We'd refurbished it, and the area was improving rapidly. However, some houses in the neighborhood were still in ill repair—like the Josephs' house next door. The houses were close together, and I looked across the driveway into their downstairs bedroom next door.

The window shade was up, and the lights were on. A crib sat by the window, and that's when I saw her. She was a tiny, beautiful baby asleep in her crib.

I started crying harder. What sort of life would this baby have? Would she wander around the bare yard in dirty diapers like her older brothers and sisters had? Richard Joseph often beat their mother. Many times, I saw Susan Joseph showing drunken affection for her kids. She probably loved them, but she couldn't even take care of herself. The peaceful sleep that precious tiny being was having might be the last happiness of her life, or at least, of her childhood. It broke my heart. How I wished I could help her!

A week later, Brock told me that we had to talk. We sat down in the living room after dinner, and my hopes were high that he'd finally decided to try to adopt.

"Things haven't been too good between us for a while now," he began, stopping abruptly. He put his hand over his eyes.

All the anger I'd been feeling toward him tumbled out of me.

This had hurt him too, so was it any wonder he had been so cold and distant, lately?

"It's been a hard time for us," I said, gently. "We've had a great disappointment. We can get through it if we just hold on to each other."

His hand dropped. "I'm going to have to put this bluntly," he said, "because there's no other way to put it. I've found someone else."

My mouth dropped, forming a perfect O. I was speechless. That was the last thing I expected.

"None of this is your fault. It's not fair that I feel so angry toward you that I can't . . . I know it's not your fault," he explained. "I'm really just angry at fate. So I started avoiding you so that I wouldn't act angry with you and well, then I fell in love with someone else!"

"Who?" I snapped. "What's the tramp's name?"

"Maryse Ashcroft," He revealed, lowering his head. His eyes wouldn't, or couldn't meet mine.

Maryse was his twenty-six-year-old secretary. "That's mighty lowdown of you," I said. "Maybe you'd better get her fertility checked before you get in any deeper."

"Don't demean yourself with nasty remarks," he barked.

"She ought to wonder whether it's her you want or her womb!"

He jolted upright in one fluid motion. "There's no sense in my sitting here listening to your sarcasm. I want a quick divorce, so I suggest that we get started. You can divorce me on the grounds of mental cruelty, adultery, or whatever Robert thinks would be best."

Robert was a friend who was a lawyer.

Brock continued. "You can keep the house, since you did most of the work on it. The money we saved, so you could . . ."

The money had been saved so I could stay home with our children, I thought. Despair and grief tore at my heart.

Brock continued his tirade, not caring how badly I was feeling inside. "You saved most of it, so you'll have that. You make almost as much money as I do, so I don't think there will be alimony involved. It should be simple."

"No child support, either," I said bitterly, as he walked out.

When I came home from work the next night, Brock had been there during the day and packed up all his things. The house was half empty, and it seemed like my footsteps echoed.

I fell into a fairly serious depression for the rest of that summer until fall. I went to work and did my job—which didn't require that I talk to others much. Friends called until I'd said no so many times, they no longer asked me out. I let the house get messy, and I lost weight. The single thing that I liked to do besides sleep was to sit in the rocker in the nursery and watch Carmella.

I didn't know her real name. Carmella was the name I gave her. I watched her sleep and cry and drink from her bottle. It was hard to watch sometimes, because she was left in her crib for so many hours. The light in her room was on most of the time, perhaps because she shared it with the other kids. Richard Joseph was either out or entertaining customers most of the evening. Susan was usually drunk, so the kids stayed up late and always fell asleep with the lights on.

Carmella was such a good baby. It would have been much worse for her if she'd been a cranky or high-strung baby. She seemed content to lie in her crib for hours. I longed to play with her and hug her.

One September evening, before dark, Carmella cried for an hour. I couldn't stand it anymore. I marched to the Joseph's home, and banged on the door. No one answered. I realized that their truck was gone. It seemed unbelievable that they could have gone out and left Carmella alone. I went to my kitchen and got a stepladder. I put it under the ground floor bedroom window, and then I slid the window up.

"Shhh, sweetheart." She looked at me. I felt her diaper. It was wet. She had to be hungry. What could they do to me? Breaking and entering to take care of a baby left alone was surely no crime.

I managed to climb into the window, stepped on the crib, and then climbed out. I picked up Carmella and she quieted immediately, nestling into my shoulder. I felt a wave of tenderness for her.

I went up the hall toward the kitchen, to find a bottle. That's when I heard the snores. Susan Joseph was passed out on the couch in the living room. The house was filthy. No one else seemed to be at home. I found a bottle, some milk, and a disposable diaper. The back door turned out to be unlocked, so I needn't have climbed in the window. I took Carmella back to my house, where I fed, changed her, and cuddled her. I couldn't seem to bring myself to take her home again, and that's when the idea came to my mind.

At first, it was just an impulse to get in my car with her and run. Then as I sat there in my kitchen with Carmella sleeping in my arms, it came to me that it would be possible to do it a different way: A way where I wouldn't be caught and they would never know I was the one who did it. Hopefully, we could disappear and never be found.

I carried Carmella back through her kitchen, and put her gently into her crib. I grabbed a stray towel and wiped the crib and everywhere I had touched. An hour had passed, the most important hour of my life. Susan was still snoring. I wiped the back door handle and the outside of the window, and I took my stepladder home. I had found something to live for.

I spent the evening in the attic. It took a while, but I finally found what I was looking for—Isabel's birth certificate and a social security card. My older sister, Isabel, died in a car crash when she was seventeen and I was thirteen. Both my parents were killed with her. It was a terrible tragedy for me. Perhaps that's why I had wanted a family so much, to replace the one I lost. Isabel was my half-sister by my mother's former marriage, and she had a different last name than mine. As far as I knew, neither Brock nor any of our friends knew that last name. The only person who knew was my grandmother. She had taken me in when my family died, but she'd been dead for many years.

My divorce was finalized in November, and the house sold later that month. Brock married Maryse two weeks after he received the divorce. I'd heard she was already pregnant.

The night before I was to move out of the house, I sat by the window watching Carmella. Dark fell early that winter night, and I could see her like she was on a stage in the lit-up bedroom. A child poked a toy at her, and she laughed. Was what I planned to do right? I knew it was illegal, about as illegal as you can get, but was it right?

Richard Joseph was not a good man, but sometimes, I saw him in the backyard, playing with the kids. Richard, and her addiction had beaten Susan, but she obviously loved her kids.

At that moment, Richard and Susan's voices rose in drunken argument. I couldn't hear the words through the closed windows, but I could hear crashes. It seemed to answer my question. Surely, God meant me to do this, I thought.

Then I winced. I couldn't know what God wanted and very likely, it wasn't something that was illegal and regarded as a heinous crime. He had put Carmella in that horrible home for His own unknown reasons. So be it. I was going to cross God, the law, and society. It seemed worth it.

The doorbell rang. For a moment, I thought it was Susan or Richard, that they could read my mind as I sat in the dark nursery. It was Brock. I let him in.

He didn't take off his coat. "I just wondered what your plans were," he muttered.

"What do you care?" I asked. "I thought you were on your honeymoon."

"We got back on Sunday. Look, just because it didn't work out, doesn't mean I don't want you to be happy."

I gave a bitter laugh. Then the anger drained out of me. What did it matter? I no longer felt hurt by Brock. I had a mission and fooling Brock was part of it.

"I'm moving to New York," I said. "I got a job there. It's only a temporary job, but I think I'll like it there. I just want a fresh start."

"It's a long way from your friends," he said. My family was dead, so my friends were the only hold on me. I didn't tell him that I'd hardly seen anyone for months.

"They can come and visit me," I lied. "How did you know I was moving?"

"From Terry." Terry was our realtor. "He said you got a good price for the house."

"Very good. The neighborhood is up and coming."

"Except for the Josephs."

"Well, I won't have to see the Josephs in New York. That's one good thing."

"Yes." He shifted awkwardly. "Good luck," he finally said, kissing me on the cheek. Then he was gone—along with ten years of my life.

17

I went back to watching Carmella. It was going to be so hard to be away from her, but the plan required it. The new owners had to be part of the neighborhood. I had to be almost forgotten. Then I would come for Carmella.

The temporary job in Newburgh and the isolated cabin in the mountains that I rented cheaply, were just going to be a way station. I bought an old van, in addition to my car, and hid it behind my house. My final goal was two states away, and I spent every weekend I could driving there and looking for the perfect town in which to raise Carmella. I finally found it in Orangeburg, a small town with good schools.

I slowly disengaged myself from my friends so no one would ask questions. I sent postcards about how busy I was and about a fictitious man in my life. Gradually, I sent fewer and fewer postcards. I knew some of them would be reporting to Brock, so this would keep him from worrying or even thinking about me. I would fade from people's minds. I'd arranged for the newspaper in my old city to be sent to me. I would need it. Hundreds of retirees did this, so it didn't draw attention to me.

At the same time, I began establishing myself as Isabel Lawson in Orangeburg. I was a widow with an infant, looking for a house, while my mother looked after the baby. I soon found a little cottage not far from the elementary school. It was tiny and needed a lot of work, so I got it for a song. The money from our old house and my savings just covered it, but I would have some time to save a little from my new job. With an address and a bank account, I was soon able to take a driver's test, and get a license with the name of Isabel Lawson. Back in Newburgh, I slipped into a parking garage one afternoon, and removed the license plates from a van. I put them in my shopping bag and walked.

My temporary job was for the owner of several nightclubs. There were some shady characters associated with that business, and one of them put me in touch with a man who dealt in phony documents. For five hundred dollars, he provided me with a birth certificate for Carmella.

Then I waited. It was only June. I wanted to wait until August. The longer I'd been gone from the house next door to the Joseph's, the more forgotten I was, the better. My temporary job would end in August. If anyone ever asked about me, it would be assumed I'd moved on. I bought toys and baby clothes. I worried. What if the Josephs had moved? Carmella would be a year old in August. Would she adapt to being with me? I knew I couldn't bear it if she were unhappy.

I worried that she might have Fetal Alcohol Syndrome or some other bad thing because her mother drank while she was pregnant. My research at the library told me that thirty percent of children who were victims of it were born to alcoholic mothers. But I wasn't Brock. I knew I'd love her, anyway.

A hot August day came, much like the one when I'd first seen Carmella. I set out for the six-hour drive over the mountains in the morning. I had the jitters. In an alley in a town across the mountains, I put the phony plates on the van. In a ladies room in a fast-food joint, I put on the wig and a pair of dark sunglasses.

I drove brazenly into my old neighborhood on that Tuesday afternoon, and pulled into the parking lot across the street. There was an old Victorian house, vandalized apartments, and the small parking lot in front allowed me to park with the rear of the van facing my old house and the Josephs' house. I climbed into the back of the van. There was a curtain behind the front seats, and a curtain over the back window.

I got out my binoculars and started watching though a corner of the back curtain. Some of the Joseph kids were playing in the hot sun in front of the house. No one seemed to be at home in my old house. That's the way it went for most of the day.

At six that evening, the people who now owned my old house came home, and worked in their front yard for a couple of hours. At eight, familiar yelling from the Josephs' home, and, a short while later, Richard Joseph bolted out the front door, spewing curses. He then drove off in his truck.

I waited and sweated in the back of the van for hours, thinking about how stupid this was, how it wouldn't work, and what it would be like when I was caught. Carmella probably didn't even sleep in the crib by the window anymore.

I kept watching. The light in the downstairs bedroom stayed on just like it used to, as the neighborhood went to sleep. Richard Joseph staggered in about midnight, but the light in the kids' room stayed on. Richard wasn't the kind of guy to check on the kids before he passed out. I took off the wig and wiggled into my black clothes.

At 3 a.m., I seized an opportunity to nose around. I got out of the van, leaving the door unlatched. I was carrying a step stool. I quickly crossed the street, pulling on a black silk ski mask and black gloves. I moved quickly under the window and up the stepladder. Carmella was asleep in her crib, and I breathed a sigh of relief. Quietly, I eased the window open quietly and picked her up as gently as I could. Kids in various states of undress were sleeping on cots crammed into the room. As I stepped down from the stepladder, I shifted Carmella so that I could pick up the ladder in my other hand. She woke briefly, and then she nestled against my neck. We were over a hundred miles away before she woke, again.

By then, I'd changed the license plates again, and I felt almost safe. My biggest worry was the one I should have had before. What would happen when Carmella wanted her mother? I thought.

She was alert by the time we were in the mountains. I stopped on a back road to feed her bottle to her. She didn't seem alarmed in any way. Several times, she said, "Katy" and "Harry." She never asked for "mama" or "dada," then or later. It firmed my resolve. I came to realize that Katy was her older sister, whose name I knew was Dee. The "Harry" question was answered the first time I handed her a hairy bear.

On the back mountain road, I moved her to the car seat in the back. I wanted to keep her in the bassinet in front, but I was afraid the police would stop me. She was such a good baby. A puzzled little frown crossed her face from time to time, but she rode in the back quietly. When I fed her, she studied me with big green eyes.

Back in the cabin in New York, I waited for the newspaper from my old city to come in the mail. That took three days. By then, I felt that even if the police came, it had been worth it to have this time with Carmella. I talked to her softly for hours. I told her of the wonderful life we would have.

The paper came at last. The story, "Baby Missing," was on page three. Police had brought in the baby's father for questioning, but refused comment when asked if he was a suspect.

It became apparent over the next few issues of the paper that the police suspected the baby's parents, but could find no evidence. The gray van was mentioned, but no one had a license plate number. A story said that Child Welfare was removing the children from the home and putting them in foster care because of reports from neighbors about the parents during the investigation. I began to feel safe, until I read the article that came the day before we left.

Detective Vows to Catch Kidnapper, the headline said. It went on to say that Richard Joseph's brother was a cop. Maybe that's what we always got so little response when we called the police on them. Robert Joseph denied that his brother had anything to do with the baby's disappearance. He wasn't assigned to the case, but he said the department was still investigating. He said something that chilled me.

"This will never be over until that baby is back with my brother and his wife," he said. "Even if the department gives up, I won't give up. I have a message for the kidnapper. Sooner or later, we will meet."

I rented the cabin monthly, and I'd already told the landlord I was leaving. I had closed my bank accounts, and put the money in the bank in Orangeburg under my new name. I forwarded my mail to General Delivery in Providence. I would never pick it up. Finally, Carmella and I drove the old van back behind the property as far as

I could go, where I took off the plates. I put Carmella in her baby carrier and walked back to the cabin. The next morning, we left for our new life.

"What a beautiful baby," the voice said behind me a few days later. I jumped. A woman in her fifties in a cardigan stood in my back yard, holding a pie.

"I'm sorry to startle you," she said. "We aren't very formal in Orangeburg. I thought I'd just stop by and welcome you." Perhaps I still looked nervous. "Is this a bad time? I'm Nancy Ryan. I live across the street."

I pulled myself together. I had to stop acting like a criminal. "I'm . . . Isabel Lawson. This is Carmella." Carmella burped. Nancy and I laughed. "Would you like some iced tea?"

"I'd love some," Nancy said, looking relieved. We sat in the yard with our tea and talked. She told me a lot about Orangeburg and her family. Her husband had died last year. Her children were all grown except her seventeen-year-old daughter, still at home. I said little except that I was a widow.

"So brave of you to start over like this," Nancy said. "But what about your family?"

"They're dead," I said.

She looked confused. "I heard that your mother was watching the baby while you were here before."

"She died last month," I said, quickly.

"How awful." Nancy's face took on a sorrowful look, and I felt guilty. It's a little late for guilt, I pointed out to myself. I was going to have to become a more skillful liar.

"But what about your husband's family?"

Even a liar as inexperienced as I was knew I couldn't tell her that everyone was dead. I was stumped and my cheeks burned. My discomfort was obvious, and I couldn't think of a thing to say.

"Oh, Isabel," she said, "forgive me for being nosy. You know, I forget that not every widow had a happy marriage like I did."

That was it! "We were about to get a divorce," I said. "When he died, I mean."

"And his family doesn't even want to see Carmella," she said, shaking her head. "How sad for you." And that was how I began the closest friendship of my life, built on a pack of lies.

Carmella thrived in our new home. I hugged and cuddled her, and she became full of laughter and fun. I took her to a big city two hundred miles away to see a pediatrician. I told the doctor that she was my dead sister's child, killed while driving drunk, and I didn't know if she'd had her immunizations. Carmella got her checkup and her shots, and then, we vanished again.

21

I had a job within two weeks of moving to Orangeburg. I was very broke by then. Luckily, Nancy was happy to make a little money taking care of Carmella. She became like an aunt to Carmella. I couldn't use my accountant's degree, so I took a general office job.

Carmella grew and flourished. She didn't look much like me, with her honey blonde hair, green eyes, and freckled nose. I told her she looked like her dead father. Nancy asked for pictures. I invented a lost trunk with the photographs. Lies, so many lies were necessary.

I had never been a criminal before, and I wondered how they lived with the anxiety. I never felt safe. I told myself I was safe, but I was always waiting for something to happen. Then one day when Carmella was in kindergarten, I picked up a national woman's magazine, and Carmella's story was in it.

I was on my lunch hour from work. I went home, called in sick, and pulled down the shades. In the dim light, my heart beating hard, I read the article. It was an interview with Detective Robert Joseph about the kidnapping. Richard Joseph had been killed in a fight the year before. The fight started when someone accused him of killing his baby. "Whoever kidnapped my brother's child is a murderer," Robert Joseph said. "I will never give up until I find the person who did this." His face was grim in the photo. They had no picture of Carmella as a baby. What caused my mouth to go dry was another picture. Robert Joseph had adopted Carmella's older sister Dee, who stood next to him in the photo. She was three years older than Carmella, but the resemblance between them was startling.

I could run again, but where would I go? Running would only draw attention. I waited and sweated. It was then that the nightmares started. They always featured Detective Robert Joseph, and I didn't stop having them until I finally met him.

I breathed a sigh of relief when the month passed, and a new issue of the magazine came out. But I was never really able to relax again. I knew old issues of the magazine were around, and every year Carmella looked more like the picture of her older sister, Dee. I knew, too, that Robert Joseph would never stop looking.

Carmella got good grades in school, and skipped the third grade. She continued to be an easygoing child, just like she'd been an easy baby. The years passed, until she was in her last year of high school. That's when the trouble came, but it wasn't the trouble I'd been expecting.

It was several months after Carmella's seventeenth birthday. She was to go to her prom, and she was very excited. We shopped hard, but we couldn't find the kind of dress she wanted, so Nancy made it for her. That afternoon, we were pinning up the dress before taking it over to Nancy to be hemmed.

"Did I tell you my date is the senior class president?" Carmella asked, swinging her skirt.

"Four times," I mumbled around the pins in my mouth. I was kneeling in front of her. "Stand still."

"Mom?"

I looked up. Carmella's nose was bleeding. "My dress!" she cried.

I ran for a towel and some ice. She had somehow managed to get the dress off, and was holding her head back.

"No, forward," I said. I pinched the bridge of her nose, but it kept bleeding. An hour later, it became clear that we had to go to the emergency room. Carmella was admitted to the hospital.

After days of tests, I sat down to talk to the doctor. Nancy was in Carmella's room with her. By now, we knew she had Aplastic Anemia, and that it was potentially fatal. My little girl was very sick, and she was starting to show it.

"How did she get it?" I asked.

"We don't know yet, and we may never know. The cause isn't clear in fifty percent of the cases."

"She didn't complain of anything. She played soccer on Saturday."

"It would have showed symptoms, soon. The nosebleed was lucky in a way. It allowed us to discover this sooner. But she's lost ninety-five percent of her bone marrow to the disease. Her bone marrow is what supplies the blood cells she needs to be healthy." He saw the look on my face. "I can't promise she'll survive, but 50% of cases are cured."

"How do we do it?"

"She needs a bone marrow transplant."

"I'll do it."

I was tested the next day, but I wasn't a match. Neither were Nancy or several others who came forward to be tested. The doctor said, "The very best results come from siblings. Carmella doesn't have any, so we'll have to try to find a match from the Red Cross. We might or might not find one. There are other things we can do, but her best chance for survival is a bone marrow transplant."

I was quiet as Nancy drove me home. I asked her to come in, and told her what the doctor said.

"It's too bad she doesn't have brothers and sisters," Nancy said, her eyes sympathetic.

I'd known from the minute the doctor said "siblings," what I would have to do. I sank into a chair and put my face into my hands. "She does have brothers and sisters," I whispered. I looked up at my friend, Nancy, who also loved Carmella. Nancy had helped me so often with Carmella. We'd gone to her house on Thanksgiving and Christmas. She'd shared her family with us. I started telling my story, slowly at first. She stood up after awhile and looked out the window.

23

That made it easier for me to tell her all of it. At last, I finished.

"So, you understand that I had to do what I did? Nancy?"

She was still standing at the window with her back to me, and she turned now, eyes brimming with tears, her mouth firm with judgment. "No, Isabel," she said. "Or whatever your name really is. I think you're a mother's worst nightmare."

"The nightmare was the way she was living, and the kind of terrible life she was going to have!" I exclaimed. I couldn't believe my friend didn't understand.

Her expression softened. "I think you did what you did when you were overwhelmed by depression and loss—loss of the family you'd wanted, and the loss of your husband. I think you've had all these years of living with your secret to tell yourself over and over again that you were right. But none of that means you were right." She sat in a chair across from me.

"You committed a terrible crime. You say you did it for Carmella, but there were other things you could have done for her. You could have pressured the law to do something about the situation. You could have ingratiated yourself with that family and become like an aunt to the children. You could have tried to help the mother. I can't begin to list the things you could have done. But none of those things would have given you what you selfishly wanted."

The truth of what she said hurt me deeply, but I recognized it. I started to cry silently.

"Whom are you crying for?" Nancy asked. "For yourself. What about Carmella? She is living in a web of lies. Everything she believes about herself is a lie. The security of her life and sense of herself is a lie. I hope to God you will do the right thing, Isabel. I hope you will think of Carmella, instead of your own needs."

She got up. For a minute, I thought she would hug me, but she turned and left the house. Later that evening, I called her and told her I was going to look for Carmella's family. I asked her to look after Carmella while I was gone.

"But where are you going? Why are you leaving me?" Carmella asked.

"I'm hoping to find some relations, back where we used to live. Someone who might be more compatible for a donation."

"Okay, Mom. Aunt Nancy will look after me." She looked at me with such trust, I thought my heart would break.

It had been many years. Richard Joseph was dead, and Susan Joseph no longer lived next door to my old house. The people living in their house had fixed it up and had no idea where they were. I knocked on the door of my old house. The woman I'd seen in the yard the night I took Carmella, answered.

"The Josephs," she said. "They've been gone for years. Are you a reporter?"

"No. I . . . need their help with something."

"I wouldn't think they could help anybody. You know that their baby daughter went missing?"

I nodded.

"We all suspected Richard Joseph or maybe even the two of them. We thought maybe they had one of their fights, and the baby got killed. The police even dug up the yard. Once the cops and the reporters got a good look at the way they were living, they took the kids. Put them in foster homes. They had one last big fight. It sounded like the house was being torn down; then, she left him, and he moved away." She shrugged. "I don't know what happened after that."

I hired a private investigator and went back home. Carmella was still in the hospital, getting transfusions. They let her come home for a few days. Nancy spent time with us. She loved Carmella, but I could see the coolness in her toward me. Carmella didn't notice that. She was trying to be brave, but missing school and the prom was very upsetting to her. Then she had to go back in the hospital so they could try a drug. The worldwide search for a matching donor continued.

Mr. Olsen, the investigator, called me a week later. "Richard Joseph died in a bar scuffle years ago," he said. "Susan had divorced him about a year after they left the neighborhood. I have her address. She lives with one of the daughters, Dee, and she works at a coffee shop."

"She works?" I was amazed.

"You wanted to know about the kids especially. Dee turned out well. She's a student at the college. One of the boys is in jail. Another one had Fetal Alcohol Syndrome and died young. The other two daughters have kids, but no husbands. I have addresses for everybody."

I got the information from him, and arranged for payment. Then I told Nancy and Carmella that I was leaving town again. I called Susan Joseph from a motel room near the state line.

"Yeah, I remember you," she said. "Why are you calling me?" She sounded sober.

"Susan . . . Mrs. Joseph . . . I'm the one who took your baby. I need to see you."

She was silent for a long moment. "You took Carol? Why are you telling me, now?"

"She's very sick. She needs our help."

"When will you be here?"

"In the morning, about ten. I have your address."

"I'll be waiting." She hung up without another word.

Susan lived in an old apartment building near the college. I got there an hour early. Her hair was dyed an obvious dark black and she looked haggard, but she was sober.

"Dee's still in class," she said. "She wanted to be here."

"I'll want to talk to her, too," I said. "It's her help, and her sisters' help that I . . . we need most."

She sat in a rocker and hugged herself.

"I guess you wonder why I took her."

"No. I don't wonder why," she said. Her tone was sad. "I was a terrible mother. They took them all from me."

I didn't know what to say to that. I sat on the couch and waited.

"After the last time he beat me up, I went to the woman's shelter," she said. "They're the ones that got me dried out. They made me see that I'd never see my kids again if I didn't dry out. It took two years to get them back, and Robert kept Dee. I still go to AA." She plucked at her sweater sleeve. "You took her because I was a lousy mother, right?"

"And because I wanted her."

Her face turned soft. "Of course, you did. She was beautiful, wasn't she?"

"Would you like to see pictures?"

The pictures were spread out on the coffee table, and I was explaining them, when the door opened. A pretty blonde girl with an armful of books came in. She looked so much like Carmella; it took my breath away.

"Ah, yes," she said, putting her books down on a table. "The kidnapper. Isn't this cozy?" She pulled up a chair and started looking at the pictures without another word. Finally, she said, "My sister, that you stole from me. My mother doesn't want to call the police, but I do."

"Dee—" Susan tried to interrupt.

"She had no right, Ma. She should be in prison. You think she should get away with it just because she lived in that fancy house and we were poor and—"

"We were a mess, Dee. I was a drunk. Richard was an abusive father."

"That still didn't give her the right to take my baby sister." Dee started to cry. "Everything changed. It wasn't so bad. We were a family until then. Then we were freaks. My father is dead because of you. Someone accused him of killing his baby, and he got in a fight. You killed him."

"That's enough," Susan said to her. "Your father got in a fight because he was a bully and thought he could beat the guy up. He hit his head when he was knocked down."

"He was still my father. Whatever he was, he wasn't a murderer, and he wouldn't have been in a fight defending himself from being called one if this woman hadn't taken his baby." Dee wiped her eyes. "Why are you back here now with your pretty pictures?" she asked me.

"Carmella needs a bone marrow transplant." I explained why. "It doesn't hurt to give it," I added hastily.

"Her name is Carol," Dee said. "I'll help her. My sisters will, too. But she has to know who I am. She has to know what you are. A criminal. Whatever we were, we didn't steal babies."

Two days later, I met them again in the hospital lobby. Dee drew me aside. Her mother followed and listened.

"I've been thinking," she said. "I wanted to turn you into the police in spite of what my mother said, but you have insurance, and we don't. Besides, it might upset my sister. Here's the deal. I'm the one who explains things to my sister. That way, you can't pretty it up and make us look like dirt. Take it or leave it, lady."

I nodded mutely, and she walked away.

"She isn't usually like this," Susan said. "She's a nice girl."

"Yes. I believe you." I knew it didn't matter if Dee didn't turn me in. Sooner or later, she would tell Robert Joseph, and I was pretty sure about what he would do.

I waited in the lounge near Carmella's room for two hours. Finally, Dee and Susan came out.

"She doesn't want to see you," Dee said.

I started to protest that I was her mother. But I wasn't. I brushed past Dee and went into the room. Carmella looked at me once, and then looked away.

"Let me tell you my side," I said.

"I don't want to hear."

"It's not all . . . I meant for the best."

She still wouldn't look at me. "Susan . . . my . . . mother, she told me how bad it was. Dee didn't want her to, but she did. It's not that. It's all those lies. My whole life is a lie."

"I was wrong, very wrong, I know that now. It's not a lie that I love you."

She turned her tear-filled eyes to me. "I believe you love me, Mom. You're not a criminal. You had to really want me to do what you did. I'm just so confused. I need to be away from you and think."

I kissed her cheek and left. I waited in the lounge every day while Nancy went in or Susan and Dee. I waited for her to ask for me. On the fourth day, the doctor found me there.

"Carmella's birth mother and her sister have talked to me about transferring Carmella to be in the hospital near them. It's an excellent facility for this problem, but I wanted to check with you." His eyes were sympathetic. "As the adoptive mother, you're the one who decides."

"She can go," I said.

"Why doesn't she want to see you?"

I didn't know what to say.

27

"It's always best to tell children when they are young that they're adopted," he said. "Many parents don't realize that, then the child is upset and angry when she finds out." He patted my shoulder. "She'll come around."

It was apparent that Dee and Susan had found their own appropriate lies to tell. I got up and went home.

Two days later, Dee and Susan waited in their old car in the driveway, while Carmella came in to pack.

I was relieved when Carmella let me hug her. She tried to smile. "I would have been leaving for college in a few months anyway," she said.

I started to cry.

"Don't cry, Mom. Please. You're always going to be my mother. Aunt Nancy says I'm lucky to have two mothers, and she's right. I still feel mixed up, but I love you."

Dee was not a match for Carmella, but one of the other sisters was. It is a simple, painless procedure to donate. It saved Carmella's life. She was cured. She got her GED, and then applied to college. Carmella and Dee got an apartment together.

Carmella wrote to me. I wrote to her even more. I went to my job, and worked in my garden. One morning, I was digging in the dirt in the backyard, when a shadow fell over me. I looked up at three men.

The one in the uniform said, "I'm Sheriff Hartman, ma'am. And this man is—"

The man with the face from my nightmares broke in. "I'm Robert Joseph," he said, looming over me as I knelt on the ground. "I'm a cop, and I'm the uncle of the little girl you kidnapped."

There was no statute of limitations on kidnapping in either state. I was allowed to "cop a plea" as my lawyer called it. Robert Joseph testified against me before the judge sentenced me, telling the damage the kidnapping had caused. Carmella and her mother testified for me, and I think that helped. I got four to six years in a minimum-security prison for women.

To my surprise, it was all a relief. Some days, usually a day when I get a letter or visit from Carmella, I am almost happy. I don't have to live with anxiety anymore, or with the feeling I had for so many years that I now recognize as guilt. I just live day to day. I try to help the younger women here, so many of them separated from their children. I work in the kitchen. I'm making a quilt for Carmella. I wait to hear from the daughter I stole.

THE END

# CAMPGROUND KIDNAPPING
Our little girl was taken in the night

Ian and I had been tent campers for years, ever since we'd been newlyweds. Even when our family expanded to include our two daughters, Chelle and Patty, we took every opportunity to spend a weekend away. It was always a relief to get out of the city, out of our daily routine, and to spend time together as a family, away from the pressures of jobs, school, and the children's activities.

But once we found out little Number Three was on the way, the prospect of tent camping lost a lot of its appeal. Suddenly, the idea of having to organize and pack everything for every trip seemed daunting. Suddenly, our minivan seemed tiny when we thought about adding a car seat and a pile of baby supplies to all the camping gear in an already cramped vehicle. We simply stopped camping. Other things seemed to take priority, and our weekend getaways now took place in hotels—on the rare occasions they happened at all.

I'll never forget that hot June day when Chelle came in from playing in the yard, her face flushed from the heat. At nine, she was an active child, always on the go. She loved the outdoors. As she got herself a cold glass of lemonade from the refrigerator, she asked, "Why can't we go camping, Mom? We used to have fun swimming at Silver Lake and hiking around the park."

It seemed surprising that she remembered, but then it had only been three years and she was definitely a child of nature. Since she'd been tiny, she had loved any living thing, from the moose we'd occasionally seen on our travels to the tiniest insect she happened upon while on a nature walk. I hadn't realized she missed it, but her wistful tone echoed her father's whenever he'd brought up the same subject lately.

"You really want to go?"

"Yes, Mommy. It's been a long time, and the baby's not a baby anymore."

I hated to admit it, but she had a point. "I'll talk to your father about it, Chelle. Maybe we can go soon." Even as I said the words, I saw the disappointment spread across my daughter's face. She thought I was brushing her off. I didn't intend to; I just didn't want to face the fetching, organizing, packing, loading, setting up, taking down, reloading, packing, unpacking, cleaning up, drying out, and putting away I knew a trip with our family would take.

Ian was always willing to help, but he had no concept of what the family needed to bring. Even if I gave him very specific lists of what to pack, we always ended up at the campground with twelve pairs of socks for each child and no jackets, or six bags of marshmallows and no wire forks to toast them with. He tried, but we both accepted the fact I was a lot better at organizing than he was. Consequently, that job always fell to me.

"Ian, Chelle wants to go camping again."

He eyed me over his newspaper that evening as we sat on our back deck watching our three girls playing in the jets of water sparkling from the lawn sprinkler. The weather hadn't cooled much, and the shade we sat in felt good. The girls' happy squeals made us both smile as they ran in and out of the cold water.

He reached for my hand. "How do you feel about it?"

"I'd like to go, too. It's just so much work."

He nodded. "I know we've talked about a motor home. Maybe now is the time."

I thought about it for a minute. "I don't think we're ready to get in quite that deep."

He eyed the paper some more, giving me no response. Suddenly, he said, "Hey, Joanne! How about this? Here's a pop-up camper for sale. The price looks good, and it's only two years old. Shall we go look at it?"

"Now that, I could handle. I like tent camping, you know that. It's just that now I want something we can throw our clothes and food into and just go, without having to think about it very much."

"Maybe this is just the thing, then."

After quickly calling to find out if we could see the camper right away, we called the teenager next door to baby-sit, and off we went.

The owner had the camper set up and waiting. I couldn't believe how compact and yet spacious it was. Each end of the trailer slid out to become a king-sized bed, with plenty of room for us at one end and all three girls on the other. As they got bigger, the dinette could be folded down into a bed as well. The canvas walls consisted mostly of windows that zipped open, letting in the great outdoors like no tent we'd ever seen. Vinyl windows zipped up over the screens for rainy days, and canvas panels unrolled down over them for privacy. The trailer contained a complete kitchen including a small refrigerator, stovetop, and sink, and there was even a small, portable toilet which would be a godsend with little children at three o'clock in the morning.

"Look at this, Joanne. These beds are huge! On rainy days, the girls can play with their dolls on the beds or play games or whatever. It's perfect."

Distracted by the clever way the cabinet containing the stove and sink flipped down for travel, I barely heard him. I'd already realized the advantage of large beds for the girls to play in, anyway. It would sure beat the tent floor on those inevitable cold, dark, damp days.

The possibilities and the advantages loomed large very quickly. Ian and the seller haggled for a bit, and then before we knew it, we were hitching up the camper to the back of our van! It all happened so quickly, we barely had time to think about it all, but it just seemed like the right thing to do.

The girls were nearly uncontrollable when they saw our new little home-away-from-home. Chelle hugged us both, refusing to let go even as her swimsuit, still wet from her play in the sprinkler, soaked both Ian and me. We couldn't have cared less. Patty, at six, was nearly as excited, but she didn't remember the camping trips like Chelle did. Three-year-old Thea didn't really understand what all the yelling and jumping up and down was about, but she went with the flow and joined her sisters in their enthusiastic response.

After we paid the baby-sitter and sent the girls in to put on dry clothes, Ian looked at me and grinned. "Well, after all that, we'd better be able to figure out how to put this thing up."

It wasn't that difficult. The seller had given us detailed instructions and provided the owner's manual as well. By the time the girls came bounding back out of the house, we had the roof raised and were working on getting the tenting all in place. In no time, our little trailer was a complete home on wheels. We all piled in to enjoy it.

"Can we sleep out here tonight, Dad?" Chelle knew which of us would be the easiest to sway. When Ian assured her that whoever wanted to sleep in the new camper could do so, her face lit up and she gave a little bounce of happiness as she sat on the front bunk, her knees tucked under herself.

By luck, we were able to take advantage of a canceled reservation at a nearby park just a week later. By then, we'd cleaned and stocked the camper with all the utensils, dishes, bedding, and everything else we'd need on a trip. It all sat waiting in the trailer, which now made its new home next to the garage.

I couldn't believe the ease with which I was able to get our family ready to go. Dry food went into a big plastic tub, perishables into the little camper fridge, soft drinks into a large cooler that stowed easily in the trailer, and clothes into duffel bags for each of us. Simple. I began to wonder why we'd used our tent for so many years, and why we'd waited so long to get back into camping.

"Campgrounds are the last safe haven, Joanne," Ian remarked as we pulled out of our driveway, our new little house on wheels following obediently behind.

That was one reason we'd quit camping—I remembered now. Ian was just too trusting when it came to the girls. His attitude was, no one who camped could ever be a bad person. For some reason, he believed all campers had only the best intentions, and no one would ever hurt anyone in a campground. In his mind, campgrounds were populated with saints.

I had never agreed, and so the endless debate had raged. I insisted on accompanying the girls to the bathrooms, for instance, even when the bathhouse was in view of our campsite. Ian, on the other hand, saw no harm in letting them go alone, something he would never do anywhere else like a shopping mall or restaurant. It wasn't that he was a bad parent—far from it. In any other situation, he watched our girls like a hawk. He simply refused to even consider that anyone in a campground could do harm to a child.

"Campers are good people." I'd heard all this before. I hoped our disagreement on the issue wouldn't ruin our very first trip with the new camper.

"Campers are just people, Ian. All kinds of people, good and bad."

He refused to give in. "Bad people don't take the time to enjoy the great outdoors, Joanne. They're too busy stalking teenage boys in the mall bathrooms. They go where it's easy—not to campgrounds where there are lots of people and the parents are nearby."

I let the issue drop, assuring myself I'd keep an eye on the girls myself, and no harm would come to them. Nothing would ever convince Ian he was wrong. I knew that. Ever the optimist, he refused to see the bad in life, focusing only on the good. It was one of his most endearing traits. I didn't want him to become a cynical person with a paranoid outlook on life. I just wanted him to face the realities for the girls' sakes.

Our two-hour journey brought us to the shore of a Great Lake, to the campground which had been our all-time favorite destination just a few short years earlier. We had been surprised to get a campsite there, as it was a very popular place in the summer, and even more delighted when, in response to our inquiry at arrival, the park ranger informed us our very favorite site in the park was vacant and waiting.

Along the way on our short trip through the park to our campsite, Chelle pointed out the things she remembered from our last trip there. Ian and I just looked at each other, amazed at her memory. Neither of us had realized what these trips meant to her.

"Look, Thea, me and Chelle used to play on that slide right there!" Patty finally spoke up, the sight of the big yellow slide attached to a gigantic jungle gym having jogged her memory. She had only been a toddler the last time she'd played there. "Daddy used to hold me on his lap and slide down through that tunnel there. See?"

Thea just nodded, too excited to speak. Patty, and even more, Chelle, had been telling her all about the joys of camping since we'd brought home the pop-up. The closer this trip had come, the more keyed up they'd all become.

I had to confess, Ian and I had gotten pretty excited as well. We'd forgotten how pleasant just the anticipation of a weekend away was, let alone the actual down time itself. With our pop-up had come not only the promise of great family memories to be made, but also a heavy-duty stress reliever on wheels.

With the playground only two spaces away from us in plain sight, we let the girls walk over to check out the swings while Ian and I started to set up. In just a few minutes, we'd gotten everything in place and ready. Ian went over to be with the girls while I stepped into the camper to start our lunch. I simply couldn't get over how easy everything was, compared to our years tent camping. The propane-fueled stove burners fired right up, and before long, lunch was almost ready.

As if on cue, Ian and the girls showed up outside as I set the plates on the picnic table. With them was a man who appeared to be about our age.

"This is Tom Richert, Joanne. He's in the park for a few days, himself. He's traveling cross-country to a new job, and just decided to take a break."

"Nice to meet you, Mr. Richert."

"Please, it's Tom." He extended his hand for me to shake. He had a nice smile, and I smiled back. I'd forgotten how much fun it was to make new friends while camping. Everything was so casual and informal, and it was easy to talk to other campers.

"Tom pushed me on the swings, Mommy." Thea scrambled up on the picnic table bench, helping herself to an apple slice from the plate I'd prepared. "He pushed me way high, too!" Popping up to stand on the bench, she stretched for the sky as she declared, "This high!"

We all chuckled at her, except Chelle who rolled her eyes. Patty grabbed Tom's hand. "You can stay for lunch. Then maybe later we can go play at the playground some more."

Tom seemed uncomfortable until I invited him, then he sat down with us and entertained the girls throughout the meal with little stories and goofy faces. He seemed to enjoy our girls' company and had a natural affinity with children.

He explained—when he could get a word in as our girls monopolized his conversation—that he'd had to leave his own family behind when he left for his new job. When he found a house for them all to live in, then they would join him. But traveling cross-country got lonely, he said. Having been through a similar separation a few years ago, Ian and I could understand his feelings. Sometimes the sacrifices that had to be made to create a better life took their toll.

Tom went back to his own camper after lunch, saying he had some work he had to do, and that he wanted to call his wife and kids.

Our family went for a nature walk, Chelle's favorite activity. Ian and I held hands as we let the girls scamper ahead, running back to us often to point out something they'd seen or had a question about. As we breathed in the fresh, pine-scented air, we could feel our hearts lighten. We were happy at home, but having some time away made us happy in a different way, somehow. It was hard to put into words, but when we looked at each other we just knew we'd done the right thing in buying the new camper. The trips we'd take in it would help create priceless memories our children would carry all their lives.

Evenings in a campground can be magical. It's a time when the fireflies come out for the children to catch in a bottle and marvel at, when a crackling campfire lights a cozy circle and chases the night chill away, and when marshmallows are toasted to gooey perfection. Watching the girls' faces as they enjoyed this timeless camping pastime was priceless.

"Howdy, neighbors!" Tom's quiet greeting from the road reached us through the darkness.

"Hey, Tom, come and join us." I would have preferred for our family to be alone our first night out, but Tom was such pleasant company, I couldn't resent the intrusion or even be annoyed at Ian for inviting him.

"It's a beautiful night for a stroll," Tom remarked, looking up at the stars that lay in the sky like a tray of diamonds on black velvet, seeming close enough to touch. "I always like to take a walk after dark through any campground I stay at. There's something so nice about seeing all the families enjoying their own company, especially those with little ones like yours."

He sounded so wistful, I had to assume his thoughts were with his own little ones.

The evening and our girls wound down as we adults talked. I excused myself to put them to bed. They were excited about sleeping in the camper the first time "for real," as Chelle put it. "That time in the driveway didn't count," she explained. But in spite of their excitement, all the day's activities had tired them out. It wasn't long before they were all asleep, three angels in a row on their big bunk. I set aside the story book I'd been reading to them and went back outside.

The men were still talking. Apparently, they'd discovered a shared love of football. Their friendly disagreement about a controversial call during the last season's big game made them seem like old buddies. As the night wore on, there didn't seem to be a subject we touched on that Tom didn't share an interest in or some knowledge about.

Meeting him had added a lot of fun to an already great trip. We'd have talked all night, I was sure, but my eyelids were drooping and I excused myself to get some sleep.

An hour or so later, I vaguely realized Ian had finally joined me. Quiet settled over our campsite. The day's adventures caught up with me and I fell into a deep, relaxing sleep.

An unfamiliar sound, one I couldn't place, brought me back to consciousness. The woods are full of strange sounds in the night, particularly for those of us used to the sounds of the city. Half awake, I didn't think anything of it and curled back up to sleep some more.

"Mommy? Mommy?" Someone pulled on my sleeve. "Mommy, where's Thea?" The sleeve-tugging stopped, to be replaced by a small hand patting my arm, then my cheek. "Mommy, where's Thea?"

Ian sat up suddenly, his abrupt action bringing me fully awake in an instant. Patty stood next to our bunk, a worried look on her little face.

Hardly awake at the other end of the camper, Chelle sat up, slapped her face, and muttered, "Darn mosquitoes!" before flopping back on the bunk and burrowing under the blankets.

"What the heck's going on?" Ian mumbled. "The place is full of bugs."

I barely noticed his observation as my gaze swept the inside of the camper. Where was Thea, indeed? Like a shot, I was out of bed and on my hands and knees checking under the dinette, the only possible hiding spot. She wasn't there. Alarmed, I frantically patted the bedclothes next to Chelle, praying one of the lumps in the blankets would be my three-year-old daughter.

To my horror, my hand slipped right through the screen on the side of the bunk, out into the morning air! I pulled the covers away from the screen to find it had been slit from one end to the other, leaving a gaping hole.

Any ideas I'd had that Thea could have let herself out to wander the campground in the night and gotten lost died a swift death. The cut screening left no doubt that Thea's disappearance was no accident.

Someone had taken my baby!

"Ian! She's been kidnapped!"

"What? That's impossible! No camper would hurt a child! Don't be ridiculous. She must have wandered off somewhere."

I showed him the screen and his face paled. In my panic, the wheels of my mind spun freely, finding no solid thought to give them traction. Until one idea entered and seemed to catch.

"Tom. Tom has her," I whispered.

"Now that's really ridiculous. Tom's such a nice guy."

But suddenly some of the things Tom had said and done started to click, pieces of the puzzle falling into place faster and faster until I reached the inevitable conclusion.

"Where's Tom's camper parked? What kind of camper is it?"

Ian's jaw dropped. I could see he was starting to put together the pieces, too. "He never said."

"And you don't find that unusual? How many campers have you met who don't want to tell you every single detail about their rigs?" I couldn't fault Ian. I hadn't noticed Tom's omission, either. I gathered up Chelle in her blankets and took Patty's hand, pulling them none too gently outside and shoving them in the van with instructions to lock the doors and not let anyone in, no matter what. To get things rolling, I leaned on the horn, sending a blast through the sleeping campground loud and long enough to wake up everyone within earshot.

I had my cell phone in my other hand, dialing for the police. I prayed we weren't too late, that Tom hadn't already left with our little girl.

"You go that way, Ian, and I'll go this way. And let's make all the noise possible. I intend to wake up this whole campground, if that's what it takes to find our daughter!"

Calling Thea's name as loudly as I could, I took off running. Lights started coming on in campers all over the grounds, and for that I was glad. Within a couple of minutes, the park ranger showed up, no doubt in response to complaints about all the noise. I quickly explained the situation to her. She checked a list she carried in her truck, and informed me that no one named Tom Richert was registered in the campground for that night.

My blood turned to ice as I realized "Tom" had planned to take a child, and he had befriended our family with that goal in mind.

Sirens screamed in the distance as the ranger left, promising to lock the park gates as soon as the police had gotten inside.

Precious minutes slipped by. I felt like I was not moving, not doing anything, when in reality I was in frantic motion. Lights were on in nearly every camper now, even in many of the tents. People peered out windows, which made it easier for me in my search. Anyone who wasn't Tom, I passed right by. Anyone with kids saved me from having to check them out.

I met Ian in the last loop. The look on his face confirmed my fears that he hadn't been able to find Thea. He'd eliminated all the campers in his search area, he said. There was only this one loop left. Farthest from our camper, this area hadn't been disturbed by our noise. Not a single light shone from any of the rigs.

Ian walked to the nearest truck, a big diesel, and tried the door. It wouldn't open, but a car alarm, the single most annoying item to be found in any campground, began to wail. Lights came on instantly in the big travel trailer behind the truck, followed by lights in all the rigs in that loop.

All but one. One camper, a nice fifth-wheel trailer with a big white pickup truck in front of it, remained dark. Either the occupants were stone deaf—or they didn't have to come out and see what the ruckus was because they already knew.

My fists and teeth clenched as I started off toward the dark camper at a run. Suddenly, it seemed ominous and vile.

A police car pulled in next to the big white truck as I banged on the trailer door, demanding to be let in. An officer tried to pull me away, but by that time I was beside myself, sure that my daughter was being held just beyond that door. Finally, he and his partner were able to restrain me. My pounding had not brought a response of any kind. The trailer remained dark, its occupants silent.

"Thea! Thea, are you in there? Thea!"

"Let us do our jobs, lady, okay?" The officer's eyes were kind as he tried to calm me down. I realized the more I carried on, the longer it would take to get the door of that camper opened, and I fell silent. The officers released my arms and I slumped back against the trailer. Ian stood beside me, his arm around my shoulders.

"Police. Open up." The authoritative voice brought a response as my pounding and shouting could not. Slowly, the door opened and Tom stepped out of the trailer, looking rumpled and sleepy.

My patience thinned rapidly as I watched him talk to the officers, telling them he knew nothing about Thea's disappearance, telling them he was a heavy sleeper and hadn't heard the noise outside his trailer. Something didn't seem right. Tom's mussed hair looked too calculated, his puzzled expression phony, his concern insincere.

"Let them look inside, Tom." Ian's statement indicated to me he'd reached the same conclusion I had, that Thea was in that trailer. "Is that a problem?"

The look in the eyes of the man who'd pretended to be our friend only a couple of hours before seemed made of ice now. "They don't have a search warrant, Ian."

"They don't need one if you give permission, Tom. Surely you'd do that, just to set our minds at ease."

Tom simply glared at us before turning his attention back to the police officers, who were now asking for his ID. The three of them walked toward Tom's truck, apparently to retrieve his driver's license.

On the campground road in that loop, half the campers had gathered around to see what all the hoopla was about. As if outside my own body, I heard the crowd muttering about a little girl being taken. Those we'd talked to in our mad search of the campground had apparently spread the word, as had the park ranger in her own search.

37

I looked at Ian and he looked at me, and in that instant, we both started racing to the camper door. In an instant, we were inside.

Tom's trailer looked new on the outside, but on the inside, chaos reigned. The floor was littered with papers and trash. The galley sink overflowed dirty dishes. Clothes were strewn from one end to the other.

Behind us, a police officer burst in.

"You people have to leave right now! This is private property! You can't just bust in here and take over this investigation! If you don't leave now, we'll have to arrest you for breaking and entering!"

I barely heard him, my attention focused on a closed door at the end of the short hallway leading to the back of the trailer. I nodded at it. "Ian?"

"Yeah, I know." He stepped between the cop and me, effectively filling the hallway to give me a chance to pull open that door, dreading what I might find. Or maybe worse, what I might not find.

What I found was my daughter.

The bed she lay in took up nearly the entire room. She lay facing the wall, her little nightgown pulled up to her neck, her panties around her ankles. Bile rose in my throat as I saw her exposed and helpless like that and realized what Tom's sick, twisted intent had been all along.

"Ian, she's here!" Behind me, the cop fell silent in his threats to arrest us. He was the least of my concerns. I couldn't tell if my daughter was alive or dead, she lay so still.

The two men joined me in the cramped bedroom doorway, peering over my shoulder. As if in a dream, I heard the cop quietly radio his partner to arrest Tom and call an ambulance.

Gently, I rolled Thea towards me so I could see her face. Tears poured down my face as I heard her let out a little sigh. I smoothed her nightgown down over her little body and picked her up. Her eyelids fluttered, but she didn't wake up. Her sleep seemed unnatural to me, her breathing slow and labored, and I prayed like I never had before.

As I handed my daughter to her daddy so he could take her outside, I looked around the bedroom for the first time. On every square inch of wall space available, Tom had plastered pictures of little girls, all about Thea's age. Most were naked, some posed like models in a men's magazine, some being forced to perform lewd acts or submit to unspeakable horrors. All looked terrified. Some were obviously crying, others just looked dazed. Some of the pictures were snapshots of the girls fully clothed and acting normally, like heartbreaking "before" shots in sharp contrast to all the macabre "after" photos.

Turning, I pushed the officer out of my way and vomited into the shower stall off the hallway, my body unable to tolerate the sickening display. In my mind, Tom became nothing more than a horrid beast. Any semblance of humanity he'd ever had evaporated in the faces of the images he'd put on his walls.

As I raised my head, a small image caught my eye. High on the shower wall above the faucets was a picture of Thea, taken the day before as our girls played with Tom on the playground. She looked so normal and happy, and I prayed someday she would be like that again. I reached for the picture. I couldn't leave that image of innocence and joy in this disgusting den of evil.

"I'm sorry, ma'am, but you can't take that. It's evidence." I'd forgotten all about the policeman.

He was kindness personified as he led me from the trailer, my legs shaking as I stepped outside. It did my heart good to see Tom spread-eagled on the hood of the cops' cruiser, still protesting his innocence. The sight of him made my fists clench again, and his pathetic attempt to lie about his sick passions infuriated me beyond words.

Having finished his pat-down, the officer cuffed Tom, who stood and faced me as I walked up. The pervert actually had the nerve to glare at me as if he held me responsible for what he'd done!

My rage boiled over. How dare this sorry excuse for a man hurt my child? How dare he do what he'd done and then take pictures of it to gloat about it all later?

"Do you know what it's like, Tom? Any idea? Huh?" He didn't have a clue what I was talking about, I could see. "What's it like to be helpless and then have someone hurt you, huh, Tom?"

His smug little grin really got to me. With all my strength and all my rage, I kicked out, catching Tom squarely in the crotch. He fell to the ground groaning and clutching himself. I felt amazed how much satisfaction that gave me.

It was probably my imagination, but the two officers and the park ranger all seemed to withdraw from the scene a bit, rather than doing their jobs and protecting this perpetrator-suddenly-turned-victim. I got the distinct impression that what I'd done was no more than what they'd have liked to do if not constrained by their oaths, their badges, and the Constitution.

"How's it feel, Tom? How much fun is it to be the victim for a change?"

My foot lashed out again, catching him in the stomach. He curled around himself, trying to absorb the blow and the ensuing pain. Watching him vomit onto the ground, as his actions had caused me to do earlier, reminded me of the bad taste in my mouth he'd left behind. I spat into his face.

The officers apparently decided Tom had gotten my message,

because the park ranger told me that would be enough. Aware the crowd of other campers had drawn in closer, I decided as much as I would enjoy seeing Tom torn apart by an outraged mob, I didn't want to be the one who caused it. However, that didn't stop me from stepping on the side of his face as I went to join my daughter and my husband. It felt really good to hear him groaning in pain.

My rage spent, I began to feel guilty that revenge had been my first concern. As I made my way through the throng of other campers, I began to realize I was not alone in my outrage, though.

"Way to go, lady!"

"You shoulda finished him off!"

"He got what he deserved!" I passed them by without responding.

Thea lay on a stretcher by the ambulance, looking tiny and helpless and so still. My tears began again as I watched the EMTs working on her. Clutching Ian's arm, I prayed for her safety and her emotional health. No one knew yet what that animal had done to her.

Suddenly, she coughed and woke up. "Mommy?"

Her voice made my heart soar. No matter what had happened, as long as she lived, we could help her through it. I had eyes and ears only for my daughter as she was loaded into the ambulance, and I was guided in next to her. Ian would follow with our other two girls.

Now, two years later, we reflect on that terrifying experience and count our many blessings. An exam at the hospital revealed that Thea had not been raped. DNA evidence showed Tom had engaged in some sexual activity while she was with him, but he hadn't actually gotten as far as the act itself. We're forever grateful that no physical injury occurred.

A drug screen at the hospital indicated that she had been given a potent sedative. She remembers almost nothing about what happened inside Tom's trailer. In fact, her only memories of Tom are that he was a nice, friendly man who came in the night to play hide and seek with her, later giving her some hot chocolate. No doubt, the drink had been laced with the sedatives, and she fell sound asleep shortly after.

The other girls are doing fine. We explained what had happened in very sanitized terms that they could understand, and none of the girls seem troubled. It helps a lot that no one from our area was at the campground that night, so there wasn't a lot of gossip around town to get back to our girls.

Tom's spending a lot of time in solitary confinement for his own safety these days, from what the prosecutor has told us. It seems prisoners don't take kindly to child molesters. We can't think of a more fitting punishment for his numerous crimes. He'll be confined for years just for kidnapping Thea and abusing her. Some digging by the authorities using the evidence in his trailer as clues has revealed what a slime he really is, and tacked on so many years to his sentence, he will never see freedom again. Thankfully, he'll never be able to hurt any family again or use his charm to fool people into thinking he's a nice guy—when he's really a hideous monster.

Ian agrees with me now that not all campers are saints. We haven't given up camping by any means, but we did trade off the pop-up for a small trailer with hard sides. Realistically, we know the odds of anything so bizarre happening to our family ever again are remote. But the point of camping for us is to be able to relax and enjoy ourselves, and having something more substantial than canvas and screen around us while we sleep allows us that total relaxation.

We're all glad we could find a way to continue enjoying the hobby we all love so much. There's no way we could allow one bad experience, no matter how extreme, to stop us from building a lifetime of wonderful camping memories. Doing so would've allowed Tom far too much control over our lives. Once we allow that to happen, the creeps have won.

THE END

# My ex's threat:
# "$5,000 OR OUR KID DIES!"

"The open house went better than I expected, Nancy," I said as I squeezed the cell phone to my ear with my shoulder. Scooping up my business cards and brochures from the small table by the front door, I stuffed them into my tote. "The house is in such a desolate area, I thought no one would come to look at it."

"From what I see of the pictures, it's a beauty and worth every penny. I'd be happy to sell a house with half that price tag." Nancy sighed.

"Your turn will come. Keep up the hard work and listings will start pouring in. It worked for me. Two months after I joined the Boston Group, I sold my first house. I can hardly believe it's been three years. Caitlyn was just a baby. Now she's in kindergarten."

"I want to be you when I grow up," Nancy joked.

I laughed. Five years my senior, Nancy recently received her real estate license. Remembering how scary those first few months could be, I decided to take her under my wing. She often referred to me as her mentor—a title I never thought to hold but which pleased me immensely. It showed how far I'd come.

"I better go," I said. "I want to get out of here before it gets dark. It looks like a storm might be moving in." The daylight had dimmed considerably, bringing a heaviness to the air.

"Are you stopping back at the office?" Nancy asked.

"No. I need to pick Caitlyn up from the sitter."

"Right. I'll see you tomorrow then. Careful driving."

"Good night." I clicked the phone off then dropped it into my bag.

Now, let me think. I tapped my finger against my lips. Have I forgotten anything? Lights off, candles snuffed and packed in my bag, windows shut—windows! I forgot to close the upstairs bathroom window.

Fresh air was a definite plus when showing a house, weather permitting. Scented candles also helped to create a warm, homey feel. Paying attention to details is what helped me succeed in business and in my personal life.

Leaving my bag in the foyer, I climbed the carpeted stairs to the top floor. No question, the house had sale appeal with its spacious rooms, vaulted ceilings, and two fireplaces. On the second floor, four bedrooms plus the bath opened onto a long hallway.

I entered the third doorway on the right. Lace curtains billowed on the wind whistling through the screen. Even the bathroom offered an exquisite view of the lake cradled in the rolling valley below. No other houses dotted the hills for a five-mile radius.

The house and surrounding area took one's breath away, but it was too secluded for my tastes. I preferred my little cape surrounded by friendly neighbors.

A glance at the swirling clouds reminded me to be quick if I intended to get home dry. I reached up to shut the window when a soft tapping stopped me cold. Slowly, I turned, my heart pounding heavily in my chest.

"Hello, Doreen. It's been a long time."

"Paul!" The sight of the tall, lanky man filling the doorway sent a tremor sliding along my spine. The eyes I'd once fallen in love with looked tired and dull. His gaze couldn't seem to stay focused on one thing, but rather darted about the room.

The sour taste of fear filled my mouth but I resolved not to show it. "What do you want? How did you know I was here?" I asked him.

"Not the warm welcome I expected for your baby's father."

I gasped.

"Surprised? So was I when I heard you kept the kid. I told you to get an abortion. I even offered to take you."

"I couldn't." It came out in a whisper. I remembered the day I first told Paul I was pregnant. The anger and disgust in his eyes cut deep. He'd insisted, practically forced me to get an abortion. When I refused, he walked out of my life—out of his baby's life—without ever looking back until now.

"A daughter. Caitlyn, isn't it?" His gaze landed on me briefly before taking flight again.

"How did you know?" I clamped my mouth shut. I refused to talk about my daughter with Paul. He'd made his choice long ago. It hadn't been easy, but I'd gained my independence both financially and emotionally. If he thought he could stroll back into our lives now, then he was sorely mistaken.

"I have my ways." He smiled.

The slight upturn of his lips could barely be called a smile. His words chilled my blood. "What do you want? Why are you here?"

"Can't an old friend stop by and say hello?"

"We aren't friends. I haven't seen or heard from you since the day I told you I was pregnant. Now if you'll excuse me, I have to go." I attempted to brush past him but he pushed me back.

"That how you want it? You too good for me now with your fancy clothes, fancy job?" His finger reached out to flick my earring.

"No. That's not it." Moving backward, I felt the sharp edge of the sink press against my hip.

Paul stepped forward, closing the gap between us. "Maybe it's time Caitlyn learned who her daddy is."

I clenched my teeth. He wouldn't dare. I'd never told anyone the name of Caitlyn's biological father. My parents may have guessed, but after their initial reaction to the news of my pregnancy we never spoke of it.

Paul Dorney had been a troublemaker even in high school. Like many of the kids who ran in his crowd, he experimented with drugs and often drank too much. At seventeen, I thought his bad-boy reputation added to his mystique.

From the look of him now, he'd failed to grow up. He didn't deserve to be in Caitlyn's life. He'd never wanted her to begin with. I would do anything to protect my daughter.

Obviously, he tracked me down for a reason. The sooner I discovered why, the sooner he'd leave. "What do you want from me?" I asked him.

"Money," he stated flatly. "Something to help me out until I find a job."

"How much?" I'd give him everything in my wallet, about fifty dollars, to get rid of him. I didn't like to, but I could write a check if we needed groceries before I could get to the bank.

"Five thousand."

"What?" My voice took on a high pitch. "I don't have that kind of money."

"Don't play innocent. I've seen you selling these rich houses, driving a new car. You with your proper house with the white picket fence."

"How do you know where I live?"

"Don't you know?" He grinned. "I've been watching you, Doreen."

My stomach churned. I was going to be sick. I bolted to the side, hoping to slip past him and out the door.

He caught my wrist, yanking me back. "I could sue for custody, you know."

"No judge would ever award you custody." Could he see the fear in my eyes? I could explain how my house was a rental, my car three years old, but my gut told me it wouldn't make a difference. Anger ripped through me. "Why do you need so much money, Paul, to feed your habit?"

He twisted my wrist and slammed me into the wall, knocking the breath from my lungs. My back struck a metal towel bar. Pain exploded up my neck.

"That's not very nice, now is it?" he sneered. "A guy falls on hard times and you put him down? It won't take much to prove I'm

Caitlyn's father. At the very least, I'd win visitation rights once I tell them how you hid the pregnancy from me. Tell me, Doreen, does Caitlyn know about me?"

When I refused to answer, he continued.

"Get me the money or I promise you little Caitlyn will get to know her daddy real well."

"You're disgusting." I lunged at him, wanting to rip out his hair. The mere sound of my daughter's name on his lips made my skin crawl.

The stinging slap of his hand caught me by surprise, making my eyes tear.

"You've got one day to get the money. Breathe a word of this to anyone and I'll make sure you never see your precious daughter again." His gaze raked my body. "I'll be in touch." Then he was gone.

If not for my bruised back and cheek, I'd swear this day had all been a horrible nightmare. I wanted to crumple to the floor, sob out my hurt, but fear drove me forward.

I descended the stairs on trembling legs, searching for any sign that Paul might still be lurking in the shadows. The house stood quiet. Only the low rumble of thunder threatened the silence.

Grabbing my bag, I jerked open the front door, fumbled with the lock, then hurried to my car. Parked alone in the long driveway, I didn't resist the urge to peer into the backseat. Finding it empty except for Caitlyn's plush teddy bear didn't relax my nerves.

Neither did the long drive back to town. It only served to push forgotten memories to the front of my mind—memories of Paul when we first met.

We'd both been juniors in high school, but we had come from opposite ends of the spectrum. I was shy with a handful of close friends. He was gregarious and knew everyone. No one was more shocked than me when Paul asked me to the junior prom.

He was polite, attentive, and made me feel like the most popular girl in school. Suddenly, people I barely knew were saying hello to me in the hallways. We dated all that summer, hitting one party after another. At first, it was hard for me to be around so many people. But being with Paul was like wearing a badge of automatic acceptance.

Most of the kids drank and used drugs. Paul more than most. But he never pressured me. In fact, I'd always thought he was proud of the fact that I didn't join in. His using never bothered me until our senior year, when it became a daily habit.

I pestered him about it but that only made him mad. More and more he withdrew into himself. Afraid of losing him, I tried to accept his excuse that this was his last year to party before entering the real world. Only the real world intruded faster than either of us planned.

The day I learned the results of the home pregnancy test, Paul was supposed to meet me at the park. When he didn't show, I went to his house in a state of panic. His parents were out, so I let myself in. It didn't take long to discover why I'd been stood up. Paul lay passed out on the bed. His room reeked of alcohol.

Disgusted, my stomach queasy, I finally managed to rouse him.

"Hey, baby, come to party?" He looked at me through slitted eyes.

"Paul, we've got to talk. This is serious." I pushed his hands away.

He frowned. "You never want to have fun anymore."

"Paul, listen to me. I'm pregnant."

That got his attention. His eyes opened wide, then narrowed again. "What are you talking about? We use protection."

"Protection isn't foolproof. I took the test this morning. It's positive." I held back my tears. "What are we going to do?" I reached for his hand, needing his strength.

He pulled away. Bolting out of bed, he started pacing the floor. "What do you mean, 'What are we going to do?' You're getting an abortion." His voice was cold. "Set up an appointment. I'll take you."

I stared at him in horror. "No!"

"No?" He whirled on me. "If you think I'm going to let you ruin my life with a kid, think again."

"This is my baby, too. You can't force me—"

"Like hell I can't." He lunged for me, but I was quicker.

Running from his room, tears falling down my face, I heard him yell after me. "Get rid of that kid, Doreen, or you'll never see me again."

With only two months left until graduation, my parents insisted I finish school. The few times I saw Paul after that, he looked right through me as though I didn't exist. The fact that he didn't care about me or our baby was devastating. He started showing up to class drunk and high. Three weeks before graduation, the principal kicked him out of school.

I lost track of Paul after that. The day after I received my diploma, my parents sent me to live with my aunt in a neighboring state. I gave birth to my daughter, went to school at night to earn my real estate license, and have been working hard ever since.

It's been a struggle and not what I'd planned for my life, but one smile from Caitlyn and I know I wouldn't change a thing. I had a beautiful daughter, a comfortable home, and for the last year, the love of a man who treated me right. Life was good, until now.

I pulled the car to a stop in front of the sitter's house. Breathing deep, I willed myself to relax. No one could know what just happened. Somehow I had to get Paul the money. Keeping Caitlyn safe and away from him was all that mattered.

I climbed out of the car, assured myself the street was empty, then hurried to the door. The wind whipped at my hair. Thunder growled above me. I twisted the knob, pushing the door open.

"Doreen, dear, is that you? We're in the kitchen."

Mrs. Sherwood had been Caitlyn's sitter for almost two years. I couldn't have asked for a sweeter, kinder caregiver for my child. I loved her almost as much as Caitlyn did.

"Yes. Sorry I'm late." Shutting the door behind me, I frowned. In all the time I'd been coming here, Mrs. Sherwood never locked her door. What had once seemed so innocent and welcoming now took on a darker tone. How easy it would be for Paul to come in here, hurt Mrs. Sherwood, and steal Caitlyn away. I twisted the lock, suppressing a shudder.

"Mommy, Mommy, come see what I made." Caitlyn raced into the hallway, her face alight with a wide smile.

Tears stung my eyes at the sight of my daughter. Not wanting her to notice my lack of control, I knelt down, opening my arms. "Come give Mommy a hug, then we'll go see."

Squeezing her small body to me, I whispered, "Mommy loves you so much, baby."

"Doreen?"

Caitlyn wiggled away.

I glanced up to find Mrs. Sherwood watching me.

"Is anything wrong, dear?"

"No." I stood up. "Everything is fine."

Her gaze shifted to the locked door, then down at Caitlyn. "Why don't you bring Mommy the present you made for her?"

Excited, Caitlyn ran off.

Mrs. Sherwood didn't say anything, but I knew she was waiting for an explanation. Even though I trusted her, I couldn't tell her the truth.

"You're wondering why I locked the door. I didn't want to scare Caitlyn, but I've been hearing reports. There have been break-ins. Last week a little boy was kidnapped." That much was true, only now it seemed much more terrifying.

"It's a mother's job to worry." She patted my arm. "I should have started locking the doors long ago. Old habits and all. Rest your mind, Caitlyn is safe here."

"I know. I don't know what we'd do without you."

"Ah, you'll get an old woman crying."

"Mommy, this is for you." Caitlyn entered the hallway, carefully carrying a plate full of cookies. "Eat one."

"Mmm. Raisin-chocolate chip, my favorite."

"Made them all by herself, she did." Mrs. Sherwood beamed with pride.

"My little girl is growing up." I smiled. "Let's save the rest for dessert, honey. Get your things and give Mrs. Sherwood a hug. I want to get home before the storm gets any worse."

Clouds continued to hover in the sky on Monday morning. My eyes stung with weariness. Sleep had been long in coming. I laid awake most of the night, listening to the storm rage outside much like the inner one tearing me apart. Already I'd lied to Mrs. Sherwood and to Blake, my boyfriend.

He called early that morning to see how we made out in the storm and to invite us over for pizza at night. Claiming a headache, I told him I'd call him back when I felt better.

I also called Nancy and asked her to cover for me at work. I couldn't handle desk duty. Not until I worked out this problem with Paul.

I thought of calling my parents and asking them for a loan. The request would raise questions. Questions I couldn't answer, not without lying. If they thought I needed money, they would worry. No, it was best to leave them out of it.

The cup of coffee I'd poured earlier sat untouched before me. How had my life taken such a wrong turn? After high school, I'd done everything I could to stay on the right path, to make a happy life for Caitlyn. I didn't worry about my own happiness.

After years of being alone, I didn't think I'd ever find a man to love both my daughter and me. I knew Blake was special the moment we met in the library. Caitlyn was helping him find a cookbook.

She turned to me and said, "Mommy, he doesn't know how to cook. We better take him home and feed him."

My cheeks had turned scarlet. Blake had laughed and said it was the best offer he'd had all week, but since he didn't want to impose he invited us out to dinner with the promise of ice cream afterward.

Caitlyn accepted before I'd even had a chance to blink.

That had been almost a year ago. Blake not only proved to be a generous and loving man, but he'd even learned to cook. We'd become a happy little family.

And now Paul was threatening that happiness. I refused to let him get away with it. I'd give him what he wanted and tell him to never come near my family again.

An hour later, with Caitlyn in school, I drove across town to my bank. Close to three thousand dollars sat in my savings account. I withdrew all but ten dollars so I wouldn't have to close out the account. It was a large sum of money, all in cash. Paul would just have to be satisfied.

I spent the rest of the day looking over my shoulder and waiting for the phone to ring. When I still hadn't heard from Paul by six o'clock, I began to relax.

I stood in the kitchen trying to decide what to pull out of the freezer for dinner. Caitlyn lounged on the floor with a coloring book, her crayons spread out before her. The TV droned on like it did every normal Monday night.

Maybe the whole episode with Paul had been a dream. Or he could've changed his mind, come to his senses. Surely, even he had a conscience. It just took him longer to find it than most.

The doorbell buzzed, dashing my hopes into one jumbled pile of nerves on the floor.

"Doorbell, doorbell." Caitlyn sang, skipping into the kitchen, a purple crayon clutched in one hand.

"I'll get it, honey." My throat dried up, making it difficult to sound normal. "Go back and finish your coloring." I gently steered her back to the playroom.

The bell sounded again. I jumped, then tried to slow my racing pulse by breathing deep. Paul wouldn't dare come to the house for money, would he?

I hurried to the door, took a deep breath, then opened it a crack.

"Doreen, what took you so long. Pizza's getting cold. Are you going to let me in?"

Blake's voice broke through my fears. The relief of seeing him standing on the stoop instead of Paul, holding a pizza in one hand and a six-pack of soda in the other, left me breathless.

"I'm sorry. Come in. I . . . what are you doing here?" I took the pizza from him, leading the way into the kitchen.

"You said you weren't feeling well so I figured I'd save you from cooking." He set the pizza box on the kitchen table. "You are looking pale. Maybe you should be in bed." He leaned forward to give me a kiss just as the phone rang.

I jumped, causing my head to bump into his chin.

"I'm sorry." I backed away toward the phone.

"Pizza!" Caitlyn ran to the table. "Hi, Blake."

"Go ahead." Blake waved toward the phone. "I'll take care of Caitlyn. Hello, sweetheart." He turned away, rubbing his chin.

I grabbed the cordless from its cradle and carried it into the bathroom, closing the door. "Hello?"

"Is that the guy Caitlyn thinks is her father?"

"Paul," I hissed, clutching the phone tighter. "Stop spying on me or—"

"Or what? You'll go to the police? I don't think so, Doreen. Not if you care what happens to that little girl."

Biting my lip, I fought for control of my anger. "I didn't think you were going to call. I'd hoped you'd come to your senses."

He snorted. "You owe me. Don't be getting all high and mighty.

I've seen the goods. You're nothing special. Now, you got the money?"

I hesitated, wondering if I should tell him I didn't have all of it. "Yes, I have it."

"You better not play any tricks." He sounded suspicious. "Meet me in the parking lot of the drug store on Second Avenue. Come alone."

"When?"

"Now."

"But—"

"Now," he repeated. Then the line went dead.

Counting to ten, I tried to compose myself before returning to the kitchen.

"Everything okay?" Blake glanced up from the table. He'd helped Caitlyn to a slice and poured her a glass of soda in her favorite plastic cup.

"Fine. I'm just going to run to the store for aspirin. My headache's come back. Will you watch Caitlyn?"

"Of course. If you feel that bad, I can go for you." He started to rise.

"No!"

His eyes widened in surprise.

"I mean, I'm fine. I won't be long." Plucking my keys from the wall hook, I grabbed my purse with the money inside and rushed out the door before Blake could question me further.

I spotted Paul the second I pulled into the nearly empty parking lot. He was leaning against a telephone pole.

His gaze darted around. Seemingly satisfied, he walked toward me.

I got out of the car, leaving the door open as a barrier between us.

"Where is it? Where's the money?" He looked past me into the car.

"Paul, think about what you're doing."

"Is this a trick?" His hands were clenched at his side. "If you didn't bring it—"

"I have it." Reaching inside the car, I pulled the thick envelope from my purse and slowly brought it out. "But there's something I need to tell you."

He jerked the envelope from my hand, a wide grin splitting his face. Tearing into it, a dark scowl replaced the grin. "I told you five thousand. What are you trying to pull?"

"That's all I had."

"It's not enough." He pushed on the door, trapping me between it and the car. "I want more. Six thousand this time."

"I told you, I don't have any more." I gasped, trying to keep the pain from my voice.

"Get it!" The pressure eased from my legs as he backed off the door. He slipped the envelope inside his shirt, then reached into his back pocket, pulling out a photo. "Sure is a pretty kid. It'd be a shame if anything happened to her."

I grabbed the picture from his hand. My body began to shake as I stared at an image of Caitlyn and me playing in the park. This was taken weeks ago. How long had he been watching us? I looked up. Paul was gone.

The moment I walked into the house, Blake knew something wasn't right. Fear left me numb. I could barely walk, much less talk. I don't even remember driving back from town.

Somehow, with Blake's help, I got Caitlyn to bed. I kissed her good night, wishing her sweet dreams. Softly shutting her door, I felt the tears finally break through the barrier I'd erected.

Blake brought me into the kitchen and made me sit. He poured me a glass of soda and handed me a box of tissues. "I knew something was wrong when I found the full aspirin bottle on the counter," he said.

"I'm sorry I lied to you. Everything is falling apart. I'm so scared." I swiped at the dried tears tightening my cheeks.

"I'm here." Blake covered my hand with his. "You know I'd do anything for you, Doreen."

I told him about Paul—the Paul from my past and the Paul presently threatening my sanity and my child's life. To his credit, Blake listened quietly, interjecting a question every now and then. Anger pulled at his muscles and I loved him all the more for wanting to protect us.

"He wants six thousand dollars this time," I explained.

"You know it won't stop there. He'll keep coming back demanding more and more. We have to go to the police."

"The money doesn't matter. All that matters is keeping Caitlyn safe."

"You can trust a guy like this, especially if he's on drugs. I don't want to scare you, but there is no telling what he might do next. Give him the power and he'll ruin your life."

"I know you're trying to help, but you don't know for sure what Paul will do."

"My point exactly."

"I can't think any more tonight." I rubbed my weary eyes.

"Get some sleep. It's been a rough day. He won't try anything tonight. Not with the money you just gave him filling his pockets. We'll talk more tomorrow." Blake brought my hand to his lips and kissed it.

The next day, all I could think about was Paul, Caitlyn, and the

51

money I didn't have, yet needed, to protect her. The thought of going to the police frightened me. What if Paul found out before they could catch him? What if the police couldn't protect my daughter?

I wouldn't be able to forgive myself if anything happened to Caitlyn. Somehow, I had to find a way to get six thousand dollars. Blake was wrong. He had to be. If I gave Paul what he asked for, this nightmare would end.

I held onto that thought as I drove to the school to pick up Caitlyn. The other mothers were already pulling away with their children.

Was I late? I glanced at my watch. School let out eight minutes ago. Caitlyn should be standing right outside the door with her teacher. Mrs. DeLorenzo was there talking to another mother, but where was Caitlyn?

Panic clutched at my heart. Throwing the gearshift into park, I jumped out of the car. The SUV behind me blared its horn. Ignoring it, I hurried past a scattering of children toward Mrs. DeLorenzo.

All sorts of scenarios converged on my mind. Around me children laughed or hugged their mothers, who'd come to claim them. Where was my child? Had Paul taken her? Would I ever see her again? Hear her sweet voice?

I'd nearly reached Mrs. DeLorenzo, who still hadn't noticed me, when I turned my head and saw Caitlyn rounding the corner of the building.

Relief so strong propelled me toward my daughter. "Sweetheart, where have you been?" I scolded. "You frightened Mommy. You know you're to stay with the teacher until I come for you."

"But, Mommy, the man said he was your friend."

My heart froze. Reluctantly, my gaze drifted away from Caitlyn toward the corner of the school.

Paul leaned against the brick building, his lips twisted arrogantly, his gaze riveted to me as if to say, See, I can get to her wherever and whenever I like.

Feeling deflated, I understood what Blake had been trying to tell me. This was some kind of power trip for Paul. Somehow, he blamed me for the wrong turn his life had taken. My success only fueled his anger. And because I had his daughter, he figured I owed him. He needed the money, but he wanted to drag my life down to his level.

I turned my back to him, took Caitlyn by the hand, and led her toward the car. With my daughter safely buckled in I started the engine, resisting the urge to check if Paul still waited by the school.

"Mommy, how do you know that man?" Caitlyn's innocent eyes, so different from Paul's troubled ones, stared at me.

"I knew him a long time ago. We were friends once."

"You're not friends anymore?"

"Things change, honey. People change. He's not the same person I used to know." Or maybe he'd stayed the same and I was the one who changed.

"I'm glad you're not friends now. I don't like him."

"Why?" Alarm bells rang in my head. "Did he hurt you?"

"No. He gave me this." She held out a wrapped cherry lollipop.

I had to force myself not to snatch if from her hand. Paul wouldn't give her poisoned candy. He wanted her alive so he could continue to blackmail me. Still, relief eased the tension in my shoulders when she placed it on the seat between us.

"He said I was pretty and that maybe someday he'd take me for a ride in his new car. Do I have to go with him, Mommy?"

My knuckles showed white against the black steering wheel. "No, you're never to take rides with strangers, even if they say they know Mommy."

"I told him, but I think it made him mad. He said he'd see me soon. He smiled but his voice was mean."

I reached for my daughter's hand, giving it a light squeeze. "You did the right thing. He needs help, honey, and I'm going to see that he gets it. You don't have to worry about seeing him again."

Caitlyn sat quietly a moment, then her face brightened as her mind shifted gears with the ease only the young possessed. For the rest of the ride, she chattered on about school, the episode with Paul already forgotten.

Once we got home, I fixed Caitlyn a snack and settled her in the playroom with a tape of her favorite movie.

Seeing Paul at the school made my decision clear. First, I called Mrs. Sherwood and asked her if she would watch Caitlyn for a few hours. Then I called Nancy at work and without going into much detail, I explained the situation at home.

"Of course I'll cover for you, Doreen. However long you need. The couple you showed the house to on Sunday would like to see it again. They're in a rush. What should I tell them?"

"Can you take them out? It could be your first sale."

"I'd be delighted to, but if there is a sale it's yours."

"We can talk about it later. Thanks, Nancy. I mean that."

"You just take care of yourself and that precious daughter. I'll be waiting to hear from you."

I hung up the phone, checked on Caitlyn, then made my last call. "Blake?"

"Doreen, is everything okay? Did something happen today?"

"Yes and no. I'll explain later. I wanted to tell you I've decided to go to the police." My voice trembled despite my conviction that I was doing the right thing.

"I'll be right there. Wait for me. I don't want you going through this alone."

"I'll wait. Blake?"

"Yes?"

"I love you."

"I love you, too, Doreen. Everything is going to be okay."

It took some time, but in the end Blake was right. The police caught Paul buying drugs from a dealer in town. He admitted to the blackmailing even though it would've been hard for me to prove.

The police said after they arrested him he just broke down. Seems his behavior had been a desperate plea for help. Help, once he was straight, he admitted to wanting.

His parents hadn't been there for him for a long time. The only friends he had were drug dealers and users. He apologized to the police for what he'd done. That he never intended to hurt Caitlyn or me. He was jealous of our life and thought if he could claim a small part of it, he'd have a chance at happiness.

Blake and I talked for a long time. In the end, we decided not to press charges with the condition that Paul relinquish his parental rights and get help. He's in rehab now. I pray for his complete recovery and hope when he's released he can find happiness.

I don't know if I'll ever tell Caitlyn about what really happened or who her biological father is. That's a decision Blake and I will have to make in the future. For now, it's enough to see the love in her eyes for her new daddy.

THE END

Tragic Mystery
# WHO'S STEALING OUR BABIES?

Fear clutched my heart as I looked down at the pink blanket in my lap. I closed my eyes, and for a moment, scents of my baby daughter mingled with the sweet memory of the early morning. Where was she? Little had I known, when I'd dropped her off at the baby-sitter's house, that it would be the last time that I'd see my precious Samantha. I blinked to keep back the tears, but they streamed down my face. My baby had been abducted!

Sitting on the edge of the sofa in my living room, Detective Morgan pulled a notebook out of his pocket. "Since there's no blood or evidence of violence, we're operating on the assumption that your daughter's been kidnapped. We found her sock by the bed," he said. "They probably took her out through the back door."

The image of a stranger holding my baby flashed through my mind. Had Samantha cried out when they'd picked her up? And, how had they muffled the sounds?

"Why aren't you out looking for my baby?" I sobbed.

"Police cars are out patrolling the area, looking for leads. An abandoned car was seen a few blocks away, but we aren't sure if there's any connection." The officer leaned forward, bracing his arms on his knees. "How long has this woman been watching your little girl?"

I reached for a tissue. Guilt sliced through me. I'd hesitated about leaving my baby with her, but several of the other women at the hospital where I worked as a technician had left their children with the same baby-sitter.

"Since she was eight weeks old," I told him.

"The sitter swears that she left the baby for only a few minutes," Detective Sullivan said. "When she came back from getting the mail out front, the little girl had disappeared."

"I believe her," I said, trying to convince myself of the truth of my words. "She has been like a grandmother to Samantha."

"Your baby's abduction has already been put in the computer at NCIC—the National Crime Information Center," Detective Morgan told me, stepping out onto the front porch. "We'll get back to you as soon as we have anything to report."

Choking back the tears, I managed to thank them. Then, I closed the door. Still holding Samantha's blanket, I walked down the hall to her room. I looked over at the crib where she'd slept. There was her stuffed lamb, and her sweet little pajamas. But, where was my baby? I leaned against the wall and cried.

Who would do such a horrible thing? Who would kidnap a nine-month-old child? And, what were they doing with her? Desperately, I fought to keep the fears that Detective Morgan had raised from my thoughts—the fears that a child molester had kidnapped my baby. But, surely those monsters wouldn't have taken an infant? I prayed to God that Samantha wasn't in any danger.

I sat down in the chair where I'd rocked my baby to sleep every night. My husband, Austin, and I had waited so long for her. College sweethearts, we'd married right before our senior year. Living in student housing, with work and studying, we'd struggled to finish school.

I'd graduated and found a position in the hospital while Austin had gotten a job with a large computer company. After waiting so long, we were thrilled when we learned that a baby was on the way.

A part of me had longed to stay at home and take care of Samantha, but since we wanted to buy a house, I'd decided to go back to work. Yet, I'd cried when I'd missed seeing Samantha take her first step. A working mother, I'd been grateful that my baby-sitter had given my baby such loving care. I prayed to God that whomever had taken Samantha wouldn't hurt her—that God would protect her, and keep my baby safe.

As soon as Mrs. Conklin had reached me at the hospital that morning, I'd called the police, then tried frantically to reach Austin. However, his job often took him out of town. The highway patrol had found Austin, though, and had escorted him back to our town.

My husband found me sitting there in the rocking chair, sobbing hysterically.

"Barbara," he called out. I heard the front door slam and I stood up. Austin ran across the room and pulled me into his arms. "What happened? Who took Samantha?"

I buried my face in his shoulder, and his strong arms closed around me. "Hush," he soothed, pulling me closer. "Don't cry. I'm here now."

Tears were still pouring down my cheeks, but I managed to tell him what the detective had said. With Austin's arm around me, we walked down the hall to the kitchen. "But, other than that, they have no clues," I finished. "No idea of who took our Samantha."

"I'm going to call the chief of police," he said, reaching for the telephone. "I want to know what they're doing to find our baby."

I closed my eyes and prayed—prayed that the police knew more about that abandoned car. Or, that they could tell my husband that they knew something more about the kidnappers. I hoped that they had some piece of information that would help us to find Samantha.

"Yes," Austin said. "I'll talk to Detective Morgan."

The memory of the morning with Samantha was planted indelibly in my mind. Clad in her soft pajamas, and snuggled under the fluffy blanket, she'd given me a big smile when I'd peeked at her in the crib. She'd kicked her feet, wanting me to pick her up. I'd fed and dressed my baby, then I'd put the sweet little socks on her, just before we'd left.

"Yes," I heard my husband say. "We'll stay close by."

Austin laid the telephone back in its cradle. When he looked over at me, his eyes glazed with tears, and my heart shattered into a thousand pieces. I hurried over and put my arms around him.

"The police don't know much more than they did when they came out to the house—at least, that's what they tell me. But, they are sending someone out from the telephone company to put a tap on our phone," he told me. "That's so the officers can monitor our calls."

"If someone would just call and tell us where we can find Samantha—" I said.

"The police told me that they have no record of any other babies being taken from Mrs. Conklin's neighborhood. Yet, three other children have been snatched. recently—one on the west side of town, and another two on the north side—all young children."

"Four little ones?" I gasped, unable to believe the news. "Four children were taken from our town?"

"It seems that the eldest was only six years old."

Visions of children being taken from their beds and shuffled into a car, swept across my mind. Why were innocent babies being taken? And, what had happened to those children? Had the police found any evidence of violence, or did a mystery surround them—just like it did with Samantha's disappearance?

"What if she isn't? What if she's hurt, or—" I couldn't finish.

Austin slipped down into a chair and pulled me into his lap. "Don't, Barbara. I can't stand to see you cry," he whispered. "We'll get our baby back. I promise."

I leaned back and closed my eyes. If I could only believe that I'd see her again.

"Why did God let them take our little girl?" I cried. "How could He let this happen?"

"I don't know the answer to that question," he admitted. "But, I do know that we'll see our baby again."

When the telephone rang, I grabbed it, hoping that it brought news—a message of hope. "Hello," I said hesitantly.

"Barbara, it's Lauren," I heard my coworker and friend say. "I'm so sorry about your baby. All of us at here at the hospital are thinking about you."

I leaned against the wall, grateful for her friendship and support. "I appreciate that."

"And, Barbara, I'd be glad to answer the telephone. Once the news of your little one is out, I'm sure that you'll be swamped with calls. I'll stay at your place so you and your husband can meet with the police," she offered.

Tears filled my eyes. "That would be wonderful. And Lauren, tell everyone that I need their prayers."

"Why don't I come on over after work?" she offered. "I can be there by seven."

"Thanks," I told her. "I'll see you then."

Austin leaned over and brushed my lips with a kiss. "Lauren can be here in case we hear from the kidnappers." He opened the refrigerator door. "Are you hungry?"

"No, I don't want food. I just want my baby," I told him.

"You have to eat," he urged. "Why don't I go and pick up a pizza?"

"No. Don't leave me," I pleaded. "I'll fix something."

Like a robot, I took out the casserole from the night before, made a salad, and set the table, but I pushed my empty plate away.

"I can't think of food now. All I can think about is Samantha," I said.

"You've got to try, honey," he said, spooning some of the casserole onto my plate. "If you get sick, how can you take care of Samantha?"

I knew that I had to give in, but worry consumed me. "I can't," I told him. "How can I eat a bite when I don't know what's happened to our baby? I don't know what she's being fed—if anything."

Austin pushed away from the table and walked to the television. "Let's see what's on the six o'clock news."

"And, in the local news—" I gasped as a picture of Samantha flashed across the screen. "If anyone has seen this child or has any information at all, please call the police station," the reporter said.

While the news reporter continued to give the details of the kidnapping, I stared at the screen in disbelief. I caught my breath as the camera panned Mrs. Conklin's house, the neighborhood, and the alley.

"They're showing the whole world how the kidnappers got away with Samantha!" I cried.

Austin reached over, turned down the volume, then grabbed the phone. I strained to hear the reporter as I heard my husband punch in the number.

While we waited, I prayed that either Detective Morgan or Detective

Sullivan would answer. I hoped that they had good news. After all the publicity, someone must know something about the disappearance of our child.

"Hello? Have you learned anything new? Do you have a lead?" he asked. Then, after a long pause, Austin sighed. "You'll call us later?" he asked. "Thanks."

I reached over and tugged at my husband's sleeve. "I don't want to sit here and wait!" I told him. "I want to go over to Mrs. Conklin's house. Maybe she knows more about how the kidnappers got away with Samantha."

Austin reached for my hand and pulled me to my feet. "I was thinking the same thing." Lost in thought, the ringing of the bell startled me. Relieved, I let Lauren into the living room.

"Thanks for coming," I told her. Scribbling the number of our cell phone on a slip of paper, I handed it to my friend. "We're going over to the baby-sitter's house. Let us know right away if you get any calls."

A few minutes later, we turned the corner and got close to Mrs. Conklin's house. Just as on television, the entire police department seemed to be at the scene. Police units and uniformed officers with their notebooks and measuring tapes filled the driveway. The news team van was still parked near the alley when we arrived, but the reporters, along with the cameramen, were headed toward the front of the house.

"Here comes Detective Morgan," I told Austin.

"I thought I told you to wait at home," he scolded gently. There was compassion reflected in his eyes, though. "We're coordinating our efforts with the federal officers. Please, let us handle this!"

"It's hard to sit and do nothing," I told him. "Especially when we don't know where Samantha is, or if she's—"

Austin slipped his arm around my shoulder. "Don't," he whispered. "Don't say that. We have to have faith."

The detective nodded. "The tracks in the alley matched, and now we have a description of the car. From a check on the license, we've learned that it's a stolen vehicle."

"Where's Mrs. Conklin?" I asked. "She must be frightened to death."

"She's gone to stay with her daughter."

When the detective left, Austin looked at me. "I think that we should try to get closer to the back of the house. Maybe we can learn something more," he said.

"What can he do?" I asked. "Scold us again?"

As we cut through the neighbor's yard, I watched as Detective Morgan walked around the house. For a moment, I felt foolish for having thought that we could help in some way.

"I'm sure that they've questioned Mrs. Conklin, but I'd like to talk to her," I told Austin. "Let's go over to her daughter's place. She lives on the corner of Monroe and Pine."

As Austin turned in at the driveway, I prayed that our baby-sitter remembered more than she'd told the police. I hoped she had some information that we could use to find Samantha.

"Oh, Barbara," Mrs. Conklin cried, wringing her hands after we'd all sat down in her daughter's den. "I wasn't gone but a few minutes. When I came back, your precious baby had disappeared."

Although I'd cried for what seemed like forever, my heart ached for the grandmother who had cared for my baby so lovingly. Blinking back my tears, I reached over and took her hand.

"I know that you've always taken good care of her," I assured her.

"Years ago, I just locked my doors at night, but these days, I lock them in the daytime, too," she told me, tears running down her cheeks.

"You had no way of knowing that something like this would happen," I comforted her. "I've never worried about Samantha when she was with you."

"I remember seeing a car driving up and down the street, but I didn't think much about it. But, for the life of me, I can't figure out how they managed to get in," she went on, her voice trembling.

"They got in by jimmying the lock," Austin told her. "The police say that it looks like a professional job."

Startled, I looked over at my husband. "Professional kidnappers? Baby thieves?" How had he gotten that information? From the police? And, what else had they told him?

"We'd better get back to the house," I said, hoping to get away as quickly as possible. I wanted to question my husband about the information that he'd given Mrs. Conklin. "We need to be home, in case someone calls."

"So, how did you know all that?" I asked Austin as we drove toward home. "And, what else are you keeping from me?"

"I was trying to protect you," he said softly. "I didn't want to add to your worries."

I reached up and touched his hand. "I love you, too, but I want to know everything that's going on," I reminded him. "We're in this together."

The news that night began with the story of Samantha's abduction.

"The stolen car has been found, but its location has not been disclosed. A suspicious blue sedan was seen in the area earlier. The police are asking everyone to stay away, and to not interfere with the investigation," the reporter said.

"We do, however, know that the police are attempting to follow the kidnappers, but it's not clear how many were involved in the abduction, or where the baby girl has been taken. Of course, as always, we will update you as more information becomes available."

As the anchorman took over, Austin exploded. "Why weren't we notified? How can they tell all of that to a perfect stranger, and not let us know what's happening? We're her parents!"

The ringing of the telephone interrupted my husband's outburst. He grabbed the receiver.

From Austin's side of the conversation, I gathered that the caller was Detective Morgan. Apparently, he confirmed the information that we'd heard on television. I wondered what other news the detective had been holding back. We were annoyed that the police hadn't kept us informed.

"What if demands for ransom are made?" I asked Austin. "What will we do?"

"Maybe the bank will give us a loan," he answered. "I don't know how we'll get the money, but with God's help, we'll find a way."

Since returning home, Austin and I had remained in our bedroom. We walked into the living room, and Lauren handed me the notepad, listing the calls that had come in.

"They were mostly sympathizers," she told me. "However, one man claimed that he'd seen a baby fitting Samantha's description being carried into a car."

"My baby?" I questioned. "Where did that man say that he saw the car?"

"Out by the outlet center," she said, slipping on her jacket. "He described the person carrying her as a woman in jeans and a red jacket, with her hair in a long braid."

"Why would the kidnappers take Samantha to the outlet center?" I asked.

Lauren picked up her purse. "It could have been just a crank call," she speculated. "Anyway," she said, touching my hand, "let me know if I can do anything else to help."

After my friend had left, I went to the kitchen and put on a pot of coffee. "The call from that man might mean something," I told Austin.

"I'll call Detective Morgan," he said, picking up the telephone.

As I poured the coffee, I couldn't get Lauren's words out of mind. I paced back and forth for what seemed like hours. Had someone really seen my baby at the outlet center? Had someone really seen Samantha? And, was the woman with the braid the same one who'd taken my baby from Mrs. Conklin's house?

Finally, I undressed, pulled on my nightgown, and got into bed. I lay there, unable to sleep. Restless, I went to the window and looked out into the darkness. Eventually, Austin came into the room.

"All I can see is Samantha's little face this morning when I left her," I whispered.

"If you'd listened and stayed home with our baby like I'd asked you to, instead of leaving her for someone else to raise while you worked, this wouldn't have happened!" he accused.

Shocked, I looked over at Austin. Where in the world had those hurtful words come from? Why was he lashing out at me? He'd promised that we'd work together to find our baby. And, suddenly, he'd turned on me?

The tears that I'd fought so hard to hold back came coursing down my cheeks.

"If you'd been here instead of running off to some other town—" I threw back at him. "I told you I didn't need a big fancy house and a top-of-the-line car to drive. You're gone all the blessed time—chasing that almighty dollar!"

"You didn't complain about the new kitchen that we just put in, or the new car that you're driving. My money was good enough for you then!"

I fell across the bed and sobbed. I cried for the baby that some evil person had taken from me. And, I cried for the husband who had turned against me. I felt as though I'd been abandoned by God—and my husband.

Austin eased down on the bed, then moved closer and tried to slip his arms around me. "Barbara—" he began hesitantly.

I drew away from him. "How could you say those terrible things to me?" I cried. "How could you?"

"Would it help if I told you that I'm sorry? That I feel guilty about Samantha, too? That you're only saying the words that I know in my heart I would never let myself believe?" he asked.

I turned and brushed a lock of hair back out of his face. "I'm sorry, too. You work hard for the things that you give Samantha and me. I love you for that."

"I love you, too," he murmured. "I wouldn't hurt you for anything in the world." He brushed my lips with a kiss.

I closed my eyes as he caressed me. With an expert touch, my lover kissed and touched me in all the sensitive places before his mouth caught mine in a hot and demanding kiss.

Our lovemaking took me to ecstasy—to new heights of rapturous delight. Afterward, we lay together, holding each other, basking in our love, clinging to each other in our fear. Our lovemaking had brought us some measure of comfort—solace. Finally, we drifted off to sleep.

I awoke a few hours later, but Austin lay asleep beside me. Carefully, I slipped out of bed and went to the window. I longed to see my baby—to hold Samantha. I shrugged off the eerie feeling of impending danger, then went to the kitchen and put on a pot of coffee.

"Couldn't sleep, either?" Austin asked when he came in and sat down at the table.

As I poured two cups of the hot, black liquid, the telephone rang.

"Who can that be at this time of the morning?" I murmured as my husband reached for the phone.

"Hello," I heard him say. "Hi, Phil."

I recognized the caller as someone who worked with my husband. I wondered why he was calling. I took a sip of coffee and waited.

"Really? Okay. Thanks," he said.

Austin sat down at the table beside me. "You'll never believe this!" he said, excitement filling his voice. "Phil said that it might not be anything important, but he had to tell us. This morning, he was working outside of town, and he saw a car matching the description given by the police, parked beside the old Rawlings mansion."

I leaned across the table and touched Austin's hand. "Maybe that's the same car that the man saw at the outlet center! Could that be where they're holding Samantha?" I asked hopefully.

"Maybe," Austin cautioned. "But it's still a shot in the dark."

"It's the best—the only—lead we have," I told him, scooting my chair over closer to his. "Isn't the mansion about eight miles out in the country?"

"Yeah, about that," Austin told me. "As I remember, the last mile or so is a dirt road." He went to the sink and emptied his cup. Austin and I decided to go out to the Rawlings mansion. He didn't want me to go, but I insisted.

The location of the police stakeout was easy to find, once we were in the general area. There were four police cars, with a giant tarp stretched over some automobiles, along with representatives from the local radio and station.

As one of the officers approached the car, Austin rolled down the window. "Hey!" he called out.

"Sorry, people, but you'll have to turn around and go back," he told us.

"I guess we didn't realize where we needed to stop," Austin hedged.

I could tell that my husband aimed to get closer to that old mansion—one way or another.

"They're going to make us go back," I whispered.

"Maybe not," he said softly. "I hate not being honest with these guys, but there's no way that they'd let us get this close if they knew that we're the parents."

I watched as the officer walked away, and I hoped against hope that he'd stay occupied long enough for us to sneak past the checkpoint. I caught my breath when the officer turned, looked toward our car, and waved.

Austin nodded to the young officer, then turned toward me. "He's telling us to turn back." He reached over and covered my hand with his. "But, we're too close to finding Samantha."

I'd heard the law officers talking while we'd waited, and I watched as men with gas masks loaded boxes into a huge van.

"Look!" I said, pointing to the van. "They're planning something!"

As Austin backed down the narrow driveway, bits and pieces of the conversation filtered through the air:

"Negotiation attempts failing. . . . Tear gas. . . . Safety of the baby. Move in!"

I fought back the tears at the thought of the authorities entering the house with tear gas and guns. What would happen to my baby?

"They're going to storm the house with guns and tear gas!" I cried, unable to hold back the tears. "I know that Samantha's in there! What if she gets caught in the middle of all of this? What if they start shooting, and Samantha gets hurt?" I laid my head on Austin's shoulder. "We've got to try to get her out!"

"Let's go!" He turned off the headlights, then headed up the drive toward the mansion. After a short distance, he stopped and pressed the switch to open the trunk of the car. Slowly, he opened the door and stepped out.

"We may need that old blanket," he whispered.

Running ahead my husband, I reached in and grabbed the blanket. While Austin closed the trunk lid, I leaned against the car and looked down the road. The police were in front of us and it seemed to me that the media had moved their equipment closer.

From seemingly out of nowhere, a car came up the road, headed in our direction. Austin grabbed my hand. We decided to go the ditch near the fence across the road.

"I'm ready," I told Austin. "Let's go!"

He pulled me to my feet, slipped his arm around my waist, and stepped forward. "I'll hold the fence up while you crawl through."

While Austin placed his foot on the bottom part, I gingerly put one leg through and stepped out on the other side of the fence.

"It'll be faster if we just cut across the pasture," Austin whispered as he crawled through the fence.

We hurried across the grassy field. When we reached the property behind the mansion, Austin grabbed my hand.

"Maybe we can make it to the porch without being seen," he whispered. "Then, we'll figure out a way to get in the back door."

I looked out across the yard at the mansion and a thousand questions filled my thoughts. Was that where the kidnappers were holding my baby? And, what about the other children that had been abducted? Could that house be where they'd been held, also? I caught my breath and wondered how many innocent little children were being kept here.

The lights were on in the mansion. As we hid in the shadows, I hoped against hope that we'd be able to get inside. We stepped onto the back porch and Austin tried the door. It was locked.

"I didn't think that they'd leave it open for us," he muttered.

As he wrapped a portion of the blanket around his fist, I grabbed Austin's hand.

"Perhaps we should go out the same way we came in and find the sheriff," I suggested softly. "After all, Detective Morgan told us to stay at home."

He smashed a small glass pane on the door, then reached inside. "We're going on," he told me, turning the knob.

While Austin closed the door, I leaned against the wall. Smells of grease permeated the air and I wondered who had been cooking there.

"This must be the kitchen," I whispered.

"Yeah," he answered, in a hushed voice. "No telling how old this place is."

I waited a moment for my eyes to adjust to the darkness. But all I could think about was my baby. Where was she?

"Let's find the stairway," I told him. "I have a feeling that they have Samantha in a room upstairs."

In the near darkness, the moonlight poured through the window, and shadows played across the walls. I took a step, then caught my breath when a floorboard creaked. With my heart in my throat, I prayed that the kidnappers hadn't heard us.

"Look," I said, pointing across the room. "Could that be it?"

"Yes, that looks like the staircase," my husband answered.

With my husband's hand in mine, we cautiously moved across the room.

"Listen," I whispered as voices came from the upstairs room. Suddenly, a baby cried out. I reached for Austin's hand. "That's Samantha!" I said excitedly. "I'd know our baby's voice anywhere!"

"Let's go!" There was urgency in his voice.

When the door opened at the top of the stairs, Austin grabbed my arm and pulled me back against the wall. Trembling, I watched as a man emerged from the darkness with a flashlight. I leaned into my husband's shoulder.

Dear Lord, I prayed, please, don't let him see us.

"I'm going on up," Austin whispered. "We need whomever's out there waiting behind those trees, to come inside now. Go for help—and hurry!" he urged.

"What about you?" I asked. "You can't take on all of them by yourself."

"I'll try to find out how many are there," he told me. "Now go!"

Quietly, I made my way back down, hurrying as fast as I dared. When I reached the bottom step, I turned around. When I couldn't see my husband on the landing, I sagged against the wall. He'd gone on up the stairs. I knew that I had to hurry before something terrible happened to Austin.

I stepped down and the darkness folded in around me. My heart pounded against my ribs. I didn't dare attempt to cross the room. If I bumped into some furniture, they'd hear me and then, surely, they'd find Austin.

"Please, dear Lord," I whispered. "Please guide my footsteps."

Suddenly, it seemed as if an angel had taken my hand. I took a step and that time, the early morning light filtered in through the window. Cautiously, I moved across the room and to the back door.

I pushed the screen open and as I stepped out, a hand reached out and grabbed my arm. My heart pounded in my throat and I caught my breath as I looked into cold eyes. I'd never seen the man before. Could he be one of the kidnappers? I squeezed my eyes shut for a quick moment, fearing the worst.

"Oh!" I gasped.

"So, there you are!" he said.

As the guy turned, I glanced at the initials FBI written across the back of his jacket.

"I was just going—" I began.

"We found your car outside," the agent told me. "And, we've been watching, but you've managed to slip by. Don't you know that you're hurting—not helping—us to get your baby out?"

"We couldn't just stand by and watch! We had to do something!" I told him. "My husband's in there!"

"Quiet," Sheriff Keeler cautioned as he walked up. "I've got deputies watching their car in case they try to get away. Several men are posted at the side entrance."

I reached over and touched the sheriff's arm. "I'm glad you're here," I told him, inching closer. "And, I want to go back in with you. I know that my baby's in a room upstairs. I just hope that the kidnappers haven't found Austin yet."

"You'd best stay here," he informed me. "Out of trouble."

Tears threatened to spill from my eyes, but I blinked them back. "My baby's in there!" I pleaded. "I've got to see her."

"Let us do our work," the federal agent ordered. "I hope that they don't grab your husband before we make our move."

Sheriff Keeler turned, pulled the screen door open, and followed the FBI agent. I waited for a moment, hoping that they were far enough ahead so that they wouldn't hear me, then, I stepped inside. There was no way that I going to stay there while my family was in danger.

I hurried across the room and up the stairs as quickly as I dared. I wondered where Austin was hiding. Where was my baby?

I looked up at the window above the stairs and suddenly, a sense of peace passed over me. I knew, at that moment, that we would find my baby. And, I knew in my heart that she would be all right.

With renewed hope, I went upstairs. When I looked in the first bedroom, I saw a woman holding Samantha. The tears that I saw streaming down my baby's cheeks were almost more than I could stand. But, when she reached out for me, relief flooded my heart and soul. With a prayer of thanks on my lips, I ran forward.

From the corner of the room, Austin lunged toward the captor, and knocked her to her knees. I reached out for the baby—my little angel. I held Samantha close until her sobbing subsided.

"Hush," I whispered. "You're safe now. Mommy's got you."

The federal agent stepped into the room, pushing another man ahead of him.

"These creeps won't be bothering you—or anyone else—again," he promised.

"My deputies have rounded up all the gang," Sheriff Keeler added. "They're ready to confess everything."

Austin rushed to me, gathering Samantha and me in his arms.

"Thank God, you're safe," he whispered as he gently kissed our baby's cheek.

The sheriff pointed at the kidnappers. "They're going to go away for a very long time," he vowed.

I turned as I heard loud cries coming from the side room. When the federal agent opened the door, I gasped. Lying in the beds were babies and toddlers.

"Dear Lord," I breathed. "The missing children!" Holding Samantha, I rushed toward the bedroom. "How could they do this to these precious babies?"

The agent stepped in front of the door. "This is our job, ma'am. You'd better let us take care of this."

Austin moved closer, then took Samantha out of my arms. He slipped his arm around my shoulder. "Let's go home."

When Detective Morgan asked Austin and me to come down to police headquarters, he explained that the kidnappers were a part of a gang who had been involved in trafficking children. He went on to report that the authorities had traced their operation and found it to be spread throughout the heartland of the country.

Many nights, I awake from a terrible dream. In the dream, I envision a room filled with toddlers and babies—all waiting to be sold. My heart breaks for all of the grieving parents who, unlike Austin and me, have searched for months—and, maybe years—and who have never found their children.

For days, I just sat, holding my baby. I reveled in rocking and singing to Samantha, and giving her a bottle—just loving her. When I called the hospital, they were understanding, and my supervisor agreed that I could have an indefinite leave of absence. More than anything, I wanted to stay home with Samantha.

I thank God every day for the angel that God sent to show me the way—the way to Samantha. And, I thank Him for helping me to realize that our children are our blessings, our gifts from God—gifts to be cherished.

THE END

# "I'M PROTECTING
A KILLER'S BABY"

## My husband and I want to raise her as our own—
but what's the right thing to do?

Hunching my shoulders against the late afternoon wind, I made my way down the snow-covered path. If I'm lucky, I'll only fall and sprain something. At worst, I'll get mugged.

When my husband quit his well-paying job to start his own business, he didn't bother to ask me if I'd mind being poor for a while. The way things were going—

Poor was looking like forever.

A week ago, Gary sold my car to save money. Today he didn't call to say he couldn't drive me to work, which was why I was cutting through the park to get to my job at the hotel.

As I came to a grove of trees, a woman ran, stumbling toward me, glancing over her shoulder. I stepped out of her way, but she kept coming at me. She was carrying a bundle. Not a bundle, a baby. What is the matter with her? One patch of ice and she and the baby will go flying. The woman stopped inches from me. Her face twisted in panic.

"Calm down," I said, trying not to catch her fear. "It's all right. I'll help you."

Her eyes brimmed with tears. Suddenly, she shoved the child into my arms. Relief flooded her face. She stared into my eyes as if she wanted to speak, but couldn't. Her meaning was clear: Take care of my baby.

Without thinking, I nodded.

Kissing her fingertips, the woman touched her baby's forehead. The child screwed up its face to cry. Terror returned to the woman's eyes. She must be afraid that someone will hear the baby crying. I cradled the child against me, making soothing sounds.

Some distance away, I saw a man running toward us. "He's coming."

The woman fled through the trees. Comforting the fussy child, I pushed into the center of a circle of evergreen bushes.

The man sped past me. He shouted, "I'll kill you! You hear me? You're dead the minute I lay my hands on you!"

My heart pounded so loudly that I wondered why the man didn't hear it. Gulping in deep breaths of cold air, I forced myself to be calm. The baby looked like a girl, maybe eight or nine months old.

She sniffled softly. What have I gotten myself into? But I didn't have time to think. First, I had to help the woman. Cradling the baby in one arm, I searched my tote bag for my cell phone. Had I left it at the apartment? Had Gary hidden it because I was using too many minutes?

Another woman came jogging by. Brushing through the thick branches, I stepped into the path. "Can you help me? I can't find my cell phone and I have to report an emergency. A man is threatening a woman."

The woman ran in place. "I saw them." She unclipped her phone from her belt and handed it me.

When the emergency operator answered, I said, "I'm in Macarthur Park near the lagoon." My hand shook. "A woman—she was frightened, panicked—a man was chasing her. He said he'd kill her. They went toward the tennis courts. Can you send someone?"

"I'm dispatching a police unit now. Stay on the line."

The baby squirmed. "No, I can't! I'll call back later."

"Wait!" the operator insisted. "Did the man have a weapon—a gun, a knife?"

"He went by so fast, I didn't see. I have to go." I hit End and handed the phone back to the woman. "Thanks."

She nodded and jogged on.

For a minute, I stood in the middle of the path, unable to think. Finally, my mind cleared. The mother had asked me to take care of her baby, and I'd agreed. Distant sirens grew louder. I hoisted the baby to my shoulder. Poor kid, she's got a right to be upset with a father like that. Watching my step, I walked toward the tennis courts. From a block away, I could see people gathering as police cars with flashing lights surrounded the area. An ambulance screamed to a stop. As I came closer, I saw paramedics load a body into the ambulance. The vehicle flew past me headed toward the hospital.

Panic gripped me. He killed her? If she was dead, the ambulance wouldn't be moving that fast. I looked at the baby, who'd buried her face against my neck. Now what do I do, turn the baby over to the police? I shook my head. I promised the woman that I'd take care of her child.

I headed back to our apartment. Obviously, I wasn't going to work. What would I tell Gary? When I got home, his car wasn't parked outside. By the time I unlocked the door, the child was sobbing quietly. Nothing I said or did would make her stop. She wasn't wet. Naptime? No, more like dinnertime. How do mothers manage? Holding her in one arm, which was getting tired, I rummaged in the refrigerator. Using one hand to spread jelly on bread is nearly impossible while a baby wiggles in the other arm. She wouldn't let me feed her but insisted on stuffing bits of bread into her mouth with both hands. She did let me give her sips of milk.

After I called the hotel, I flipped on the radio to the all-news station. While I spoon-fed the baby applesauce, the newsman said, "An unidentified man was found near the tennis courts in Macarthur Park, stabbed in the chest. He died on the way to the hospital. The police are looking for a woman who called 911 about the incident. They ask that the caller contact them immediately."

I felt cold all over. She killed him. Now I have to call the police. I looked down at the little darling eagerly waiting for another spoonful. She grinned, flashing two gleaming bottom teeth. If I called the police, they'd want me to describe her mother so they could arrest her.

As I wiped food off the baby's face, Gary burst into the kitchen.

"Geez, Audrey, you could have walked to work. Now you're going to be late." He did a double take. "What is that?"

"What does it look like?" I said, searching my mind for the right words.

"You're babysitting? Are you crazy? Unless you're getting paid a ton of money, you can't afford to miss work."

Since I'd heard the news report, I was trying frantically to invent some cover story so that I could keep the baby until I could reconnect with her mother. Suddenly, I knew that I couldn't go behind Gary's back, not after he did the same thing to me by springing his new business on me as a done deal. Our marriage was in enough trouble without heaping on more dishonesty. Unfortunately, if I told Gary the truth, he'd insist I call the police.

"I need to talk to you."

"After I make some client calls." Instead of hurrying off like he usually did, Gary leaned over the baby. She flashed him a grin so sweet it would melt cement. "Hello, sweetie," he cooed. "She is so cute. A girl, right?"

I nodded.

"What's her name?"

I took a ragged breath. "I don't know."

He did another double take. "What do you mean, you don't know?"

"Gary, we need to talk. Right now." I was about to find out how shaky our relationship really was.

He pulled a chair up beside me. "What's going on?"

The baby reached toward him. He made a goofy face as he covered her hand in his. If he'd paid this much attention to me lately, I wouldn't be thinking about leaving him.

I shifted her weight. "Would you like to hold her?"

Gary is a high-energy person. When I first met him, I was

attracted to his enthusiasm. Sometimes, he bordered on hyperactive. But as he reached to take her from me, every bit of tension drained out of him. Folding her into his arms, I swear he purred.

"This afternoon, I cut through the park on my way to work." He was so wrapped up in making faces at the baby that I wasn't sure if he was listening. "A woman ran up to me and dropped this baby into my arms." That got his attention. I told him the rest. "The radio said a man was stabbed to death near the tennis courts. If she killed him, it was self-defense."

"The police are coming here to pick up the baby?"

"I didn't tell them about the baby."

He frowned. "But you will."

I grabbed his arm. "They'll turn her over to Child Protective Services. The mother has enough problems without having to deal with that misguided bureaucracy." For years, the news has reported horror stories of what happened to some of the children in their care.

He let out his breath. "Audrey, sooner or later, the police will find the mother."

"When they do, I'll come forward and tell them what I saw. Then I can return the baby to her or to her family."

"The cops will want to know why you didn't tell them right away."

"I'm not shielding the mother. I don't know where she went or who she is or even what really happened. She gave me her baby because she was afraid that the man would hurt her child. I promised I'd protect the baby. And I'm going to."

He shook his head. "How are you going to take care of this kid? You have to work. If you lose your job, we lose our health insurance."

I started to lash out that if he hadn't quit his job, we'd have even better insurance. But I bit back my words. "I work three evenings a week, four to four, so a lot of the time you're at home when I'm out."

His mouth dropped open. "You expect me to take care of her?"

I could feel the ice cracking under my feet, but I kept plodding on. "You seem to like her."

"Watch her every minute? Feed her?" He made a face. "Change her diapers? I have a weak stomach."

"Never mind, I'll find someone else."

He put up his hand. "The kid sleeps a lot, right?"

Mentally, I crossed my fingers. "I can come home on my dinner break."

Gary looked like he was seriously considering it. He loves a challenge and believes he can do anything he sets his mind to. "What if the guy she killed is a drug dealer? Or worse?"

"He's dead."

"He's got friends."

I squared my shoulders. "I will not call the police. If you want to hand her over to Child Services and let her disappear into that uncaring bureaucracy which may never reunite her with her loving mother, that's up to you."

Gary looked at the baby, who was trying to pull his thumb into her mouth. He rubbed her chin. "This isn't right."

"It wasn't right for you to quit your job and start your own business without telling me. It changed our lives drastically, but I've gone along with it."

"That didn't involve murder."

"Self-defense," I snarled. "Besides, quitting your job was permanent. This is only temporary."

"Okay, that was my decision and I guess this is yours. Does that make us even?"

I wanted to shout: No, it does not make us even. Reluctantly, I nodded.

"We have to try to find her mother." Gary was taking charge again, leaving me out. I let him only because he's better at planning than I an.

Gary shifted the baby on his lap and she snuggled against him. "We'll go to where you met the mother in the park. Same time of day, maybe leave her a note. We can use what's reported in the news as an excuse to ask a few questions around the neighborhood."

"That sounds good."

"There has to be a time limit. If we can't find the mother after, say, a week, we call the police."

"Two weeks."

"Split the difference."

I nodded. That was the longest conversation we'd had about anything important since he started his own business six months ago. If Gary talked to me like this about everything else, I wouldn't be so angry with him.

We brainstormed a cover story that my cousin had gone into the hospital for tests and the doctor was keeping her for observation. Then we bundled up the baby—we called her Angela since she was such an angel—and took her to the Salvation Army thrift store. There we bought clothes and a combination car seat, carrier, and stroller, along with bedding and a walker. Next stop was the grocery for food, bottles, and diapers. At home, Gary rearranged the bedroom furniture to make her a bed on the floor that she couldn't get out of.

The next day was Saturday. Gary and I spent more time together than we had in forever. Angela could pull herself up and sidestep around the coffee table. She crawled almost as fast as I walked. She also popped everything within reach into her mouth. By the time she took a nap, Gary was so far behind with his paperwork that he let me help. He was surprised that, with a little instruction, I could handle the orders almost as well as he did. That evening, I went to my job as the hotel's night cashier. I called home as often as I could and drove home on my dinner break. Gary was a little frazzled, but he managed. I got Angela to sleep before I went back to work.

News reports didn't mention a missing baby, only that the police were looking for a dark haired woman—possibly foreign—as a suspect. Maybe that was why the mother hadn't said anything to me. The man was still unidentified. The woman whose cell phone I borrowed had described me to the police. That made Gary nervous, but he kept his word about not calling.

Sunday afternoon, we took Angela to the park at the same time I'd met Angela's mother. Gary had taken the baby's picture with his digital camera and printed several copies. I wrote a note on the back of a picture and put it in a plastic bag. Gary tacked it to a tree.

On Monday after shopping for the baby and eating lunch out, we went back to the park. Gary seemed to be avoiding the grove of trees.

"It's not time yet," he said, jostling Angela on his hip.

"You don't want to give her up, do you?"

He shrugged.

"Even after last night?"

Gary looked indignant. "She had a bad dream. The poor kid's been through so much. I think she's being really good, considering."

Last night Angela woke up crying just when we were about to make love, which we hadn't done for I don't remember how long. When we got her calmed down, she wanted to play and, of course, Gary obliged. Then I had quite a time getting her back to sleep. Naturally, she was awake bright and early.

He shifted her to his other arm, making her giggle over his silly faces.

"Put up her picture," I said. "Then we can play with her."

Gary handed me the baby. She made gurgling sounds. Some of her gibberish sounded like 'mama' though Gary had been trying to get her to say 'dada'.

He took out a small hammer. "Considering we've had no practice, we make pretty good parents."

"We're not her parents," I reminded him. "We're just babysitting."

"But we would be good parents, don't you think, Audrey?"

Was Gary hinting at having a baby? Over the past three days, we'd talked and shared more than we have since our wedding. However, we were nowhere near being ready for that big a step.

"Hello," a deep voice said.

I jumped. A young man, dressed in a heavy overcoat, stood next to me.

"Cute baby. How old is she?" Angela was busy pulling off her mittens.

I wanted desperately to run, but what if he knew who Angela was? "Eight months."

I grabbed for the plastic bag on the tree, but he beat me to it. "That's mine," I insisted.

"It just became evidence." The man pulled out a policeman's badge. His ID said he was Sergeant Rick Pinella.

"I suppose hammering a tack into a tree is illegal?" Gary snapped.

The policeman shrugged. "Probably not, but I work homicide. We're investigating a murder that happened near here last Friday. Someone called 911 to report a man chasing a woman through the park."

I clutched Angela tighter. "It sounds like the man was threatening the woman. If she killed him, it must have been self-defense."

"We won't know until we find her. The 911 call is on tape. They do amazing things with voice matching these days. If it turns out that you're the woman who called, we can charge you with obstruction."

I glared at him.

He looked at the baby. "Hello, Tiffany."

At the name, Angela looked around. "Tiffany," he said again. "Is that your name? Are you Tiffany?"

Angela pointed at the policeman. "Do you know who this baby is?" I asked, trembling.

"The deceased was her father, Phillip Paulson. But you'd know that if you were in on the kidnapping."

"Kidnapping?" Gary asked. "The baby was kidnapped?"

Officer Pinella narrowed his eyes. "Why don't you tell me your version of how you came to have this baby?"

I sighed deeply. Gary tried to stop me, but I told the man every detail from my arriving in the park on Friday until I took Angela to my apartment.

"If all this is true," the policeman said, "why didn't you tell the police about the baby?"

"Her mother wanted me to take care of her. You would've turned Angela—I mean Tiffany—over to Child Protective Services. The mother had enough problems without having to deal with them."

"Except the woman who gave you this baby isn't her mother."

My mouth fell open. "She has to be." But Angela didn't look anything like the woman.

Officer Pinella said, "The woman you met was the nanny. The California police believe she helped the father steal the baby. Either he paid her or he threatened to turn her over to Immigration. She has a green card, but she barely speaks English. She may have run away with the baby when she figured out how much trouble she was in."

"Or when she discovered how violent he was. There was nothing on the news or in the papers about a baby. If I knew she was kidnapped, I would've brought her in immediately."

"We learned the whole story this morning after we got a fingerprint match on the deceased. We sent out the information, but maybe you missed it. One of your neighbors called to say you'd suddenly acquired a baby and that sometimes you cut through the park on your way to work. Tiffany's mother flew in this morning. Her name's Maggie Lester. She's at the station now identifying her ex-husband's body."

"Take me to her," I insisted. "She must be frantic."

"That's an understatement," he said.

When we walked into the police station, a woman ran up to me. She screamed, "You stole my baby!"

I clutched Angela closer. Gary put his arm around my shoulder.

The woman stopped in front from me. "I'll have you in prison for the rest of your life!"

She didn't even look at her baby. Angela buried her face against my neck, holding on for dear life. "This is not helping Angela—I mean Tiffany." My heart beat so fast that I could barely get the words out. "Please, calm down. You're upsetting her."

"What do you care?" the woman cried. "You kidnapped her."

Officer Pinella took the woman's arm. "Let's go into an interrogation room and sort this out."

Maggie looked confused. "I want my child."

He glared at her. "Now." He pointed for Gary and me to follow. Inside the small windowless room, Pinella motioned us all to sit down. "You two tell Ms. Lester what you told me."

I repeated the details, and Gary added how we'd taken care of Angela the past three days.

She jumped to her feet. "Are you're stupid enough to believe this pack of lies?" she raged at Officer Pinella.

He glared at her. "I know the story sounds odd, but I believe her. You should, too."

The woman seemed to crumple. "You took care of my baby?"

I nodded, puzzled that she hadn't once reached for her child. Tiffany refused to look at her mother. I coaxed the baby's chin up to look at me. "She acts like she doesn't know you."

Maggie looked frightened. "She hasn't seen me in three weeks. She's forgotten."

"She remembers her name." I turned to Tiffany. "Honey, everything's all right. Your mommy is upset. She missed you so much. Do you want to go to mommy?"

The child didn't seem to know what I was talking about. I started to put her in the woman's arms, but Tiffany pulled back. I glanced at Officer Pinella. "You have proof this woman is her mother?"

He nodded. "Pictures, birth certificate, a police report."

The woman started crying so hard she slumped against the wall. I put my arm around her shoulder. Tiffany reached her hand toward her mother as if trying to comfort her. She looked at her baby but didn't touch her.

"Could we be alone for a minute?" I said to Officer Pinella. He shook his head slowly but moved to the far side of the room. I turned back to Maggie. "Take your baby's hand."

Cautiously, she twined her fingers around Tiffany's.

"Smile at her," I suggested. "She's frightened and confused."

A shuddering sob escaped the woman. "I can't."

"You have to. She's your daughter."

Maggie straightened her shoulders and forced a smile. Tiffany offered a shy grin in return. The baby wiggled her hand free and reached for her mother's face. Maggie started to pull back, then made herself relax. She let her daughter put her hand in her mouth. Maggie kissed the baby's fingers. Tiffany studied her, puzzled.

"I'm a terrible mother."

"This baby is very well cared for," I said, shifting Tiffany higher so she could put both hands on her mother's face.

"By Rosa," Maggie said. "Her nanny." Near tears again, she added, "Tiffany loves Rosa. My baby doesn't know who I am."

She closed her eyes for a moment. Tiffany found her mother's earring and was pulling on it. Maggie gently took her child's hand and rubbed it against her cheek. Tiffany smiled at her, showing all her teeth. Maggie smiled back, and this time it was genuine.

"I left my husband when I found out I was pregnant," she whispered. "I didn't want her."

"You could have gotten rid of her. You didn't."

"I got as far as the door of the abortion clinic, but I couldn't go through with it. I couldn't give her up for adoption because Phil would've demanded custody. He's so vicious. I couldn't let him have her."

I nodded. "So you let the nanny take care of your daughter. Rosa did an excellent job. Tiffany is happy, sociable, and well behaved. She's been loved."

Maggie began sobbing again. "But not by me."

I patted her hand. "You wouldn't be this upset if you didn't love her."

She pulled herself up straight. "I didn't care about her before. I mean, I hardly know her." She stroked Tiffany's cheek.

"Let's sit down."

Gently, I placed Tiffany on her mother's lap. Maggie put her arms around her baby, rocking her a little. Tiffany reached for me. I held her hands.

"She'd rather be with you," Maggie sniffed.

"She belongs with you. You'll be a good mother now."

Maggie's lip quivered. "I kept myself busy; my career, the house, anything so I wouldn't have to be with her. I always saw Tiffany as a part of my ex-husband."

"She's part of you, too. Mainly, she's just herself."

Maggie started to cry again. Tiffany snuggled against her as if trying to give her a hug. Maggie took a deep, relaxing breath. "After he took her, I began to realize what I'd lost. I'd see her a few minutes, maybe an hour a day. But those were the only truly happy minutes I had. I missed her so much. I know that sounds selfish. Well, I guess I am selfish."

"It sounds like a loving mother," I said.

Officer Pinella had a few more questions before he let us leave. He offered to drive us home, but Gary wanted to walk.

Coming down the steps of the police station, Gary said, "You were terrific with Maggie."

I smiled. "Thanks. I know I shouldn't, but I miss the baby already."

He put his arm around my shoulder. "I love you, Audrey."

A week ago, those words would have astounded me. "I love you, too."

"All the things we've been fighting about, I mean sort of fighting and sort of not talking about. . . ."

"We need to talk about all of them."

"I'm going to give up my business. See if I can get my old job back."

I cocked my head at him. "Wait a minute. We said we'd talk about this."

"You never wanted me to go out on my own. I just did it. I wasn't fair to you."

I put my hand on his chest. I'd waited months to hear these words from my husband. Instead of bringing me satisfaction, they raised new questions. "Why did you want to have your own business?"

"It doesn't matter."

"Yes, it does. Tell me."

He started walking again. "Because I wanted to be my own boss, to use my imagination and talents. I know you haven't seen the results yet, but I've earned some pretty good commissions. I just have to wait until the customers take delivery and pay."

"You love the work you're doing, don't you?"

"Not if it makes you unhappy."

Ever since I met him, Gary told me he wanted to be self-employed. Every time he brought it up, I'd say I couldn't live without a steady paycheck coming in and he'd drop the subject.

"I need to know more about what this business entails. What the consequences will be." It was hard to admit that I was wrong, too. "I didn't listen before."

He grinned with excitement. "Not only will I tell you, I'll show you. We can work together. You're good at all the things I don't like to do; writing up orders, follow-up, billing, and filing."

"Then neither of us would have a steady job."

His face puckered into a frown. "Mmmm. And we couldn't have a baby." Gary was going overboard talking about important things, but that's what I'd asked for. "We could put some money aside," he went on. "When the baby comes, you can stay home and run the office."

"Gary—"

"I know; I'm making all the plans again."

"At least you're discussing them with me first."

A baby, working with Gary, running our own business—it was a lot to take in. But the experiences of the past few days made me realize that what was important weren't money or even security. It was sharing life with the man I love.

The police never found Tiffany's nanny. She probably returned to her native country. I talked to Maggie often over the next few months. In June, Gary and I went to California to visit them. Tiffany is happy and Maggie is a devoted, if overindulgent, mother. Gary and I have started our business. We save a little from every commission check. We're planning to buy a house and, in a couple of years, to have a baby.

THE END

# SWITCHED AT BIRTH
## I want my real baby back

For a moment, I thought I was home in my own bed, trying to wake up in time to get breakfast for Darryl before he went to work. Then, as I became more fully awake, I remembered I was at St. Francis. Last night I'd had my baby—a little girl. A sigh of happiness breathed through me.

"More medicine?" I murmured drowsily to the nurse who was shaking me.

She shook her head, and I'd noticed that there was a funny look on her face. "No, Mrs. Desidario. We're going to take you for a little ride." Suddenly, blankets were swept around me, and I was lifted onto a stretcher. Puzzled and startled, but still groggy, I'd grasped the stretcher with both hands as it was whirled through the door. It was dark, not yet morning. What was going on?

Then, as I was rushed down the hall, I smelled a great, choking wave of smoke, and I knew what was happening.

"Fire!" I gasped, trying to sit up. "The hospital is on fire! My baby—bring my baby to me! The orderlies who were pushing my stretcher didn't answer.

All around me, I heard the sound of running feet, voices calling, and the wailing of new babies. And the smoke—that black, awful smoke! I struggled against the blankets, but they held me as tightly as a straitjacket. Suddenly, a door was pushed open and clean, cool air hit my face. The stretcher bounced down a ramp and into the yard. The orderlies left me there, under some trees, a long way from the building. I couldn't see any fire yet—only that pitch darkness—but I knew that other stretchers were around me and that there were nurses, running back and forth. More cries and moans joined mine.

I didn't cry out after the first few seconds. I just stared at that dark building where death lurked, and I prayed. Once, two years before, I'd lost a daughter—my Daria Rose had died when she was only six weeks old. Only a woman who had lost a child could have understood how I'd longed for another baby.

Then, the night before, my second daughter had been born. I'd had a hard time, and my memories of the experience were jumbled, but I remembered Dr. Christiansen telling me that my baby was a girl. I'd begged to see her, and he'd said something about waiting until she'd been cleaned up. Then darkness had fallen over me again. But, I'd heard her lusty cries even as I'd drifted off to sleep.

80

Later, Darryl had bent over me and whispered happily that we'd had a girl.

"Did you see her?" I murmured.

He'd laughed. "Not much of her, Laurie. The nurse whisked right by me into the nursery. But, she was really yelling. Our little angel sure has a good pair of lungs!"

I'd giggled a little at that, and gone back to sleep. And, suddenly, I had awakened to a nightmare! With horror, I saw the flicker of fire at a window. Was it the nursery window?

"My baby!" I screamed again.

As if in answer to my cry, a nurse, scrambling between the lined-up stretchers, dropped a cocoonlike bundle into my arms. Then she ran off, but my panic ebbed. I struggled to raise myself on one elbow, and unwrapped the baby's blanket. I had to know if she was all right. In the blazing searchlight of the fire truck, parked nearby, I looked down at her for the first time.

Of course, all new babies looked somewhat alike, but when I'd looked at her sweet face, she'd reminded me so much of the baby that I'd lost—my precious Daria Rose.

I was oblivious to everything—just holding her—when a nurse had come up and taken her from my arms. "You're being sent to another hospital," she said briskly. "The babies are going in another ambulance." She looked down at me and smiled kindly. "You'll see your baby in the morning."

Then, I was being hustled away, trying not to cry out in pain as I was lifted more swiftly than gently into the ambulance. How I'd wished that they'd let me hold my baby until I'd reached the hospital. I told myself, though, that they knew what was best for my baby. I was so weak that I might have dropped her.

As soon as I was settled into a bed at the new hospital, I was given another sedative, and once again, I'd drifted into sleep. When I'd opened my eyes, Darryl was there, holding my hand.

"Oh, honey—last night was hell," he said. "When they told me—"

"What happened?" I whispered.

"No one knows yet. There'll be an investigation, of course. Just relax, baby—don't talk about it anymore." He brushed his lips across my forehead. "The doctor just let me come in to see you for a minute. I have to go right out and let you rest." He tucked the covers around me and kissed me again, that time on my lips.

"I've seen Hope," he told me.

Hope was the name that we'd chosen for our new baby—if it was a girl—when I'd first learned that I was pregnant. It was the perfect name, because we'd done nothing but hope since we'd learned of the precious new life that was growing inside of me. We'd hoped and prayed that our new baby would be born healthy. While I was sewing baby clothes I'd murmur over and over, "For Hope!" Somehow, it had helped me to hold back the fear that I'd lose my new baby, just as I had lost my Daria Rose.

Despite all of the stress that Darryl must have experienced in the past few hours, he gave me a wide grin. "She came through everything just like a little trouper. Not even a day old, and she takes everything in stride," he boasted. "She's so cute." He hesitated a little. "She doesn't look much like Daria Rose, though."

I frowned, puzzled. "I thought that she looked a lot like Daria Rose."

I would have said more, but a nurse came in and told Darryl that he had to leave. I learned later that they were afraid that he might tell me more details about the fire, and that it might upset me. Despite the hospital staff's courage, not everyone had been as lucky as we had been: Five patients and one infant had been lost in the flames. It was the greatest tragedy that had ever hit our little town.

The nurses told me that my baby was doing fine, but that, for the first day, all of the babies would be kept in the nursery under observation, while the mothers rested. That made me uneasy, but Dr. Christiansen dropped in to see me and calmed my fears.

"She's one of the biggest, healthiest babies in the nursery," he told me, smiling.

I had never really liked Dr. Christiansen much, but that day, even his crisp manner hadn't bothered me. I loved the world, because my daughter was safe.

That day, the last peaceful day that I was to know for years, passed in drowsy daydreams. How complete my life had seemed— at last. It was almost worth the heartbreak and loneliness that I'd endured in the past.

I'd been a change-of-life baby myself. When I was born, my father had been nearly fifty, and my mother was forty-four. I had a sister, Susannah, who was sixteen years older than I. In many ways, it was like being an only child. Susannah seemed more like a younger mother than a sister to me, except that she wasn't the least bit motherly.

When I was five, she'd gotten married, and had gone to live in another state. My folks had worried a lot about Susannah. Mom had cried every time she'd read one of her letters. A year later, Susannah had given birth to a baby boy. She'd named him Anthony—after Dad. Mom, though, had been feeling sick and hadn't been able to go to stay with her when the baby was born.

Then, before the baby was a year old, Susannah had told us that she was getting a divorce. Susannah had said that she was sure that she could support Anthony better than her husband ever had. Susannah's divorce just crushed Mom. Her health went downhill quickly that. A few months later, she died.

Dad and I lived alone for a few years, and then he married Bella Morgan, a woman who lived on the farm next to ours. She was very unattractive, and had a cold, clipped voice, but she was a wonderful housekeeper. She was a lot younger than Dad. She was never unkind to me, but she never showed me any affection, either.

After that, we'd received letters from Susannah once or twice a year. She'd married another man who seemed, from what she'd written, to have been good to her, and that had made Dad happy. But, to me, she was still like a dream person. She sent Christmas cards every year, and once, there was a pretty necklace for my birthday. But, by that time, I could hardly remember what she looked like.

When I was sixteen, Dad had died of a heart attack. Susannah had come back for the funeral. I felt very shy around her.

"Things are kind of tough financially for Seth and me," she said. "But, we'll take you in, honey, if you've got nowhere else to go."

I wasn't sure that I wanted to go with my sister or not—she seemed like a stranger to me—but Bella settled it by saying, in her tight-lipped way, that she'd do her duty by me. Dad had left a small trust fund for me, that I'd receive when I was eighteen. Until then, she'd go ahead and continue to care for me.

So, Susannah had gone home, and I'd stayed with Bella. But, by the time I was eighteen, I couldn't wait to get away, and I believed that she was just as eager to have me go. She gave me the money that my father had left me. She told me that she hoped I'd spend it wisely, and that was that.

I took the money and went to Huntington, a town several hundred miles away, and entered business college. My high school teacher had gone there and had told me that it was a fine school. But, within three months, I'd realized that school didn't interest me, because I had met Darryl Desidario.

Darryl owned a dry cleaning business that was located a few blocks from my furnished room. From the minute that I first entered the shop, with an armful of skirts, pants, and sweaters, Darryl had caught my eye. But, it was his mother who'd really brought us together. She was wonderful—a sweet woman who had the nicest, warmest smile in the world. She and Darryl lived in an apartment above the shop. After I'd been there a few times, she'd learned that I was all alone in the world, and her heart had just melted. She'd invited me for Sunday dinner.

I would have accepted her invitation, anyway, but because Darryl was there, nothing could have kept me away. I forgot my shyness and just sparkled that first day, and Darryl began to notice me, too—enough to ask me to a movie that evening.

In a few weeks, we were going steady, and a few months later, we were married in a simple ceremony at Darryl's church. We had a short honeymoon in the mountains. Oh, the magic of that time, when we'd discovered what it was really like to belong to the one you loved. Darryl was so gentle and tender that I never knew a moment's fear.

Maybe ours wasn't as exciting as some marriages, but it was fine for me—warmly comforting for a girl who'd been lonely almost all of her life.

For a while, we'd lived with Mom Desidario, but when I'd become pregnant, we'd bought a little house of our own. Even though it was a very modest home, I was still a little scared, because it had taken so much of our savings to make a down payment. But, Mom Desidario had told me that we could save in a dozen different ways after the baby was born—and, she'd offered to show me how to cut corners.

But, after Daria Rose arrived, there were even more expenses. She was such a beautiful baby—tiny and frail, but like a little doll.

"You sure can tell that this little beauty belongs to the two of you," Mom Desidario said, the minute she looked at her. "Darryl looked just like her when he was a baby."

Daria Rose didn't belong to us very long, though. She'd been born with a heart problem, and when she was only six weeks old, she died. Almost all of her short life had been spent in the hospital.

Oh, the agony of those days—and nights. The doctors had told me that there was no reason why I couldn't have a healthy baby, and I couldn't wait to get pregnant again. My arms actually ached to hold a living, healthy child.

Well, the baby had been born, and God had been good to us: He'd brought us safely through the delivery, and even the fire. But, I knew that I wouldn't feel really secure until I could hold my daughter again. I remembered a thousand times how she'd felt in those precious, dangerous moments when I'd cuddled her close.

In spite of my happy daydreams, it was the longest day in my life. When the nurse finally brought my baby to me that evening, I gave a cry and stretched out my arms. She smiled back at me and placed the baby in the crook of my arm. With swift fingers, I pulled back the blanket. Then I gasped.

The baby that I held looked nothing like my daughter had.

"Nurse!" I cried. "You've brought me the wrong baby!"

The nurse wheeled around in the doorway and looked down at the baby, lying in my arms. Then she smiled. "She's yours," she said. "Look—" She pulled up one of the baby's tiny wrists, and showed me the identification bracelet, which had my name, and my daughter's, on it.

I pushed the baby from me. "No!" I cried again, in a panic. "This is not my daughter. She looks nothing like my daughter. During the fire, I held my baby for a while and she—oh, please, take this child away! I want my daughter! I want my child!"

I was screaming by then. The nurse snatched the baby out of my arms and almost ran down the hall. I lay there, sobbing, and pounding my pillow with clenched fists.

In a few minutes my doctor appeared, shaking his head as if I'd been a sick child.

"My dear," he said, "of course, this is your little girl. Last night, they didn't even try to put the babies with the proper mothers. They just dropped them down in any safe place while they went back to get the others."

"Don't lie to me!" I yelled. "You're just trying to hide some awful mistake. What happened to my baby?"

He sighed and rang for the nurse. "No wonder you're upset," he went on, in his patient voice. "You've been through a terrible ordeal. I'm going to give you something that will help you to sleep."

I glared at him. "I don't want to sleep," I insisted. "How dare you tell me that—that this baby is mine! Why, the hair color is different, her skin is a different shade—everything—"

The nurse came in with a syringe. Paying little attention to my struggles, the doctor thrust the needle into my arm.

"Mrs. Desidario," he began, more gently than he'd ever spoken to me in the past, "you're hysterical. I delivered your baby and I know what she looks like. As for that hair, it's baby fuzz. She may turn out to have the same color hair as everyone in your family." He patted my shoulder. "Try to get to sleep. When you wake up, you'll see just how silly you've been."

I slept, all right—the medication took care of that. But, I had awful nightmares about my helpless, beautiful baby being pulled from my arms. I awakened screaming and that time, after a few nurses had tried to quiet me down, Darryl was standing by my side.

"Oh, Darryl," I whispered, clutching him, "the baby that they've brought to me isn't ours! You saw her. Tell them!"

"Honey," he said, his face white, "I didn't see her before. She was just a little bundle, all wrapped up, when the nurse carried her from the delivery room. Today, I looked at the—the baby that they showed me, and I never doubted that she was ours. Sure, she doesn't look like anybody in our family, but doctors don't make mistakes like that."

I could feel myself getting hysterical again. "They can! They're just human. You've got to find our child!" I cried.

85

Darryl tried to soothe me, and then, the doctor came again. At last, I slept, but when the nurse brought the same baby in for an early-morning feeding, I wouldn't accept her. I cried and begged for my own child.

For the first day or two, they treated me as if I were hysterical, and I'd soon come to my senses again. But, after a while, I convinced them that I really didn't believe that the baby was mine. The doctor tried to reason with me. The identification bracelet with her name had been placed on her right after she was born—fire or no fire, he assured me that it wouldn't have been taken off.

I just shook my head. In the confusion, tiny bracelets could have slipped off, and been replaced. Anything could have happened.

And, Darryl—good, trusting Darryl—he believed all that he had been told by the doctor. He believed that I was hysterical, and that I didn't know what I was talking about. He figured that the shock of the fire, especially after the loss of my first baby, had caused me to act that way. But, when he'd tried to reason with me, I'd gone crazy.

"I'll prove that this isn't my baby," I told him. "Get the baby's footprint records."

Unfortunately, those records had been lost in the fire. Then, I demanded to talk to the other parents who'd had babies in the nursery that night, and with that, Dr. Christiansen became stern and cold.

"There's been enough suffering caused by this fire," he told me firmly. "There were over thirty other babies in the nursery that night. I will not cause all of those parents any more uncertainty because of your hysteria."

During that time, the nurses kept bringing the baby to me for feedings. After the first day, I'd accepted her simply because I'd wanted to study her face, and see if I could find one trace of Darryl's or my features. I found none. My fear became an acidlike dread—eating into my very soul.

While everyone was trying to convince me that I was mistaken—deluded—only God knew where my real baby was. The mothers and their children had been moved to many different hospitals after the fire that night. Because I was so upset, I was kept in the hospital for days longer than I should have been. Who had taken my baby home? Where had they taken her?

Finally, I was discharged, and I took the baby home with me. I knew that I had to. They might have kept me there, in the hospital for observation, for weeks if I hadn't outwardly accepted the child that was not mine. I knew that I had to get free before I could begin my search to find my own baby and bring her home.

The first night at home, Darryl and I stood beside the crib, looking down at the sleeping baby. His arms went around me.

"She is ours," he announced strongly. "Surely, you can't doubt it now."

I looked at him steadily. "I don't doubt," I said firmly. "I know. She is not our daughter. No matter what Dr. Christiansen says, I know that I held my baby in my arms on that stretcher. And, I'll find her."

Darryl's face was pale. "But, honey, you can't still think that the doctors and nurses have all tried to deceive us."

"Maybe they didn't mean to," I said, trying to be fair. "I guess, to someone like Dr. Christiansen, who has delivered so many babies, one child looks pretty much like another in the delivery room. Maybe he truly believes that this is our child. The nurses say that they can't remember who placed that baby in my arms, when I was lying on the stretcher—or, which baby it was. It was a night of such horror, Darryl. But, there is one thing that I know—I held my real baby then." I clung to him, trying to make him understand. "There was such motherly love," I whispered. "It's an instinctive thing, Darryl. I felt it, the moment they placed her in my arms. I've never felt it with this baby."

A shadow of doubt crossed his face. He put his hand into the crib and rubbed the baby's soft fist. Such a fierce one she was—even in sleep, her fingers closed around his thumb and clung.

"I don't know about mother instinct," he murmured. "But, this little girl—I've never really doubted that she was ours. Still—do you still want to keep fighting, and looking?"

"I have to," I insisted. "I'll care for this child because she's a baby, and she's helpless. But, I'm not her mother!" My voice rose sharply and she stirred restlessly at the shrill sound. "And the woman who has my baby is not the mother of my child." I threw my arms around Darryl's neck. "The world is against me," I told him. "You have to stand by me. You're her father, honey—wherever she is. Help me to find her—please, help me," I begged.

"I'll help you, Laurie," he said at last—slowly and seriously. "But, promise me this: If you discover, without a doubt, that this baby is ours, you won't build up any crazy arguments in your own mind. Promise that you'll accept her."

I nodded, because I knew in my heart that they could never prove, beyond a doubt, that the child was mine.

I could say so much about my fight and my search to find my own baby, but it all boiled down to one thing: It was hopeless.

I'd heard about blood tests. One of the first things that I did was ask for them, but they proved only one thing: We could have been the parents of the baby that we'd brought home. But, that didn't satisfy me, because I'd read that blood tests couldn't prove the negative, only the positive. If she'd had a completely different blood type, our problems would have been solved. But, she could have had the same blood type, and still not have been our child. DNA testing was expensive, and Darryl thought it was unnecessary after the blood tests.

If there had been any doubt in Darryl's mind, it was swept away by the blood tests. I couldn't make him see how little they could be depended upon. By that time, he and his mother both thought that I was a hysterical, foolish woman. Mom Desidario was very gentle and understanding—at first. She told me that my fears were natural enough, due to all that I'd been through. But, she adored the baby and kept saying how much she looked like Darryl had, at that age. After all, coloring wasn't everything, she said. I listened, and kept my thoughts to myself.

When the baby was eight weeks old, she was baptized. I wouldn't go to the church. I couldn't bear to see that strange child be given the name that I'd chosen for my own precious baby. That was the first time Darryl and his mother had really gotten angry with me. I was half out of my mind with despair by then, though, and I didn't care what they thought. I was beginning to believe that they were kind, easygoing people, who were content to take the simple way out— weak. I couldn't hate Darryl for his blindness, but I reached deep inside myself for the strength to go on, and to find my baby by myself.

But, I still had a child to take care of—to bathe, feed, and dress. No matter how hard I tried, though, my very hands shrank away from her. Where was my Hope? Was she being cared for? Was she being fed properly? Was the woman who thought she was her mother kind to her?

As soon as I was well enough, I turned the baby's physical care over to Mom Desidario and became a detective. I talked to people who had worked in the hospital, and I tracked down the birth announcement columns in our local newspapers for that whole week. I even went to the city department where birth records were kept, to get all the names of the babies who'd been born at the same time as mine. But, that didn't work very well. Despite all of my efforts, I only found about twenty names.

I went after those families ruthlessly, disguising myself in any way to get into their homes. I pretended to be a saleswoman, a survey taker, even a talent scout for a baby beauty contest. And, I saw all of the babies—but, none of them was the baby that I'd held in my arms that night. Oh, I knew that, even in a few weeks, babies changed, but I was sure that when I'd found my Hope, I would know.

In desperation, I went to the police. They told me that they were sorry, but Dr. Christiansen was a respected man in the community, and I'd have to respect his word. When I'd insisted, they'd said that the only way for me to proceed would be to hire a lawyer to handle the case.

The problem was, I couldn't get a lawyer to take the case, even though I was willing to use all of our savings to pay the lawyer's fee. Every lawyer that I contacted had told me that they couldn't do anything for me—that I had to believe that the infant I'd brought home was my baby. One man even insisted that, for some reason, God had given her to me to care for.

Oh, it sounded sensible, but the words did nothing to ease my heartache. How could a mother lose her child as I had? But, it had happened. All I had left was a strange baby and Darryl. And, I wasn't sure that I even had Darryl anymore. He had stopped asking me how I spent my days. His face was a stranger's face across the table. A great wall had grown up between us. I couldn't understand how he could so easily accept that child and not even try to find his own, and he couldn't understand why I didn't accept the child as mine. I hated him for what he would not see, but I loved him because he was Darryl, and because he was the only person who truly belonged to me.

Finally, I made up my mind. It was a bitter decision, but it had a sort of twisted strength. I'd make him think that I'd accepted the baby as Hope. I'd win back his love, because I could not live without it. And, all the time, I'd go on looking for my daughter—somehow. He wouldn't need to know about my search, and if I never found her, at least I'd have his love. I couldn't lose everything else and that, too.

The weeks after I'd made that decision were the hardest of my life, for I felt as though I'd betrayed my own baby. I took care of my home and the baby that everyone said was mine, but inwardly, I was like a frantic creature in a cage. I was so desperate that I'd even thought of writing to Susannah. But, how could you share your deepest problems with someone you only got a Christmas card from once a year—even if she was your sister? So, I flung myself into everyday living and hoped that no one noticed how deeply I resented Hope.

Oh, I cared for her well enough. I made lovely dresses for her, gritting my teeth as I sewed the fabrics in colors that went so well with her skin and hair.

Darryl and Mom Desidario were crazy about her, but for a child's curious reasons, it was I—the cold, standoffish one—that she clung to. It seemed as if, in her innocent way, she was trying to win me over. Well, I did feel a certain fondness for her. But, love her as a daughter? Oh, God forgive me, I'd tried, but I just couldn't bring myself to love her.

And then Dr. Hollander, my new doctor, gave me the news: I was going to have another child.

The three of us drew closer than we had ever been during the months of my pregnancy. Somehow Hope, Darryl, and I were almost a family unit. Then, during the last weeks of the pregnancy, I felt quite ill, and Mom Desidario took Hope home with her to care for her until after the baby was born. After that, we never quite recaptured that closeness.

I knew that Darryl had wished that the baby would look like Hope, to erase my doubts. But, Tyler looked just like my first baby, Daria Rose. If anything could have made me sure that I was right, that was it. From the beginning, I'd poured a flood of maternal love onto Tyler. I couldn't help it. Two babies had been snatched from my arms, but Tyler was mine.

The day I brought him home, Hope, almost three then, was there to welcome me. She had picked some weeds from the yard to make a bouquet, and she'd come in singing a welcome-home song. I'd hushed her sternly, afraid that she'd wake up Tyler. Then, I'd started to take her in my arms, but just at that moment, Tyler had begun crying. His diaper had needed changing and somehow, in all the confusion, Hope had been forgotten. Later, when Mom Desidario was leaving, Hope took her hand.

"I think I'll go home with you, Grandma," she said quietly.

Darryl started to protest, but I interjected quickly. "Oh, Mom, would you mind keeping Hope for a week or so more?" I began. "I'm going to be busy with Tyler, and—"

Her steady look cut off my words. She gathered Hope up in her arms. "I don't mind taking care of Hope. She's welcome to stay with me whenever she wants to," she said. "I love her. But, you haven't changed, have you, Laurie? I can only pray that God will help you to see the truth, and to do right by your little daughter."

"I'd give my life to do right by her," I burst out, "but I don't even know where she is." I burst into tears.

Hope gave a startled gasp and wriggled from Mom Desidario's arms. "I'm right here, Mommy," she told me. "I'll stay with you."

I put Tyler down and hugged her tightly. In a moment's insight, I realized that even though God had seen fit to take my own child from me, he had sent me another little girl, who was one of the warmest, sweetest children in the world. And, I did love her—I did. But, once more, that very love had made me feel guilty—as if I had betrayed my own daughter. I cuddled her for a few minutes, then gently put her down.

"You run along with Grandma," I told her, smiling and kissing her cheek. "As soon as I'm stronger, I'll come and get you, honey."

She hesitated. "Can't I stay here and help you?" she suggested shyly.

"Later, when Tyler's bigger," I promised. "When he's older, you'll be Mommy's little helper."

If only I could have remembered that promise. True enough, Hope did come back in a couple of weeks, but Tyler was a fretful baby, troubled every night by colic. During the day, I tried to keep the house very quiet so that he could nap. I was tired, too, and more irritable than usual. Sometimes, when Hope forgot herself and laughed or yelled loudly while she was playing, I'd scold her until I was ashamed of myself. After all, she was still a baby, too.

So, during the first six months of Tyler's life, Hope spent more time with Darryl's mother than she did with me. After that, I did try to let her help me with Tyler, but she was too little to do more than get in my way, and, of course, she didn't know that doing certain things might hurt a baby.

Once, when they had both been down on the floor, playing, she'd thrown a block at him, expecting him to catch it, as an older child might have done. It had hit his forehead and left a dark, swollen lump. I was paralyzed with fright. She could have killed him. After that, I tried even harder to keep them apart.

When Tyler was fifteen months old, I got pregnant again. That time, to my delight, I had another girl. I named her Caleigh, and there were no words to describe how much I loved her. Hope was happy to have a little "sister," but she'd learned to stay out of my way. That time, she didn't try to help me with the baby.

Outwardly, everything was smooth and happy. I was so thankful that I had two beautiful babies, and I tried very hard to be nicer to Hope than I had ever been before. I didn't even scold her as much as I did Tyler—even though she was becoming more difficult as she grew older. She had temper tantrums, and often, she was stubborn and demanding about the smallest things. When I reprimanded her, I tried to be very fair and firm. Instead of being strict, as I would have been with Tyler, I was more lenient. In a way, it was as if Tyler were my own child, to be disciplined as I saw fit, while Hope was a child that I was keeping for strangers. I felt as though she were a visitor in the house.

As she grew older, she continued to change. On her bad days, she was sullen and angry with me, and, on her good days, she was carefully polite. Even with Darryl, she was a little aloof. Only with Mom Desidario did she cuddle up and speak affectionately.

Even so, I'd believed that things had been going along well enough. The business was doing better than ever. Darryl had enlarged the space and added another processing room. Mom Desidario had rented a town house with a yard, and an extra bedroom, which she'd fixed up as a pretty room for Hope. Hope had started kindergarten that year, and I'd bought her a lot of cute outfits. It almost seemed as if I felt that I could ease my guilt by giving her material things, to make up for the love that I couldn't give to her.

When Darryl had seen the bill for the clothes, he'd grinned and hit his forehead with the flat of his hand. "Take it easy," he teased. "You'll break the old man." But, I could tell that he was pleased.

Soon, though, despite our good fortune with the business, we'd started experiencing a host of other troubles. Caleigh was teething and it had been giving her a hard time. Then, Hope had caught the chicken pox and passed it on to Caleigh and Tyler. Right after that, Hope had come down with strep throat, and the whole miserable pattern had repeated itself.

All of the children's diseases seemed to be passing through the school at that time, and Dr. Hollander himself had suggested that Hope stay with Darryl's mother for awhile, to safeguard the other two children. We all thought that it would be better for everyone, especially since Mom Desidario lived nearer to the school.

Deep within me, though, I'd realized that I was beginning to neglect Hope a little. In the past, I had left the babies with Mom Desidario on Saturday afternoons and had taken Hope to the movies. Recently, though, I'd begged off more and more often. Hope had accepted it quietly enough, and I'd thought that she'd understood. Once, though, I did a really bad thing to her, without meaning to.

Hope's school was having a play, and Hope had been chosen to play the part of the princess. Mom Desidario made her costume—all lace and sequins—and all Hope could talk about was the play. For the first time in months, she'd seemed like her old, vibrant self.

"Just wait until you see how pretty I am, Mommy," she told me, over and over again.

"I'll see, all right," I promised. "I'll be right there, in the front row!"

The play had been planned for a Friday, but at the last minute, the time of the performance had been changed to Thursday night. Maybe that was why I'd forgotten. Truthfully, though, I didn't really know how I could have forgotten. I'd planned so carefully to attend. Darryl had been working until nine every night, but I'd decided that just once, I could take both babies out with me.

The whole week had been hectic. First, I'd caught a miserable cold. Then, the toilet had overflowed and I'd had to have a plumber come in. On Thursday morning, my next-door neighbor had gone to the hospital to have her baby, two weeks early. I'd taken care of her other three children until her mother had arrived to take over.

None of that, though, excused me. Those were just the things that had happened. Somehow, in the chaos, I'd forgotten all about Hope's play.

I was in bed, my hair wet from the shower, blissfully relaxing with a magazine, when Darryl had come home from the shop.

"Hey," he asked, "is the play over so soon?"

My hand flew to my mouth. I had forgotten all about Hope's play. "You didn't even go!" he yelled.

"I—I forgot," I stammered.

"How could you?" His face was dark with anger. "That poor little kid has been looking forward to it for weeks." He really lit into me then. A lot of the bitterness that I'd hoped had been buried forever flared out in the open. Once more, he'd accused me of never really accepting Hope—of not loving her. And, in my guilt, I got angry, too, and screamed a lot of things back at him.

It was one of those tearing-apart arguments. It ended with him yanking me out of bed and telling me that we'd have to go over and say something to Hope. I'd tried to protest that the babies were asleep, and that Hope herself would probably be in bed, but he wouldn't listen.

"For once, you're not going to put Tyler and Caleigh before Hope!" he told me angrily. "It won't hurt them if you wake them up. And, I can almost bet that our poor little girl isn't asleep—unless she's cried herself to sleep, thanks to you!"

He was right: Hope was awake—and, she was crying. Still dressed in the princess costume, she was sprawled on the sofa, crying her heart out, while Darryl's mother tried to comfort her. I sat down beside her and smoothed her hair back.

She hiccoughed and sobbed again. "I kept thinking that you'd come," she whispered. "The whole time—I forgot my lines because I was looking for you." She grasped my hands with cold little fingers. "You told me that you'd be in the front row!"

I tried to explain. I told her about my cold, and the plumber, and the neighbor's new baby, but, of course, she didn't really understand any of it. She only understood that I had forgotten. I hugged her and rocked her as if she were no older than Caleigh. Over and over, I whispered how much I loved her—and, I realized for the first time, that it was true. The shadowy memory of my own daughter still stood between us, but I did love her, too. I would have cut my heart out before I would have purposely hurt her.

At last, Darryl and had I taken her home, and she'd slept in our bed that night, cuddled in my arms. I didn't make her go to school the next day. All weekend, I'd kept her close to me, trying in a million ways to make up for the way that I'd wounded her. By Monday, I felt that I'd erased the wrong I'd done. When she went back to Mom Desidario's on Sunday night, she was as cheerful as a little sunbeam.

Hope's birthday was in May. Darryl's mother had planned a party for her. I told myself that it was easier for Hope's school friends to travel the few blocks to Mom Desidario's town house than to come all the way out to our house. Besides, I thought, there's more room there.

Mom Desidario had made a big event out of that party. She'd trimmed her living room with crepe paper and all kinds of party decorations, and she'd baked a big, elaborate cake, fit for a princess. Two days before, I'd bought Hope's party dress, in a shade almost the same color as her princess costume. She was so excited! But, as we'd left the store, she'd clutched my hand and looked up into my face with those serious eyes.

"Now, don't forget, Mommy," she said, almost shyly.

"Silly," I tried to tease. "How could I forget your birthday!"

I left her at Mom Desidario's door with an especially tender kiss, but as I drove home, an old pain burned in my heart. How could I ever forget Hope's birthday? It was a date that would always torture me. That was why I'd never given Hope a birthday party before. I just couldn't have stood the pain. I'd always know that somewhere, another little girl was having a birthday—a precious child who belonged to me, and yet, who would never be mine.

I had planned for the new dress to be my birthday present to Hope, but the morning of the party, I'd awakened with the sudden knowledge that a dress wouldn't be enough. Darryl had bought a bicycle for her—it was at Mom Desidario's, with a big bow, and both of our names on the card. But, I'd decided that I wanted Hope to have a gift that was just from me.

It was a rainy day. I'd stared out the windows and watched the rain pelting down against them. I'd wished that there were time to order something and have it sent—something special. But still, that wasn't what I'd wanted to give—a gift that I'd bought carelessly by phone.

As I hurried through my chores, I mulled over the problem. After the babies had been bathed, fed, and put down for naps, the answer came to me: The old, soft doll that Caleigh was hugging had belonged to Hope. She'd named the doll "Rosie," and she'd adored it. Once, though, Mom Desidario had said that Rosie was old and ugly, and Hope had burst into tears.

"I won't take Rosie to Grandma's house!" she had told me, with that unique fierceness of hers. "Grandma doesn't like her."

As if it were pure inspiration, I stared at the tattered old doll. Moments later, I was ripping Rosie down the back and flinging away the materials that had stuffed her. Then, I carefully washed the limp rag of a body. She came out all clean and fresh, her eyes as bright as ever. True, her hair was matted and ugly, but I could rip that off. There was more yarn in my knitting bag. I'd make her new hair, and tie it back with two of Caleigh's hair ribbons. The mouth had faded completely, but I could sew another one—a bright, red mouth with an impish smile on it. For stuffing I'd use the foam rubber that I'd planned to make sofa pillows with.

I worked furiously. A little while later, a plump and clean Rosie, with a pretty, new hairdo, sat on my sewing machine. Suddenly, I felt the strangest, loveliest happiness that I'd ever known. I was doing something for my Hope—for both of my Hopes, really. And, I'd done it not out of duty, but because I'd wanted to.

The party was scheduled to begin at three o'clock. I realized that I didn't have much time. But, Rosie had to have a new dress. I went and got Caleigh's christening dress and began ripping it up ruthlessly. I'd thought I would save it forever, but suddenly, that idea had seemed foolish. Why make a keepsake of a bit of lace and nylon when it could be put to such good use?

I cut and sewed until my eyes ached, and for once, I didn't even stop for Tyler and Caleigh when they whined for my attention. It was a few minutes after three when I'd finished, but I had to admit, Rosie was a real work of art. I gave a final, satisfied glance at the billowing dress and the ribbon-tied braids—then I sailed around, washing and dressing the babies and getting myself ready for the party. My eyes flew guiltily to the clock. It was already four o'clock. I was an hour late! I figured that Hope would forgive me, though, when she saw Rosie.

Oh, what a fool I had been—doing too little, much too late. But, my heart had been singing as I'd zipped up my dress. In just a minute I'd bundle the babies into the car and we'd be off.

That was when I'd heard the knock at the front door.

How could I ever describe the blinding panic of that moment— when I saw two policemen, and a white-faced Darryl, standing at the front door.

The policemen tried to tell me gently, but Darryl just blurted it out: "Hope's in the hospital. The doctor thinks that she might die."

I sagged and would have fallen, but one of the policemen grabbed me. "How—what—" I faltered. "The party—"

"She was at the party," Darryl said angrily. His red-rimmed eyes accused me. "She snuck out and tried to come here, because she thought that you had forgotten again."

"It seems that you were late, ma'am," one policeman put in gently. "The little girl ran off while the other kids were busy playing. Her grandmother didn't notice that she was gone at first—there were so many kids there." He cleared his throat. "It seems as though she was trying to come here to remind you about her party. At Front Street, she darted across the street right in front of a pickup truck. She was so quick, and in the mist and rain, the driver didn't see her until it was too late." He cleared his throat again. "She's clinging to life. We'd better get you over to the hospital as quickly as we can."

If I'd thought that I had suffered before, suddenly I realized that I hadn't known how bitter pain could be. At the hospital, I was only allowed to look into Hope's room for a moment. They were giving her blood transfusions and oxygen. She was unconscious, in a state of shock, and very near death. In fact, I couldn't even tell if she was breathing or not.

Her color was bad, and her lashes were like shadows against her poor, bruised little face. Her leg had been broken, but the emergency room doctor told me that that was the least of her injuries. A fractured rib had pierced her lung, causing it to collapse. She was in deep shock and the doctors believed that blood had escaped into her chest cavity. If the hemorrhaging continued, they would have to operate—open the chest cavity, and stop the bleeding by tying off the blood vessels, or by removing the damaged portion of the lung. The doctor said that it was a very serious procedure, especially in a child as young as Hope.

The doctor could give us little hope. He had Dr. Worthington, a specialist, working with her, though, and he told us if anyone could save her, Dr. Worthington could. The only encouraging thing that the doctor could say was that we were lucky that her heart and bronchial tubes hadn't been damaged. If that had happened, he explained, she probably would have died within minutes.

We waited outside her room, not daring to hope. Darryl's mother was there, too, sobbing uncontrollably. She blamed herself bitterly, but from the set look on Darryl's face, I knew that he blamed only me. And, in God's truth, I blamed myself much worse than even Darryl could have. Why hadn't I have realized how Hope might have felt? Poor little baby, worried sick—sure that I'd forgotten her again, just as I had at the school play.

In those moments as I stood at the window, praying as I'd never prayed before, I learned what it was to be a mother—Hope's mother. At last, it was unimportant whether she was child of my blood or not. She was mine. In her heart, I was her mother—the only one she had—and with her fire, warmth, and sweetness, she had given me the love due a mother. Time and time again, I'd pushed her away, but she had always forgiven me and come back, begging that I return her great, unselfish love—even just a little bit.

Please, let me keep her, Lord. Let me have another chance to care for her, and to show her how much I love her. Let me prove that I am her mother, in every way a mother should, I prayed fervently.

When the door to Hope's room opened, my head jerked up, and my mother-in-law leaned against Darryl as if she had no strength left. Dr. Worthington came out. He looked very tired, but he smiled kindly at us.

"I can't give you a definite answer yet," he said, in answer to our unspoken questions. "But every minute—every hour—counts in a case like this. Luckily, most injuries like this aren't as serious as they seem at first." He paused.

"Any chest injury is bad," he went on. "But, if the patient can pull through the first few hours, we have every hope for recovery. Usually surgery isn't needed, because there is a wonderful healing power in a person's body, where the lungs are concerned. I have a lot of hope that your little girl's hemorrhaging will subside spontaneously, so that we won't need to operate. We'll know pretty soon." He smiled again and went back into the room. None of us dared to look into each other's eyes. Our hope and our fear were too great.

Those next few hours—in fact, the next few days—were a blur of mental anguish and physical exhaustion. Our neighbors were wonderful. They helped take care of the two younger children, and after the first day, Mom Desidario, Darryl, and I worked on shifts. One would stay in the hospital, one would sleep, and the other would care for the babies.

Then, four days after the accident, Dr. Worthington brought me the wonderful news: Hope was out of danger! I was selfishly glad that I was the one who was at the hospital then. I had those first few precious moments with my little girl. Kneeling by her bed, I kissed her limp hand again and again, and then, I placed Rosie into her arms.

"This is why Mommy was late for your party, honey," I whispered, trying not to let the tears slip down my cheeks. "See—I made Rosie just like new. And—and now you're going to be just like new, too, honey."

I was rewarded by her faint smile. It was the most beautiful thing that I'd ever seen.

Hope was in the hospital for nearly a month. During that time, Darryl treated me almost like a stranger. That hurt—badly. But, I knew that I deserved it, and I was humble and grateful that Hope had been spared. I knew that all of our other problems could be faced later. For the moment, just to have her alive was enough.

Finally, the day came when we were able to bring her home. The weather, though, had been wet and cold, and Hope didn't get strong as quickly as we'd hoped that she would. The dampness left her uncomfortable, and I was always afraid that she'd catch a cold, or pneumonia—which was one things that the doctor had warned us about.

One day when I was making her scrapbook of old greeting cards, I came across a Christmas card that Susannah had sent me the year before. I stared down at the brilliant desert scene and, all at once, I felt as though I had the answer. The desert! Maybe the dry, hot climate was just what Hope needed. I'd felt too distant from Susannah to ask her for any favors, or even to confide in her before, but at that point, I would have asked even a stranger to help me—for Hope's sake.

When I told Darryl my idea, he looked at me in surprise. "You mean, you'd go away and leave Tyler and Caleigh?" he asked.

"Just for a while. Besides, your mother can help you with them," I told him. "They don't really need me now, but Hope does."

For the first time since the accident, a look of genuine warmth came into his eyes. "I never thought that I'd see the day when you'd put Hope ahead of your own two children," he told me. His eyes were on my face, testing me.

"Hope is mine, just as much as they are," I said defensively.

To my surprise, he began to smile. "It's like a miracle," he murmured softly. "As much of a miracle as Hope's getting well. At last—after all these years—you finally believe that she's yours!"

I nodded. I decided that there was no need to tell him that there might always be doubts in my mind, as to whether or not Hope was my biological child. After her brush with death, I'd realized that she was the child of my heart, and that was enough. And, it was more than I had ever hoped for, when Darryl took me in his arms and kissed me—at first, with forgiving tenderness, and then, with the passion that I'd thought I would never know again.

Of course, the wall between us couldn't dissolve that easily. The years when our wills, silently and without words, had been set against each other—well, those years had left their scars. And, Darryl would never forgive my blatant neglect of Hope. But, he told me that he still loved me, and that he was willing to try to work on our marriage. He wanted us to be joined together, as a family, once more, and that was the most important thing. I clung to him, and our love eased old heartbreaks as nothing else could have done.

I wrote to my sister the next day, and she called as soon as she'd gotten it.

Come and visit, she wrote. Our place isn't fancy, but you say that you want sunshine—and that, we've got plenty of!

Hope was very excited about the trip. I was afraid that it would be hard on her, but she managed to do very well. On the plane, she snuggled up to me.

"It's so nice to be going someplace with you, Mommy," she murmured. During her stay in the hospital she'd begun calling me "Mommy" more often. There seemed to be so much more warmth and meaning in the way that she said it, too.

Susannah and Seth met us at the airport. Seth was handsome, with an easygoing grin. And, Susannah—well, I wouldn't have known her. Or, maybe I would have. The years had taken her early, rather hard, prettiness away. She was pleasant looking and warm—almost like the memories that I had of my own mother. She hugged me and cried, and then she'd scooped up Hope in her arms, as gently as if she were a porcelain doll.

"Well, if you aren't the spitting image of your cousin, Anthony!"

She grinned. "Both of you certainly take after your great-grandfather."

Hope giggled and wrapped her arms around her aunt's neck, but I just stared, my mouth open.

"What did you say?" I asked.

Susannah put Hope down and her forehead in surprise. "Mom's father? Oh, sure, you never knew him. He looked just like Hope. It's funny how he—and she—look so different from the rest of us."

"Yes," I agreed faintly, trying not to show her how dizzy and shaken I felt. "It's funny."

I was silent all the way to my sister's house. I supposed that Susannah thought I was tired from the trip, and she kept up a running fire of chatter, but I just couldn't answer her.

My mind was in a perfect storm. Dear Lord—had I wronged that poor child, for so many years? My arms closed around her with fierce tenderness.

Dr. Christiansen had been so sure that she was my baby. The identification bracelet—Darryl's fervent belief—the police—the lawyers. Had I been the wrong one, all along? Oh, why hadn't I written to Susannah sooner? Why hadn't I at least sent her a picture of Hope? I closed my eyes against the glare of harsh sunlight, but I was chilled to the bone with new and painful emotions.

At last, we pulled up at the house, which was just as shabby, and cozy, as I'd thought it would be. Anthony came running to meet us. He was young and handsome, and his grin was like his mother's—warm and good. As he grasped my hand, I gazed at him searchingly.

Did he look like Hope? Heaven help me, even then, I didn't know. There could have been a resemblance, but I wasn't sure.

I stared at him, then drew my eyes away. And, in that moment, I stopped searching. It was in God's hands—just as I'd put our lives in His hands in the hospital.

Really, our lives had been in His hands long ago, on the fateful night when Hope was born. She was alive, my precious daughter, when she could have died in the fire. She was alive, when she could have died just a few short weeks earlier, on an operating table.

Most important, she was mine. That was enough for me. I would not question His wisdom anymore. The search had ended. I had my daughter.

I smiled suddenly and my joy, deep and enduring, was in my voice. "Hope, honey, you've got to soak up lots of this good sunshine. We want to get you well and strong enough so that we can go back to your sister, brother, and daddy. So that we can go—home."

THE END

# A COP TOOK MY BABY
# ON A HIGH-SPEED CHASE

An officer walked toward me. "What type of car were you driving, ma'am?" he asked.

"Can you tell us who the name of the officer?" another questioned.

"Can you describe the vehicle, ma'am?" the first officer added.

Their questions were like buzzing bees inside my head. I knew I was close to fainting, but the thought of my baby in the backseat of a car that was involved in a high-speed chase kept me conscious. Barely.

The thought of how my husband would react, however, made me want to close my eyes and let the blackness overtake me. I could just hear him: "How could you have been so stupid?" He'd be furious.

Their questions were like buzzing bees inside my head. I knew I was close to fainting, but the thought of my baby in the backseat of a car that was involved in a high-speed chase kept me conscious. Barely.

The thought of how my husband would react, however, had made me want to close my eyes and let the darkness overtake me. I could just hear him: "How could you have been so stupid?" He'd be furious.

"Ma'am, are you okay?"

Numbly, I'd stared at the female police officer. Didn't she realize how stupid her question had sounded?

"No, I'm not okay!" I practically shouted. I'd glared at the other officers who were standing in a circle around me, asking their inane questions. I decided that I'd give them the answers they wanted. First, I'd described my vehicle.

"No, I don't know who the officer was," I snapped.

As one, they'd backed away. Maybe it was the note of hysteria in my voice. Or maybe it was the growing madness in my eyes. I didn't know, and I didn't care. I was just glad that they'd given me some breathing room.

I'd tried breathing deeply, but that didn't seem to help my light-headedness. I knew I should probably have called Shane the minute I'd finished calling the police, but every time I'd considered it, my teeth had begun to chatter. Our two-month-old baby girl, Olivia Rose, was his life. We were both in our late thirties, and her arrival had been an unexpected surprise.

That I had been careless with her life would be a big issue with Shane—one from which I wasn't sure our marriage would be able to recover. Shane didn't believe in mistakes, and I had made a big one.

Suddenly, someone had thrust a glass of water into my hand. I'd barely had time to close my fingers around it before the hand had disappeared.

"Just be calm, Mrs. Prentiss," a sympathetic voice droned in my ear. "Our officers are trained drivers."

Her flimsy assurance fell upon deaf ears. I had watched the real-life chases on television, and I knew that no matter how good they were, they couldn't always control what happened.

There was another thing I knew, too—something that I had yet to admit out loud. I had a terrible secret—one that I couldn't bring myself to reveal.

As if she'd read my mind, the female police officer had begun to interrogate me again. "Now, tell us again how the officer could have missed seeing the baby in the backseat. We're all trained to look for these things," she insisted.

I'd wet my dry lips and stared at the glass of water in my hand. "I, um, had been grocery shopping, and the bags were stacked all around her. I'm sure that's why he missed her."

The female officer frowned, then shook her head. "A baby that small would have been rear-facing, right? I don't know how he could have missed that."

My stomach quivered, and for one awful moment, I'd thought that I was going to vomit on her shiny shoes. They were close to discovering my shameful secret. Just the thought of Shane finding out had made my stomach wrench ominously.

At the risk of incriminating myself, I'd said nothing. Eventually, when the officer arrived at the station with my car and my baby, they would find out the truth. I didn't see any reason to volunteer the information. I knew that I had enough on my mind, worrying about my baby.

An officer in plain clothes joined the group. He thrust out his hand. "Ma'am? I'm Agent Morrisen with Internal Affairs. Would you mind telling me what happened?"

"I've already told—" I began.

"I know, ma'am, but I'd like to hear it again, if you don't mind," he said.

Being married to Shane had made me sensitive to demands, and I'd sensed immediately that Agent Morrisen wasn't asking—he was demanding. Reliving the confusing horror over again, I'd begun to explain what had happened.

"I was just finishing up loading the backseat with bags of groceries when I saw a black van speeding by. A few seconds later, a police car screeched into the parking lot. He had a flat tire. Before I could react, he jumped out of his car and pushed me aside, then took my car."

I'd shuddered and closed my eyes, praying that Olivia would be okay. She usually slept in the car, but if the car was driving fast and jerking around, she might wake up. What if her sudden cry startled the police officer into losing control of the car? What would happen to her, if he was still driving at that speed?

"You didn't get a chance to tell him about the baby in the backseat?" Agent Morrisen asked.

I shook my head. "By the time I got over the shock and started screaming at him, he was too far away to hear me." I'd started crying again, and my nose began to run. I wiped it with my sleeve, too overwrought to care how crude the gesture might have been. Oh, my poor baby! "You—you have to find her!" I urged. "Don't you have a radio or something?"

"Ma'am, the radio would have been in his police car. You don't have a CB radio in your vehicle, by any chance?"

I knew that he was talking about a trucker's way of communicating—with a CB radio. I hadn't been aware that they still used them. "No, of course not," I told him.

"A cell phone, maybe? Some people hook them to their dashboard."

Again, I shook my head. My cell phone was in my purse, which had been hanging on my shoulder. It was now lying beside my chair. Shane had given me strict instructions about cell phone use while I was driving. It just wasn't allowed.

"How old is your baby?" Agent Morrisen asked, pen poised over a small notebook.

"Two months old. She's—she's just an infant." My only child. Shane's pride and joy. Our big surprise. I'd held back a sob.

"Does she usually sleep when you're in the car?" he asked.

"Yes. Always." I'd hesitated, then turned an imploring gaze his way. "This police officer—he'll stop if he realizes that she's in the car, won't he?"

"Of course. He would never endanger a civilian, ma'am," he assured me.

But I'd seen the doubt in his expression, and it had filled my veins with the icy flow of terror—as if I weren't already terrified enough.

"What if he crashes the car? I've seen it happen on television," I said.

The agent's mouth tightened grimly. "In real life, most police officers don't take unnecessary risks with their lives."

Most police officers. I'd caught that, despite the panic that was clawing at my insides.

"What about this police officer?" I demanded.

The female officer put a soothing hand on my shoulder. "We don't know who's driving your car, Mrs. Prentiss. He'll either catch the perp or give up the chase, then he'll report back to the station. We've already got a man waiting on him in the parking lot where he left the patrol car."

My fingers dug into the chair arm. "How many high-speed chases can there be? Surely he reported it before he took my car!"

"This is a big city, ma'am. We have a dozen high-speed chases going on at the moment. We're trying to track him down, but chances are, he'll get in touch with us before we can find him."

And so, it was back to the waiting game, I realized. My throat felt as though it were going to close up in panic. I'd swallowed hard and reached for my purse. I knew that it was time to call Shane. I hated the thought of telling him, but I knew that the longer I put it off, the angrier he would be.

"I need to call my husband," I murmured.

"That's a good idea. You should have someone here with you," she agreed.

My fingers trembled as I dialed his cell phone number. When he answered, I blurted out the whole story.

"Shane, it's Marie. I'm at the police station." I'd had to take a moment to swallow another sob before I could continue. "I was putting groceries in the car when a police officer commandeered the car. Olivia was in her car seat. He—he took off before I could tell him about the baby."

There was dead silence.

I took the phone from my ear and stared at it to make certain that it hadn't gone dead. It hadn't. Putting it back to my ear, I'd continued to speak.

"Shane? Are you there?" I asked hesitantly.

"My God, Marie!" he exclaimed.

His voice whipped through me like a hot wire. I'd flinched and closed my eyes.

"How could you be so stupid?" he yelled.

"Shane—" I began.

"Where are you?" he asked coldly.

I told him, and he hung up without saying good-bye. My eyes met those of the female police officer. Heat stung my cheeks as I saw the pity in her eyes.

It took twenty minutes for Shane to reach the police station, and we still hadn't heard from the officer who had taken my car—and my baby. The furious look on Shane's face as he'd strode toward me had made my knees weak.

Shane had never been violent toward me, but I knew what he was capable of doing. He'd discovered other ways of being abusive and had, so far, kept his temper in check. I'd never known how powerful and painful words could be until I'd married Shane, though.

I knew that what I'd done could very well push him past the limit. And, for one awful moment, I'd actually wanted him to hit me. He didn't know the half of it yet, and when he found out, I feared that our marriage would be over. With his connections, I'd be lucky to be awarded even partial custody of Olivia.

We'd sat in silence. I could feel his furious, condemning gaze on me, but I refused to look at him. I knew I'd be subjected to a barrage of Shane's verbal abuse later, and right then, I was already near the breaking point. Olivia was due for her scheduled feeding, so I was worried that she'd be getting hungry. Just the thought of my helpless baby made my breasts ache.

Just when I thought I would go out of my mind, I saw the dispatcher making his way through the crowded police station. He looked excited, and my heart gave an answering leap. Shane and I stood as he reached us. Agent Morrisen had been talking to an officer at a nearby desk. He'd joined us the minute he'd noticed the dispatcher.

"Officer Martin just called in!" the dispatcher exclaimed breathlessly. "He's on his way to the hospital. He said he had a baby with him."

"Hospital?" I echoed, my heart thundering. "Why is he going to the hospital with our baby?" My voice rose hysterically.

Shane wrapped his fingers around my arm and squeezed hard enough to leave bruises. "Did he say if my daughter is all right?" Shane demanded.

"He didn't say. He just said he was on the way to the hospital with a baby and asked if anyone had called in," the dispatcher explained.

Shane's fingers tightened even further, making me cry out. Only then did he release me.

"Let's go," he muttered.

My waking nightmare had continued at the hospital. We weren't allowed to go to our daughter, so we were forced to pace the waiting room.

When the doctor finally came out to talk to us, my knees had buckled at the grim expression on his face.

"Are you the parents of the baby that Officer Martin brought in?" he asked, looking directly at us.

We'd rushed to him. I was hanging on to Shane's arm to hold myself upright. I didn't think I've ever known such terror in my life as I'd felt at that moment.

"Olivia. Her name is Olivia," I managed to whisper.

"We're doing all we can, but we don't yet know how severe her brain injuries are," the doctor stated bluntly.

I'd had to grab at Shane to keep from fainting.

Shane didn't seem to remember that I existed. "Brain injury? What the hell are you talking about? Did the cop have an accident with my daughter in the car?"

The doctor frowned and shook his head. "No, he didn't wreck the car, but since she wasn't properly secured, we think she suffered what is commonly known as the 'shaken baby' syndrome. Officer Martin was involved in a high-speed chase—"

Shane cut him off, his voice cold with fury. "We know that. What do you mean, she wasn't properly secured?"

My gaze dropped. It felt as though my heart had actually stopped beating as he spoke the damning words.

"When Officer Martin realized that there was a baby in the backseat, he pulled over. He said the car seat wasn't rear-facing. That's why he didn't see her in the first place." The doctor hesitated before continuing. "I'm afraid the trauma from the high-speed chase, combined with the fact that she wasn't properly secured in a rear-facing car seat, resulted in severe injuries. Her brain was bouncing against her skull, causing internal hemorrhaging. We're not sure yet about the extent of the damage. I'm sorry."

That time when my legs buckled, I didn't hang on to Shane. I didn't deserve to live—much less stand up. My baby was dying. I could see it on the doctor's face—hear it in his voice. He didn't have much hope that she would survive. And, in case I hadn't already sensed the grim truth, he'd confirmed it.

"I'll be honest with you. The prognosis doesn't look good. A child rarely recovers from this type of injury, and if they do. . . ." he trailed off.

"Isn't there something that you can do?"

I'd felt sick to my stomach at the pleading note in Shane's voice. Unlike Shane, I had read about the shaken baby syndrome—generally, in conjunction with child abuse—and knew, without asking, that there wasn't much that they could do.

"We're prepping her for surgery right now. We're going in to try and stop the bleeding, but after that, we don't know."

He'd left us then, and, while Shane went to call his parents, I'd gone in search of the hospital chapel. Once there, I'd gotten down on my knees and begged God to help us—to help my baby girl. I'd begged for Him to take my life, instead.

Shane found me in the chapel, sobbing on my knees. I could feel his coldness before he spoke. We were alone in the chapel, but I doubted that it would have mattered if we hadn't been.

"How could you have been so stupid, Marie? There's a reason why it's the law that an infant has to be in a rear-facing car seat."

Although he'd spoken softly, his condemning words had fallen upon my ears like screams. I'd remained silent. What could I say? I had condemned myself long before he'd voiced the words.

"It's bad enough that you were too stupid to let the police officer know about Olivia being in the car. Why wasn't she facing the right way?" he demanded.

I'd tasted my salty tears as I'd stood up and sat on the bench. My knees were numb, like my heart. "She was spitting up, and I was afraid that she'd choke. I couldn't see her, so I thought that, just that once, I could seat her facing forward so that I could keep an eye on her in the rearview mirror." My voice dropped to a self-loathing whisper as I'd voiced the pitiful excuse. "It was only a few miles to the house."

My husband's voice was ragged as he'd sunk onto the bench beside me and put his face in his hands. "I can't believe that this is happening to me again. What does God have against me? What did I do that was so terrible that he'd take another child from me?"

A strange, keening sound had risen in my throat at his agonized words. I had known from the moment my car raced out of the parking lot with Olivia and the police officer that the pain would reopen old wounds for Shane. The fact that our daughter lay near death had only intensified his memories.

When I'd first met Shane, I'd been hired to develop his company's website. As managing art director of his advertising company, Shane was the man I'd been told to consult. I'd been warned ahead of time that he could be difficult to work with, and he could be picky to the point of exasperation.

Surprisingly enough, we'd hit it off right away. I supposed it had helped that I was easy to work with, and eager to please. After a few weeks, Shane had asked me out, and I'd told him that I'd love to have dinner with him.

Six months later, we were married. By that time, he'd told me about losing his son, and his subsequent divorce. His awful story had made me fall more deeply in love with him. And, it had made me more determined than ever that he would never have a reason to talk about me with the loathing that he used when he referred to his ex-wife.

I didn't blame him for blaming his ex for his son's death. When their son had drowned, his ex-wife had been holding a bridal shower for one of her friends. She had sent their two-year-old son outside to swim in the pool with the older kids—one of who baby-sat for them occasionally.

"The stupid woman should have known," Shane had told me,

his voice raspy with pain, "that when you put teenage boys and girls together, they don't pay attention to the younger kids. By the time they noticed him floating in the water, it was too late. My son was dead. As far as I'm concerned, she should have gone to prison for what she did."

Hearing the story from Shane's point of view, I couldn't have agreed more. I'd always wanted a baby, but I'd been told it was unlikely after a bout with endometriosis. When I'd told Shane that I couldn't have kids, he'd seemed relieved.

"Good," he'd muttered. "I don't think I could handle worrying about another child. I'd be crazy all the time, thinking something was going to happen to them."

After being married five years and edging close to forty, nobody had been more shocked than Shane and I when I'd learned that I was pregnant. The shock had worn off quickly, however, and we'd been almost giddy with joy. In his heart, Shane had truly wanted another child. Once that the decision had been made for him, he was more than happy about the fact that we were expecting a baby.

From the moment Olivia was born, my life had changed, and not exactly for the better. Shane had become a different man. He was moody, paranoid, and sometimes downright ugly with his criticism. Suddenly, it had seemed as though I could do nothing right where Olivia was concerned. When he came home from work, he would check her diaper and if it was the least bit damp, he'd come unglued.

One night, Olivia had woken up screaming. Before I could stir, Shane had gone to check on her. She was soaked to the skin. For the next hour, Shane had ranted on about my carelessness with Olivia. He'd claimed that I had neglected to change her before bed. He was wrong, of course, but nothing I'd said had seemed to get through to him.

I'd become obsessed with being the perfect mother. I'd gone through dozens of diapers a day, and I'd changed Olivia's clothing each time she'd spit up or drooled, which was often. I'd lay awake at night listening for her. I was terrified that Shane would hear her before I did. Then he'd find something to scream at me about. Eventually, I'd become as paranoid as Shane that something would happen to Olivia. I knew that there could never be an accident—not in Shane's eyes.

His obsession and my paranoia were the reasons I had been afraid to leave Olivia facing away from my view. What if she'd choked to death on her own vomit? It would have been my fault. I would have been devastated. Shane would definitely have divorced me.

I loved my daughter every bit as much as Shane loved her, but his obsession was brewing a resentment I couldn't control. I was suspended in a perpetual state of anguish. The joy of motherhood and everyday life had been replaced by fear and trepidation. The possibility of living my life in fear that something would happen to Olivia and bring Shane's wrath down upon me had kept me depressed.

I'd considered divorcing Shane, but I truly loved him, and couldn't imagine my life—as miserable as it had become—without him. When he wasn't obsessing and accusing me of bad motherhood, he was charming, caring, and loving.

Somewhere along the way, I supposed I'd convinced myself that he would eventually relax about Olivia. I'd tried to believe that he would eventually realize that I was a good mother, and that I'd never do anything as thoughtless as what his ex-wife had done.

As I'd sat beside my raging, grieving husband, I'd realized that I had done exactly that. I'd done something extremely stupid and unforgivable—at least, in Shane's eyes.

And so, I didn't try to explain, or to make excuses. I knew that it was hopeless. Instead, I'd concentrated on my daughter. She had to be okay. She was the miracle—the baby I'd thought would never happen. She was my precious gift.

I was in the nurses' station, using a breast pump to relieve the pressure, when the doctor came in. He was still dressed in scrubs. I'd focused on a spot of blood on his shirt and tried to calm my thundering heart, even as I'd wondered if the blood belonged to Olivia.

"Where's your husband?" he asked, looking haggard and defeated.

I didn't like that look, and I'd refused to speculate on its cause. I was already hanging onto my sanity by a thread.

"He's in the waiting room." My voice was hardly a whisper, my throat was so dry.

The doctor sent a nurse out to get him. When they returned, he'd motioned for Shane to sit down. Shane shook his head and clenched his jaw.

I'd closed my eyes and prayed.

"The hemorrhaging in her brain was worse than we anticipated. I'm sorry. We lost her," he told us.

We lost her. I'd felt like screaming at the doctor. People "lost" dogs and cats, and sometimes, car keys. They didn't "lose" babies.

"She's dead," I heard myself say in a flat, emotionless voice. It was as if I'd felt compelled to verify his statement, just in case Shane didn't understand.

"Yes. I'm sorry." He hesitated. "I know this might sound harsh, but she's probably better off. The brain damage was extensive. If she had lived, she would have been severely disabled."

"This is your fault," Shane snapped harshly. I didn't have to look up to know that he was talking to me. "Because of your stupidity, our daughter is dead."

With those awful words ringing in my ears, he'd stood up and left. I'd sat there for a long time, numb with shock and grief. The nurse had stayed with me, rubbing my shoulders and offering to call someone for me. I shook my head. My mother lived in another state. I knew I'd have to call her, but, at that moment, I didn't want to move. To move would end it for good. It would make Olivia's death final.

Eventually, I'd gathered my purse and walked out of the hospital. I didn't know where I would go, but I knew that I couldn't go home. I had just lost my infant daughter. The last thing I needed was to hear Shane's hurtful accusations.

I walked aimlessly for a while before stopping at a bench, where I'd taken out my cell phone. I'd called my mother and told her the news. She broke down, and I'd sat there, still numb with shock as she cried. Finally, she'd stopped crying long enough to tell me to check into a hotel and wait for her. She'd seemed to realize that I was moving on autopilot.

I'd hung up and called a cab. I gave him the address of the hotel that my mother had suggested. Once in my room, I lay across the bed and stared at the ceiling. My eyes were dry—my heart numb with grief and guilt. Was Shane right? Was I responsible for killing our daughter? But how could I possibly have known that the one time I'd made a mistake, a police officer would grab my car and take off with Olivia?

My breasts ached, reminding me that Olivia should have been nursing. The nurse at the hospital had carefully sealed the breast pump in a sterilized bag and put it in my purse, but I didn't use it. I'd welcomed the pain. I'd felt as if I deserved to suffer. My marriage was over. I'd never doubted it for a moment. I'd lost my daughter and my husband in the same day.

Eventually, I'd slept, still lying in the same position on the bed. A knock at the door had woken me. It was dark in the hotel room. I'd turned on the light and gone to answer the door.

It was my mother, her eyes swollen and red-rimmed from crying. She'd only gotten to see her granddaughter once in her short lifetime, right after she was born. I'd fallen into her arms, my tears flowing. We'd cried together until my throat and chest hurt and my eyes were nearly swollen shut.

When my shuddering sobs had subsided, Mom had brought me a cold washcloth and a glass of water.

"Here, darling. Drink this and wash your face. You'll feel better," she murmured soothingly.

It was on the tip of my tongue to tell her that I would never feel better again, but I'd held back the words. Recognizing the small overnight bag that she'd set beside her suitcases at the door, I glanced at her.

"You stopped at the house before you came here?" I asked.

"Yes." She bit her lip. "Shane let me get some clothes for you."

"What did he say?" I'd stared at her, willing her not to lie. It was clear that she wanted to avoid the subject.

"He said that you couldn't come home. He told me that he doesn't ever want to see you again." She'd grabbed both my hands and offered me a watery smile. "I'm sure it's just the grief talking."

"No, it's not." When her gaze slid from mine, I knew that she hadn't told me everything. "What is, Mom? What else did he say?" She shifted on the bed, then tried to stand up. I'd stopped her by grabbing her arm. "Mom? Just tell me."

"He claims that you're going to be charged with endangering a minor."

My eyes widened. "But the police officer was the one who—" I'd closed my eyes and let the words trail into silence. What were they trying to say? That if Olivia hadn't been facing the wrong way, she wouldn't have gotten injured? Or, that the police officer would have seen her sooner?

Either way, the blame was going to fall solely upon me. I knew that it was inevitable, and right then, I didn't care. The facts were simple: I had made a mistake, and because of my mistake, my daughter was dead. Maybe I deserved to go to jail—to have everyone know what a terrible mother I had been.

"Don't, Marie. I know what you're thinking, and you're wrong. What happened was a fluke—a bizarre accident. It wasn't your fault." She'd squeezed my hands for emphasis. "When you were a child, we never used seat belts or car seats."

Although she'd meant to make me feel better, she hadn't been successful.

Mom rose and headed for the phone. "I'm going to call my lawyer right now. Don't worry, honey. We can beat this thing." She shook her head. "I can't believe that you're having to deal with these accusations right now. You just lost a child, for heaven's sake! And that police officer, thinking that he doesn't have to shoulder any of the blame! He should have taken the time to look in the backseat."

I had already considered that, and the answer had made me flinch. In all likelihood, the cop wouldn't have seen Olivia at a glance—surrounded as she had been with the groceries. I would have known exactly where she was and would have been able to watch her in the rearview mirror. I'd doubted that the officer would have spotted her, though, unless he was searching for her. The truth was, he hadn't even been aware of her existence.

"They're trying to save their own hides by blaming you," Mom ranted as she searched her address book for a number. "We'll just see about that."

At another time and place, I might have felt good about Mom's obvious love and loyalty, but at the time, I felt nothing but guilt and grief. I had a huge, gaping hole in my chest.

My baby was gone. She was dead—forever. Nothing else seemed to matter.

The next three days had passed in a blur. Mom took care of everything that I should have been doing. She worked with Shane on the funeral arrangements. She chose the outfit that Olivia would be buried in, and she decided where everyone would meet after the funeral. I didn't know how she did it, but she'd managed to convince Shane to let me come home the day of the funeral.

Later, when I'd begun to emerge from my fog of grief, I'd realized that Shane had agreed because he didn't want to pass up the opportunity to let everyone know that he blamed me for Olivia's death. I think he also knew that the district attorney's office was waiting until after the funeral before they pressed formal charges against me. He was hoping that he'd get to see the show.

He did get to witness my shame, as it turned out. It was late in the evening and just about everyone had gone home. Mom was with me, thankfully, when there was a knock at the door. I'd been packing more clothes to take back to the hotel with me. Mom's lawyer had arrived the day before, and Mom and I were supposed to meet him later at the hotel.

I'd gone calmly with the officers who'd come to get me. I'd suspected that something like that would happen. Standing a few feet away, I could feel Shane gloating over my arrest. My heart felt like a stone. We had just lost our child. It was a time for unity, not hatred. What I needed most right then was Shane's support, and he couldn't give it to me.

Mom assured me that she would post bail the moment she was able. Still numb with grief, I'd barely remember the ordeal that I'd had to endure. Later, I stared at the ink stains on my fingers, trying to remember how they'd gotten there.

The next morning, Mom had posted bail, and we'd met with her lawyer. It was painful, telling my story again, but I knew that I had to do it. Mom's support meant a lot to me during those dark hours. I couldn't begin to explain the terrible grief I'd suffered over losing my baby, and the added guilt I'd felt made it worse.

The day I had to appear in court before the judge, Shane was there. He hadn't changed. He'd still stared at me with accusation and hatred. I was beginning to feel sorry for Shane. How could he ever be happy, with so much hatred in his heart? Didn't he know that if I could have traded my life for Olivia's, I would have?

In a monotone voice, I told the judge what had happened. I'd explained why I had disobeyed the laws and turned the car seat to face the wrong way. My lawyer then made excuses for my actions, playing up the part of the officer who had taken my car without giving me a chance to warn him about the baby in the backseat. He didn't try to say that I was blameless, but he did his best to shoulder part of the blame onto the officer.

Mom was a rock through the entire thing. The judge ruled Olivia's death as an accident. Then he slapped me with a ticket for having her wrongly secured, and she was there to lead me out of the courtroom. But not before Shane had screamed at me, accusing me of murder. He'd accused me of ruining his life.

I might have gone on blaming myself, hating myself, if I hadn't gone for therapy. My counselor helped me to forgive myself for my part in Olivia's death, and to work toward forgiving Shane for blaming me entirely.

In the end, I lost my husband as well as my daughter, but I'm getting stronger. I still think of Olivia, and I still miss her. I always will. As for Shane, I pity him, mostly. There's a small part of me, too, that blames him. But I know that blaming him won't bring Olivia back, so I try not to think about blame at all.

About six months after Olivia's death, I got a phone call from Shane's ex-wife. She'd heard about our tragedy and wanted me to meet her for lunch. She explained that she wanted to tell me her side of the story about what had happened the day their son had drowned.

I came very close to refusing to meet with her. Why would I want to open wounds that had just begun to heal? But something had urged me to go, so I had.

I'd seen pictures of Christine, but I'd never met her in person. It was strange, meeting the woman that Shane had taught me to hate. If not for her, Shane might not have been so tough on me.

Then Christine told me her story, and opened my eyes to the possibility that Shane had lied.

"I can tell by your expression," Christine said, "that Shane didn't tell you he was there when it happened."

I shook my head, my throat clogged with tears. "No, he didn't."

Christine sighed. "I think he's convinced himself that he wasn't, but that doesn't change the fact that he was. I know what he told everyone, that it was my fault, and at first, I let him convince me. Eventually, I got over it. When I saw the obituary and found out that you'd lost your daughter, I couldn't shake the feeling that you were going through the same turmoil that I'd gone through—thanks to Shane."

"But it was partly my fault," I admitted, to be fair. "I had the car seat turned around to face the front so that I could keep an eye on her."

"Yes, I understand that. But don't you realize that if that police officer hadn't taken your car, she would have been okay? And if Shane hadn't been so paranoid and picky about how you took care of Olivia, then you wouldn't have turned the car seat around in the first place?"

She shook her head. "I know how convincing and hateful he can be, and how he hates to take responsibility for his own actions. Yet, he's very quick to accuse someone else. I'll bet he's never told anyone that he was upstairs taking a nap when Timmy drowned. I had asked him to watch Timmy, but he'd refused. He'd said that there were plenty of teenagers around to keep Timmy busy during the party."

I'd sat in stunned silence until she'd spoken again.

"So you see, I could have blamed Shane for taking a nap, instead of watching his son. He never gave me the opportunity. Instead, he took advantage of my grief and guilt to convince me that it was all my fault Timmy drowned." She put her hand over mine. "Don't let him destroy you, Marie. It was a freak accident. Get on with your life."

And so, I did. Christine's confession helped me to do that. I'll always be grateful to her for giving me the gift of inner peace.

THE END

# BLACK MARKET BABIES
## Our town is full of them

I thought my life was the most ordinary life in the world until a strange disease, a chance encounter, and an old rumor came together to uncover a family secret that changed not only my life, but the lives of almost everyone in my hometown—forever.

I grew up in a small town in Oklahoma, one of those rural communities where everyone knows everybody else. Most families have lived in the area for generations, so we not only know each other but each other's kinfolk. Though there were times, especially as a teenager, when having so many people poking their noses into my business drove me crazy, for the most part it was a good place to grow up.

When I went away to college, I thought I was going out into the big, wide world to live a whole new, exciting life. But the joke was on me when I fell in love with a boy who had lived down the street from me half my life. Josh and I married the day after we both graduated from college and moved back home, where Josh had a job working for the county appraiser. I went to work in the billing department of the local hospital, and life was good.

We had our first baby, a girl we named Genevieve, a month after our third anniversary. She was a beautiful child, with brilliant eyes like mine, and a halo of soft red hair. I heard more than a few jokes about "the milkman's baby," since neither Josh nor I, nor anyone in our families as far back as we could remember, had red hair. But we laughed it off. Anyway, nobody had delivered milk in our neighborhood in thirty years.

Two years later, we had our second baby, Riley. Right away things were different. Even in the hospital nursery he cried and cried. He seemed happier when we brought him home, but the slightest bump would cause a bruise on his little body. Once, when I accidentally scratched him with my fingernail, he bled and bled. It got to where we were almost afraid to touch him, he seemed so fragile.

I worried, too, that people would see the bruises and think we were abusing our baby. The thought horrified me, but I knew how people in small towns liked to talk. It wouldn't take any time at all for our reputations to be ruined.

So I insisted our pediatrician run tests to find out what was wrong with Riley. "Genevieve never bruised like this," I said, pointing to a plum-sized bruise on the baby's arm. I didn't have any idea where it came from. "People are going to think I'm hitting my baby."

"You sure you're not being a little rough with him? Having two little ones to take care of can get the best of anyone sometimes."

The question shocked me. Dr. Truman had been my pediatrician when I was a girl, so I thought he knew me better than that. "No! I would never hurt my children." I burst into tears.

Dr. Truman patted my shoulder. "Now, Janine, there's no need to get upset. I believe you. We'll run some tests and see what we can find out."

So they took some blood samples to send out to the lab. Even Dr. Truman was alarmed when it seemed to take forever to stop the bleeding after they pulled out the needle from my baby's arm. But he tried to be reassuring. "You go on home now, and don't worry. We'll get to the bottom of this."

I figured we'd know the test results in a couple of days, but when three days went by and we didn't hear anything from Dr. Truman's office, I started to get really worried. When I couldn't stand it any more, I called and talked to Dr. Truman's nurse, Elizabeth. She and I went to school together, so I trusted her to tell me the truth.

"That is odd that you haven't heard," she said. "Let me check."

She came back to the phone in a few minutes. "Doc says he sent the results to Children's Hospital in Oklahoma City for review. Sometimes it takes a while to hear back from them. But he'll call you as soon as he knows something."

As I hung up the phone, I knew we were dealing with something out of the ordinary. Thoughts of leukemia, or rare, incurable disorders, filled my head. I bowed my head and said a silent prayer that everything would be all right. That my baby would be made well.

That afternoon, Elizabeth called me back. "Dr. Truman wants to see you and Josh in the office tomorrow. Is eight-thirty okay?"

"Sure. Eight-thirty is fine. Elizabeth, what's going on?"

"We got the test results back, and Doc wants to go over them with you. That's all I know. Really."

Of course I didn't sleep much that night, and Josh and I were at the doctor's office early the next morning. We'd left the children with Josh's mother.

Dr. Truman ushered us into his office and sat down behind his big oak desk. He must have seen how anxious we were, because he didn't waste time with pleasantries. "Well, we know what's wrong with Riley," he said. "And the good news is that, with treatment, there's no reason he can't live a normal life."

"What is it?" I leaned toward him. "What's wrong with my baby?"

He opened a file and glanced at a page of notes. "Have you heard of hemophilia?"

"That's where people can't stop bleeding, isn't it?" Josh asked.

"That's right. They lack a clotting factor in their blood. When most people cut themselves or fall down and get a bruise, clotting factors within their own blood will stop the bleeding naturally, and they'll go on to heal. Hemophiliacs lack this clotting factor and can bleed to death from a relatively minor cut."

He must have seen how pale I'd become, because he hurried to add, "Today, we can administer the clotting factor regularly to keep this tendency to bleed freely under control. And there are a lot of things you as a parent can do to help your son grow up as normally as possible."

Josh reached out and took my hand. "It's a lot to take in," he said.

"I have some literature for you to take home to read, and I suggest you get in touch with some of the organizations for hemophiliacs and their parents. They'll be a lot of help to you." He smiled. "I think Riley is going to be just fine. We'll do everything we can to make certain of it."

"Thank you, Doc." I managed a weak smile. "I'm glad to know there's a treatment."

He closed the folder and rested his hands on top of it. "I'm curious, Janine. I've checked my records, and I don't find any other instances of hemophilia in your family. Do you know of any, perhaps in other branches of the family?"

I was surprised. "No. Not that I know of. I mean, all three of my brothers played football. They got banged up so many times we would've known if they had something like this."

"I don't think there's any hemophilia in my family, either," Josh said. "Why?"

"Most of the time hemophilia runs in families. Although it can skip generations. And sometimes it shows up unexpectedly. There's a theory that sometimes genes spontaneously mutate."

"You say it's genetic." Josh frowned. "Does that mean Riley got this from me or Janine?"

"From Janine, actually. The genetic anomaly that causes hemophilia is in the X chromosome a boy receives from his mother."

"You mean I gave this to Riley?" A chill washed over me.

"You passed it on through your genetic material. There's a chance Genevieve is a carrier, too. She should probably be tested before she has children of her own."

"And I got this gene from my mother?"

"Possibly. Are you sure none of her brothers—your uncles—had it?"

"Of course I'm sure. Both of my mother's brothers are still alive. Uncle Danny owns the feed co-op, and Uncle Bernie is principal of Long Ridge Elementary."

"Well, then maybe you're one of the cases in which the gene mutates on its own." He smiled again. "I wouldn't worry about it. The important thing now is to take care of Riley."

Dr. Truman sent us home with a lot of information about hemophilia and instructions on caring for Riley. "It's going to be a little challenging at times," he said. "But I know you're up to it. And Riley is going to be all right."

I stood over my baby's crib a long time that night, looking at him and wondering. To think I'd been carrying this genetic time bomb around in me all my life and never knew it. If I'd known about it, Josh and I could've been tested.

And then what? I wouldn't trade Genevieve and Riley for all the other babies in the world.

Josh found me there by the crib and gave me a hug. "Don't beat up on yourself about this. You had no way of knowing."

"But why didn't I know?" I gripped the crib railings. "If this disease runs in families, someone in my family must have known about it. Why didn't they say anything?"

"You heard the doctor. You might be one of those who have the gene for no reason."

I nodded. "I know. It's just hard to look at him so helpless there and know there's nothing we can do."

He squeezed my shoulder. "We can be there for him, and we can follow the doctor's directions. We can help him grow up to be a fine young man. We can do all that."

I leaned down and tucked the blanket more tightly around Riley. "You're right. I worry too much. Everything's going to be all right."

Maybe if I said those words enough, I'd begin to believe them.

The next morning, I called my mother. She's almost seventy, and since my dad died five years ago, she's lived in a little house a few miles away. She was quiet when I told her what Dr. Truman had told me.

"I don't know what to tell you, dear. There's never been anything like that in our family. Maybe Josh's family—"

"No, Mama. Dr. Truman said the gene is passed through the mother."

"Well, that just can't be."

Then, before I could explain about genes mutating, she did an amazing thing. She hung up on me!

I told myself Mama was just upset about Riley, that she hadn't meant to slam the phone down in my ear. I'd call her back later and we'd laugh about it.

Meanwhile, I had errands to run in town. I found myself at the store right down from my uncle's feed co-op. On impulse, I went inside.

"Janine! What a nice surprise!" Uncle Danny came out from his office and gave me a hug. "And look at these gorgeous children." He gathered Genevieve into his arms and smiled down at Riley. "Did you just stop by to say hello to your great uncle?"

"We came to say hello. But, also, can I talk to you about something?"

He must have heard something in my voice. His face sobered. "Sure, hon. Come on into my office."

Uncle Danny's office hadn't changed since I was a little girl. The same stack of stock magazines teetered in the corner, and the same antique saddle doubled as an ottoman in front of a sagging recliner. A moth-eaten deer head served as a hat rack for a half a dozen feed company caps advertising chicken scratch and horse cubes, and Danny had to move a pile of invoices off the chair before I could sit down. The familiar smell of molasses and grain filled the air.

While Genevieve played with Danny's keys, I told him about Riley's hemophilia.

"That's a hereditary disease, isn't it?" he said.

"Usually." I cradled Riley against my shoulder. "Do you know of anyone in our family who had it?"

He shook his head. "No, I sure don't. Both my uncles were in World War II, and I don't think the Army would've let them in if they'd had something like that. I had six male cousins and I don't recall any of them being sick."

"Then I guess it's one of those genetic anomalies Dr. Truman talked about."

"Did you ask Nancy about this?"

I fussed with Riley's shirt, pulling it down over his little belly. "She said she didn't know anything about it. And then she hung up on me."

"I reckon she's just feeling bad, thinking she might've passed this on to you, and you to little Riley. She thinks a lot of her grandbabies, you know. Thinks a lot of you, too. Especially since she waited so long to have you."

I nodded. I'd been born late in my mother's life—when she was thirty-seven and Daddy was forty. My youngest brother, Nick, was ten when I was born. I guess most people assumed I was a surprise baby, but I was always told Mama kept trying to get pregnant because, more than anything, she wanted a little girl.

I left the co-op and decided to go see Mama. I wanted to reassure her that she didn't have anything to do with Riley having hemophilia. It was just one of those unlucky things that happen in life sometimes.

When Mama answered the door, I was struck again by how frail she seemed. Like most of the women in our family, Mama is small and dark, with olive skin and hair that was jet black well into her forties.

Of course, I'm the exception to the family rule. I tower over Mama by a good six inches, and I have a lighter complexion. Daddy's people were all dark too, as were my brothers, so I always stood out at family gatherings.

Even though I don't look anything like my mother, people say I act just like her. Which made for some rocky goings on sometimes. We were both so stubborn, neither one of us liked to give in to the other.

"Janine, come in! Oh, and Genevieve, give Grandma a hug." Mama gathered Genevieve into her arms, then straightened and reached for Riley. "And let me see this beautiful boy."

I followed Mama and the children into her living room, where Genevieve immediately headed for the toy box Mama kept stocked for the grandchildren. Mama sat on the sofa, Riley in her lap. "Oh, he's such a sweet baby," she cooed.

I waited for her to ask about his hemophilia, but she didn't say anything. I decided I was going to have to be the one to bring it up.

"The doctor says with treatment, there's no reason Riley can't have a relatively normal life."

"I don't know if that old fool knows what he's talking about." She smiled at Riley. "There's nothing wrong with this little darling."

"Mama, Riley does have hemophilia." I leaned toward her. "We don't know why, but there's nothing we can do now except see that he gets the best care possible."

Mama raised her eyes to meet mine. "I'm sorry, dear. I wish this hadn't happened."

"I wish so, too, Mama. But it will be all right. Really it will."

It's amazing what you can get used to when you have to. Before long, dealing with Riley's illness was almost normal for us. The first time I took him in to be treated with the clotting factor, it was hard to listen to his cries as they threaded the needle into his vein, but the doctor and nurses were all so supportive, and that helped a lot.

Our families all rallied around us. I hadn't expected less. We've always been close, living in the same town and visiting each other often. They, too, accepted Riley's disease as a fact in our lives, just something to be dealt with.

Except Mama. She refused to talk about hemophilia and tried to pretend it didn't even exist. I mentioned this odd behavior to my oldest brother, Chris, and his wife when they were over at our house one evening.

"She's old, sis. Maybe this is too much for her."

"Uncle Danny said maybe she feels guilty, thinking she might have passed this gene on to me. I tried to tell her since nobody else in the family has it, that's probably not the case, but she won't listen."

He shrugged. "You were always extra-special to her. The only girl, and she waited so long to have you." He looked at his wife, Carole. "Mama had three miscarriages between Nick and Janine."

"That must have been terrible for her," Carole said.

"Finally she changed doctors, started going to a doctor who specialized in women who couldn't have children."

"An infertility doctor," I said.

He shook his head. "I don't think they called it that. Just another gynecologist." He grinned. "Guess it did the trick. Next thing you know, we hear we're going to have a baby sister."

"You mean a baby," I said. "She couldn't have known back then I was going to be a girl."

"Guess she was pretty sure. She even had the name picked out. We always talked about you as Janine. One day she went to the hospital and when she came home a few days later, there you were."

I hadn't known about Mama changing doctors, but then, why would I? I imagined what it must have been like for my mother, wanting a baby so badly, and waiting so long. I'd been so lucky, not having the slightest trouble conceiving or any problems during my pregnancies. Even Riley's hemophilia was turning out to be manageable.

I was still thinking about all this the next day at work. Who was the doctor who had helped Mama? It seemed I owed him a debt of thanks.

On my lunch hour, I walked over to Medical Records and talked to Viola Lyman. Viola had been in charge of Medical Records for the past thirty years. She had a mind like a computer and could tell you everything about everybody.

"Well, Janine Curtis, what in the world brings you over to my neck of the woods?" she said when I walked into her little office.

"I wondered if you could help me find out the name of the doctor who attended my birth," I said.

"Well, let's see here. I'm sure we can find that." She led me down a narrow aisle between shelves piled high with storage boxes. "Now let's see, you were born in seventy-five, is that right?"

"Yes, ma'am. March fourteenth."

"That would be right . . . here." She reached up and hauled down a box. After a few seconds of flipping through the contents of the box, she pulled out a folder. "That would be Dr. Virgil Mason." She smiled. "I remember Dr. Virgil. He had a very busy practice. His patients loved him."

"I understand he specialized in infertility."

"That's right. Woman who wanted babies and couldn't have them would go to him and next thing you know, they'd be bringing home a beautiful baby."

"Is he still practicing?"

"Oh, no. He retired years ago." She replaced the folder and reshelved the box. "I believe he still lives in town, though."

I looked around us, at the rows and rows of file boxes. "Are all the records filed by dates?"

"That's right, dear. All the births for March of 1975 are in this section." She smiled at me. "Do you need anything else?"

"No. Thank you. You've been a big help."

I went back to my desk, but my mind kept straying back to those stacks of medical records. What else could they tell me about my birth? Was there anything in there that might point to some genetic damage—something that might've led to my son being born with hemophilia?

I waited until I was sure Mrs. Lyman was on break, and then I slipped back into the records room. I found the right file box and pulled out the folder labeled with my mother's name.

As I read through the cramped lines of notations made by the obstetrics nurse, my mouth dropped open. Here was something I'd never known. Apparently I wasn't born at the hospital after all. According to the nurse's notes, I was born in route to the hospital.

Why hadn't my mother told me this? It seemed like the kind of story that would become family lore.

I stuck the record back in the box and the box back on the shelf. I couldn't wait to ask Mama about this one.

I had my chance that afternoon, when I stopped by to pick up the children. My mother and Josh's mother took turns watching the children, which worked out great for us and gave them both plenty of time with their grandchildren.

"Mama, why didn't you tell me I was born on the way to the hospital?" I asked as I watched her change Riley's diaper.

She gave me a puzzled look. "What are you talking about?"

"My medical record at the hospital says I was born before you ever got to the hospital."

She looked away. "That was a long time ago, dear. You can't expect me to remember everything. Besides, why does it matter?"

"Mama, how could you not remember something like that? Especially when you'd waited so long to have me."

"I don't see what difference it makes now." She fastened the snaps on Riley's jumper and smiled at him. "Isn't he a handsome little fellow?"

"Mama, how did you know I was going to be a girl?"

"What was that, dear?" She pulled her attention away from Riley to look at me.

"Chris said you talked about me being a girl from the first. He said you always called me Janine."

"I just knew, dear." She picked up Riley and cradled him to her shoulder. "Don't you think you'd better go home now? You don't want dinner to be late."

I could take a hint. For some reason, Mama didn't want to talk about my birth. But the more she stonewalled, the more I wanted to know. Having Riley had awakened a desire in me to know as much as I could about what had happened that long-ago March day.

I went back to Medical Records the next day to talk to Mrs. Lyman some more. "Did you know I wasn't born at the hospital?" I asked her. "I was born on the way to the hospital."

"That wasn't unusual for Dr. Virgil's patients. Quite a few of them were born on the way to the hospital, or in the doctor's office, or even at home." She smiled. "I think he was so insistent that they not come to the hospital too early. He didn't like to get here and wait around."

"Isn't that a little odd, though? I mean, what if something had gone wrong?"

"Things were different in those days, dear. We didn't have all these managed care companies telling us what to do. And Virgil Mason had an impressive reputation around here. The women whose babies he delivered loved him. People would drive from five counties to see him, too. Women who'd been told they'd never have a baby would end up with the child they always wanted after seeing Dr. Virgil. He didn't need all these fancy drugs and medical procedures they put women through these days, either."

"How did he do it?" I asked.

She shook her head. "No one knows. Maybe he just knew how to get the women to relax. Whatever he did, it worked. For a while there you couldn't walk down the street of this town without seeing new babies everywhere."

I decided I wanted to talk to Dr. Virgil Mason. If he knew that much about bringing babies into the world, maybe he could shed some light on the reason Riley had been stricken with hemophilia.

It was easy enough to find his name in the phone book. I finally worked up the courage to call him.

"Hello, Dr. Mason?"

"No one's called me that in a while, but yes, this is Dr. Virgil Mason."

His voice was warm and friendly. I began to relax. "You don't know me, but my name is Janine Curtis. When my mother, Nancy Piermont, wanted a little girl so desperately, you were the doctor who helped her."

"Nancy Piermont. Yes, I remember her. A very pretty, dark-haired woman. She had four sons."

"That's right. But she wanted a little girl. And you helped her."

"And now you want me to help you, too."

I was surprised. "Why yes. How did you know?"

"I get these calls from time to time. I'm not really in practice anymore, but I like to help when I can. Now tell me, do you have any children already?"

"Yes, that's why I called. I—"

"Do you want a boy or a girl this time?"

I frowned. "Why are you asking me that?"

"It's up to you, dear. I can arrange either one. As I said, I don't do much work anymore, but since you're second generation. . . ."

I understood now. He thought I wanted him to help me, the same way he'd helped my mother. I smiled. "Dr. Mason, I didn't call you because I'm having trouble getting pregnant. I called because my son was born with hemophilia and there is no record of hemophilia anywhere in my family. I was hoping you could help me understand why that it."

"I don't know what you're talking about. Why would I know anything about that? I don't want to talk to you anymore." Then, like my mother, he hung up on me.

I stared at the receiver in my hand. What had I said to make Dr. Mason so angry? He acted almost like I was accusing him of something. Something wrong.

Had Dr. Mason done something wrong? Something that could've damaged me and thus, damaged my son?

I decided to have another look at the hospital records. I thought Mrs. Lyman might be suspicious if I showed up to talk to her a third time, so I waited until she was away from her desk and slipped into the records room. If anyone stopped me, I'd say one of the billing supervisors had asked me to fetch a chart, as sometimes happened.

I went straight to the box that contained my file and pulled it. But this time, I also pulled files from boxes on either side—any babies who were listed as being delivered by Dr. Mason. I knew what I was doing was wrong—patient confidentiality is sacred in hospitals. If I was discovered looking in other people's files, I could be fired. But something told me things weren't right with Dr. Mason. He'd acted too defensive on the phone. And what kind of doctor routinely encourages his patients not to show up at the hospital until the last possible moment? The only way I knew to find a pattern was to look at other births he'd attended.

I had just enough time to copy the records and return them to their proper places before Mrs. Lyman returned from lunch. When I passed her in the hall on the way back to my desk, I looked away and hoped she hadn't noticed me. I felt guilty but excited, too. Was I going to learn something that would help me to help Riley?

When I looked over all the records that night, I noticed a few similarities right away. All but one of the babies in question had been born away from the hospital—two at home, three on the way to the hospital, and two in Dr. Mason's office. Other than that, the babies themselves seemed pretty normal. I re-read the names, most of which were people I knew. Jon Hartwell, Henry Holbrook, Coretta Langford, Cheryl Hendricks, George Robertson, Kathy Harper, and Lloyd Marlowe. Cheryl was the only baby who'd been born at the hospital. She and I had been in the same grade. She was a freckle-faced cherub who went on to be the high school valedictorian. Certainly nothing unusual there.

I decided to make a list of what I knew about each of these people—what they looked like, what their parents did. Part of me worried I was being silly, that I was making a mystery where there was none, but something drove me to continue.

Only when I'd written down everything I could think of did the pattern emerge. Four of the eight were only children. Cheryl had two older brothers and a younger sister. George was like me, much younger than his older siblings, all of whom were girls. Coretta and Lloyd both had younger brothers, born several years after them. So it seemed a good bet that most of their mothers had turned to Dr. Mason for help in conceiving—either a first child, or a much-wanted later child.

Then there was the matter of appearance. Except for Cheryl, none of the other seven really resembled the rest of their family. Lloyd Marlowe especially stood out in my mind. His dusky skin and curly hair were so different from everyone else in his family of fair-haired, red-faced farmers. In high school, a particularly nasty rumor had circulated that Lloyd looked like he did because his mother had had an affair with the family's farmhand. In fact, Lloyd had dropped out of school and joined the Navy, probably to get away from that kind of talk.

So what did any of this tell me?

Not much, I had to admit. Maybe something shady had been going on with Dr. Mason, and maybe he was what everyone said he was—a very good doctor who had a talent for helping women conceive.

The next day, I was entering some routine billing paperwork into the computer when a name jumped out at me. Kathy Harper had recently been admitted to the hospital. I scanned further down the page for her diagnosis. Breast cancer.

I knew Kathy. She and I had been partners in ninth grade home-ec class. We'd had to work together to plan a household budget and prepare a five-course meal. We'd lost track after graduation, though I'd heard she'd recently moved back to town.

At lunch, I took the elevator up to the fourth floor surgery wing and found Kathy's room.

"Kathy? It's Janine Curtis. I used to be Janine Piermont. Do you remember me?"

"Janine?" She reached over, put on a pair of glasses, and squinted at me. Then a smile wreathed her face. "Janine! Of course I remember you. What are you doing here?"

"I work here. When I saw your name on the admitting sheet, I had to come up and see you."

"Well, come over here and tell me what you've been up to." She motioned toward a chair by the bed. "Pardon me if I don't get up."

I sat and told her about marrying Josh, and about Genevieve and Riley. She told me about her husband, Mike, and their two girls. "And now this." She nodded toward the bandages swathing her chest. "I thought thirty years old was too young to have breast cancer, but the doctor tells me I've got this nasty, aggressive kind. He says most people who have this kind of cancer have a family history." She made a face. "Guess I'm just lucky."

Her words sent a chill through me. "You mean, no one else in your family has ever had breast cancer?"

She shook her head. "Can you believe it? Of course, the doctor mumbled all kinds of stuff about 'genetic anomalies' and such. The bottom line is, I've got it and we're going to treat it aggressively, and hopefully I'll beat it."

"I hope so, too." I hesitated. "What do your parents say?"

"Oh, Mama's all torn up about it, of course. Daddy is, too, but he tries not to show it. I'm their only child, so I guess that makes it harder."

We talked a little more, but I could see she was getting tired. I promised to stop by again later, and left.

I couldn't get my conversation with Kathy out of my head. What she'd said about her cancer usually being hereditary and the doctor's mention of genetic anomalies was eerily similar to what Dr. Truman had said about Riley's hemophilia.

Kathy was a short, olive-skinned woman in a family of redheaded Irish. I was a tall blonde in a family of short, dark Italians. My son had a disease that was usually hereditary.

I kept trying to shove a strange, frightening thought out of my mind: What if I'm not my mother's daughter after all? What if someone else gave birth to me, someone who's tall and fair, who has a history of hemophilia in her family?

I decided I had to confront my mom. If I was wrong, I would apologize to her. But if I was right, I had to know.

We sat on the sofa in Mama's house. Riley was still down for his nap, and Genevieve was absorbed in a puzzle on the floor between us.

"Mama, what really happened when I was born?" I asked. "How did Dr. Mason help you to have a baby girl when you never could before?"

All the color went out of her face and she looked away. "I don't know what you're talking about," she said softly.

I reached over and took her hands in mine. They were ice cold. "Mama, I know something happened. Why don't I look like anyone else in the family? Why does Riley have this hereditary disease no one else in our family has ever had?"

"It's not always hereditary," she protested. "The doctor said—"

"I know. In some cases hemophilia shows up for no reason. But is that really the case here? Mama, tell me what happened. Why wasn't I born in the hospital? Why were you so sure I was going to be a girl when you'd had four boys before?"

She started shaking, silent sobs wracking her body, big tears running down her face. I gathered her close, my heart breaking. "Mama, whatever it is, I'll understand. Please tell me."

I found a box of tissues and brought them to her, along with a glass of water. Still not looking at me, she began to talk. "I wanted a baby girl so badly. I tried everything. After my third miscarriage, my doctor told me my body wasn't capable of having more children. I should be happy with my boys and go on with my life."

She sniffed. "I tried to do that. I really tried. But I kept dreaming about a little girl. About you." She smiled through her tears. "Sue Ramsey told me that Dr. Virgil Mason could help me. She and her husband had tried to have a baby for years. Thanks to Dr. Mason, they had a beautiful little boy."

"But what did Dr. Mason do to help them?" I asked. "What did he do to help you?"

She shredded the tissue in her hands. "He was really doing a great service. Women who were pregnant and couldn't keep their babies would come to him and he would find homes for them with families who wanted babies. And his fees were very reasonable."

I gasped. "You . . . you bought me from this man?"

She looked at me, her expression scolding. "It was a private adoption. They do it all the time these days, don't they?"

"But they don't try to pass the baby off as their own." I stood and began to pace. My mother wasn't really my mother? The words would not sink in.

"We thought it would be easier that way."

"That's why I don't look like the rest of the family. Why my kids don't look like their cousins." I stopped and stared at her. "My mother—the woman who gave birth to me—she carried the hemophilia gene."

"You don't know that, dear."

"No, but what else don't I know that I might need to know someday? Does this woman have cancer in her family? Or heart disease or diabetes? Or some birth defect I might unknowingly pass on to my children?"

"I really think you're overreacting. Dr. Mason helped lots of women, and I haven't heard of any problems before now."

"So Michelle and Maggie Ramsey were 'adopted' through Dr. Mason?"

"And Emma Robertson's boy, George, and that sweet Jon Hartwell, and Henry Holbrook. Oh, you can't imagine what a blessing it was for us when Dr. Mason came to town. And for the poor girls who needed homes for their babies, too."

I sank down onto the couch beside her. "But, Mama, it was wrong." I looked at her. "Don't you see? Those babies—me—we've been living a lie, thinking we were one thing and being another. What other time bombs are we sitting on? Who else is carrying a genetic defect they could pass on to a child, or a family history of some disease they need to know about?"

"We never meant to hurt you, dear."

"I know that, Mama. But I have to tell the truth now. Maybe I'll protect somebody else's child."

She frowned. "I think you're going to hurt a lot of people."

"A lot of people have already been hurt. I have to try to keep more from being hurt."

I went home and made a list of everything I knew—names, dates, and what details I'd been able to piece together. Then I looked it over. While I thought deliberately deceiving all these people was unethical, was it really against the law? Or was it as Mama had said, merely a different kind of private adoption?

I decided the best thing to do was to send the information to the state police and the state medical examiner, and let them decide. With shaking hands, I typed two letters and put them in the mail. Then I waited.

I didn't have to wait very long. A week later, a man and a woman in dark suits showed up on my doorstep and introduced themselves as investigators with the state police. While these two were talking to me, other agents were interviewing Dr. Mason and some of the other people involved. They also went to the hospital and subpoenaed the records associated with every birth Dr. Mason had attended.

My first feeling was one of triumph. Justice was being done. The investigators were going to do their best to track down the birth mothers of all the babies. They wanted to find these women to build their case, but I saw it as a chance for all of us to learn our families' medical histories.

The next morning, I wasn't feeling so happy. The story made the front page of every paper in the state, and my phone never stopped ringing. Most of the calls were from the press. After the first half dozen, I refused to talk any more.

The calls from friends and neighbors were harder to deal with. Sue Ramsey was one of the first. "Why did you do this?" she demanded. "Why couldn't you leave well enough alone? Do you know how many people you've hurt?"

"I've helped people with this," I said. "We have a right to know the truth."

"The truth is that we did what was best for our children. Everyone would've been fine if you had just kept quiet."

I thought the other 'adopted' children would understand what I'd done, but that wasn't the case with everyone. Coretta Langford called me in tears. "Do you know what you've done?" She sobbed. "I don't even know who I am now."

"Now you have a chance to really find out," I said. "I'm not saying our mothers didn't love us. But we have a right to know the truth."

"I don't want to know the truth," she said. "Things were fine until you started meddling."

I was feeling pretty low by then, wondering if I really had done the right thing. A lot of people's lives would never be the same because of this. Did I have the right to change so much this way?

Then Kathy Harper called. She was crying, too, but her words to me weren't angry. "I just wanted to thank you," she said. "I know it wasn't easy for you."

"You seem to be in the minority with that opinion," I said. "I've been hearing all morning how I should've minded my own business and kept quiet."

"They're wrong!" The strength of her voice surprised me. "What you've done may have saved my life. The doctors tell me if my cancer doesn't respond to chemotherapy, my best chance for recovery is a bone marrow transplant. And the best donors are members of your immediate family." She started crying again. "You've given me a chance I wouldn't have had otherwise."

Her words kept me going over the next weeks, as people I'd thought were my friends publicly shunned me. I was vilified as a troublemaker and a busybody.

The hospital put me on disciplinary leave while they investigated my breech of patient confidentiality. I admitted my wrongdoing and resigned. Though I felt what I had done was worth the end results, I also didn't want patients to have to worry that their privacy might be violated. The hospital's policy was the right one.

But good things came from all of this, too. A man contacted me and thanked me for helping him to understand why he always felt like an outsider in his own family. A young woman wrote that she'd spent twenty-five years searching for the daughter she'd given away and thanks to me, they'd been reunited.

Despite the hurt I know they suffered, my family stood by me. My mom and I had a long talk and she said she thought she understood. My brothers told me this didn't change the way they felt about me, but they were proud of me for standing up to everybody. Josh said he never knew I was so strong, and it made him love me even more.

As for Dr. Mason, he was caught trying to destroy the records from his practice—records which contained the names of many of the birth mothers. He was charged with fraud and taken to jail, though he continued to protest he had done a great service for his patients. It will be up to a jury to decide if he was right or not.

A few months after the story broke, a letter came to me from the state police. The agent in charge of the investigation thanked me for my help.

"I hope you'll find the enclosed information useful." Included was a card with a woman's name and address.

I sank into a chair and stared at the card. Stephanie Stewart. My birth mother. What did she look like? What did she think about me?

With a lump in my throat, I sat down and wrote a letter. I introduced myself, told her a little about my life and my family. I wrote about Riley and his hemophilia. "I don't want to intrude on your privacy or disrupt your life," I wrote. "But I would very much like to know about your family's medical history. It would help me and my family so much. I would especially like to know if anyone in your family has hemophilia."

A month went by. Then two. I began to think that my birth mother didn't want to have anything to do with me. When she'd given me away, she'd cut the ties completely. Though this saddened me, I tried to accept it. After all, I had a family that loved me very much. I had lived a blessed life so far and had no complaints.

Then one day, I received a letter addressed in an unfamiliar, feminine hand. My heart pounding, I slit open the envelope and unfolded a single sheet of paper.

Dear Janine, I read.

You can't imagine my shock—and yes delight—upon receiving

your letter. It saddens me to tell you that my daughter—your mother—died three years ago in a tragic automobile accident. She was away at college at the time of your birth, and I never knew of your existence. I can't imagine how, or why, she kept such a secret from me, but to hear from you now seems like an extra blessing. As if I had a piece of her back in my life.

You asked about hemophilia. Yes, there is a family history of the disease. In fact, it is one reason my daughter never had any other children. I don't know of any other diseases that run in our family. We have generally been a very healthy bunch.

I know I have no right, but will you send a picture? And if you would like to stay in touch, I would welcome that very much.

The letter was signed, Shannon Carter.

I was crying by the time I finished the letter. But I couldn't wait to pick up the phone and call Shannon—my grandmother.

Later, Shannon came to see us. Though the visit was a little awkward at first, we soon settled down like old friends. The children were delighted with the gifts she brought them. Best of all, she and my mother really hit it off. They were almost the same age and have a lot in common. I couldn't believe I was so lucky.

Things have finally settled down around here. I have a new job, working for a lawyer. He said he liked the fact that I was a good investigator.

Genevieve and Riley are doing well. I've joined an on-line support group for parents of hemophiliacs, and my new friends there have helped me so much. I've had my tubes tied so I don't pass the hemophilia gene onto anyone else.

Kathy Harper and I have stayed in touch. She did require a bone marrow transplant, but her sister—whom she'd never met before—was a perfect match. She's made a full recovery, and I've gained a very special friend.

There are still people in town who won't talk to me. I respect that there are families that are trying to heal. But I know I did the right thing. There's no reason for anyone to live a lie. In the end, lies always hurt one way or another.

THE END

# STOLEN!
## Will I ever see my baby again?

"Sarah? Sarah? Are you okay?" My coworker, Jane Wilcox, was snapping her fingers in front of my face.

"Girl, where are you?" she asked when I finally realized she was speaking to me. "You seem like you're a million miles away, and we have a lot to do today!"

We both worked as secretaries at a small law firm in town. Usually I enjoyed her company, but today all I wanted was to be left alone.

"Sorry," I told her. "I just have a lot on my mind today. You know how it is . . ."

Suddenly, her eyes grew wide and her hand flew up to cover her mouth. "Oh, no," she breathed. "It's the anniversary of the kidnapping, isn't it?"

Not only my coworker but my best friend, Jane had known me long enough to know the details. In fact, it was shortly after the kidnapping of my three-year-old son, Alex, that I met her when I started working at Harriman and Smith.

"It's been seven years, Jane," I said. "Seven years to the day. And it just never gets any easier."

Jane's usually sparkling eyes dimmed as she studied my face. "Go home," she said. "You don't need to work on a day like today. It's a special day." I began to protest, thinking of all the work we had to do. She insisted and even said she'd notify Mr. Harriman for me. "I'll just say you're sick," she said. "No sense going into detail."

Gratefully, I left the office without argument. When I got home, I went into what had been Alex's room, lay on his little-boy bed—which was still covered with his many stuffed animals—and allowed the memories to engulf me.

When I married my high-school sweetheart, Sandy, at the age of nineteen, we were both sure of one thing: We wanted children. An only child myself, I longed for a home filled with happy laughter, dozens of toys, and sticky hands.

When Alex was born a year later, he was more wonderful than we ever could've imagined. From the day we brought him home from the hospital he was a happy, sunny child, always smiling, rarely crying. In fact, his first words were, "I wuv you." He was like an angel.

I quit my job to devote my life to Alex, and the three of us enjoyed so many happy times. As Alex grew up, he seemed to grow even more cheerful and was always delightful to be around. When he was three, he would meet Sandy at the door each evening demanding a hug, and he refused to go to sleep without at least ten kisses from both of us.

I'll never forget the evening before what was to be the worst night of my life. Sandy was working late and Alex and I spent the entire evening together. I made his favorite dinner, hot dogs and macaroni and cheese, and we baked cookies together.

After Alex had eaten a few cookies and had his bath, he slipped into his favorite pajamas—the ones with little trucks on them—and scrambled into bed.

"Come tuck me in, Mommy!" he called, giggling.

I went in his room and sat on his bed, then brushed the hair off his forehead. "You know how much I love you, don't you, sweetheart?" I asked my baby.

"Yes, Mommy!" Alex exclaimed. Then, seeming to grow more serious, he echoed me, "You know how much I love you, right?" Seeing the smile creep across my face, he said, "Really, Mommy. I love you a billion times, and I will never, never forget you." I was touched, but also thought it seemed a curious statement for a three-year-old.

"You'll never have a chance to forget me, sweetheart," I told him. "Mommy will always, always be right here. No matter what." And I tucked Alex's small quilt around his warm little body and gave him another kiss for good measure.

Alex was snatched from our lives the very next day. He was often allowed to play in our fenced backyard, as long as he stayed within view. I checked on him every five minutes, but the last time I checked, he was gone. I raced around the neighborhood and called everyone I knew, but it was no use. Alex had vanished without a trace.

An extensive search involving police officers, volunteers, and a private detective went on for months, but Alex was never found. The only clue the police had was footprints in our muddy yard, but the police officer in charge said it was no use trying to trace them.

"The prints are from generic tennis shoes that can be purchased at any shoe store," Detective Marlin told us, shaking his head. "They won't help us. Now, do you have any enemies?" he asked for the thousandth time.

Our lives fell apart completely and I was overtaken with despair. The only consolation was knowing that Alex could possibly be alive somewhere, and I took comfort in the fact that no body was ever found.

Maybe he's alive somewhere, I thought. Maybe someone else just took him to be their little boy. Whatever happened, I vow to never stop searching for my son.

Sandy and I had an amicable divorce a year after Alex's

disappearance. Our little boy had been the sunshine in our lives and without him, we had nothing. We were both simply too sad, too emotionally drained, to continue our marriage, but we still kept in touch and spoke regularly.

Sadly, Sandy died in a car accident a year after our divorce. Neither of us had had any other family, so my life became emptier than ever. As the years dragged by, my lonely days settled into a steady pattern. I threw myself into my job at the law firm and tried not to think about the pain of losing my baby.

The ringing of the phone interrupted my reminiscences. I scrambled into the kitchen to answer it. It was Jane.

"Honey?" she said. "Are you doing okay?"

"Yes," I replied. "Thanks for getting me out of work today. I just needed to be alone for a while."

"I have a question," she began slowly, "and stop me if you want."

"Okay," I answered, a bit intrigued.

"My brother, Vic, and his son just moved to town, and I promised him I'd take him on a few errands this afternoon. He needs to get a few things for his new place, buy some groceries, and get his phone and electricity set up—except he flew out here and his car's not arriving until tomorrow."

"So?" I asked.

"I hate to ask," she said slowly, "but I was supposed to take the afternoon off to help him. But since you left work . . ."

"Mr. Harriman won't let you leave, too," I guessed. Our boss could be a stingy old coot sometimes.

"Yes," she said. "Unfortunately, that's exactly what he said."

"I'll come back," I told her immediately. "I feel better. I'll come back to work and you can go help your brother."

"There's a problem," she said. "I told Mr. Harriman you were sick, and if he sees you back at work . . ."

She didn't have to finish her sentence. Mr. Harriman constantly complained about employees abusing their sick time. If he even had an inkling that one of us had "faked" being sick, there'd be heck to pay.

"I'm really sorry, Jane," I said. "What do you want me to do?"

"Can you please help Vic today?" she said. "I hate to ask, but you do have a car and it would only take a couple of hours and I'd be so grateful and he's a really nice guy—"

"Whoa!" I cut her off, laughing. "I'll do it. Anything for a friend."

She gave me Vic's address and I promised to pick him up shortly. No harm done, I figured. I'd been alone long enough and if my best friend needed a favor, I wanted to be there for her.

Incredibly, I enjoyed the afternoon with Vic more than I'd

enjoyed anything in a long time. I felt drawn to him the moment I saw him. He was one of those classically handsome men who didn't seem to know that they were good-looking. He was strong, but also had an inherently gentle quality that made me want to cling to him and feel his arms around me.

We spent the afternoon taking care of the small details that go along with moving. I drove him around to various stores and companies and we had plenty of time to chat. I discovered that he was a regional manager of a welding company and had moved to town after being transferred by his company.

He was also a single father who was divorced. He told me about his son, a ten-year-old named Chris, and how thrilled they both were to be moving closer to Jane.

"Ever since Millie, my ex-wife, left us a few years ago, it's been tough on Chris," he said soberly. "He deserves a mother, and wants one so badly. I figure if he can't have one, being near Jane is the next best thing."

My heart broke as I thought of the little boy. Vic changed the subject and after that we mostly discussed pleasant things, like how our town would compare to the big city he'd lived in before. We told silly jokes and discovered we had much in common, like a love for fast food and a dislike for stuck-up people.

We topped off our pleasant afternoon of errands with a leisurely dinner at a local diner. I felt like a kid again as we polished off cheeseburgers, onion rings, and chocolate milkshakes while listening to the oldies that played on the jukebox. I hadn't had so much fun in years.

When I dropped him off in front of his house, Vic surprised me with a quick kiss on the lips.

"Sarah Crittenden, there's something special about you," he said. "I haven't been out with anyone since my divorce, and that's because I've never met anyone I felt anything for. But you—you're different."

My heart pounded in my chest. "I feel the same way," I told him. "There's just something about you."

When he kissed me again, I felt my heart grow so large I thought it would burst. I knew I'd love Vic Wilcox for the rest of my life.

The following months were among the happiest of my life, of course not counting my all-too-short time with Alex. Vic and I grew closer every day. We were both tied up with work and he was busy with his son, but we managed to see each other at least three or four times a week, often meeting for lunch in the park, or for a meal or coffee while Chris spent time with Jane.

I was eager to meet Chris, but Vic wanted to hold off. "He's been through so much," he told me. "I promised myself I'd never let him get close to a woman until I was sure the relationship would last." I completely understood.

But we continued to grow closer and shared more and more with each other. I confided to him about the pain of losing Alex, and he was so sympathetic it almost made me cry. "Oh, honey," he said. "I can't imagine that kind of pain. I wish I could take it away for you!" He, in turn, confided in me about his unhappy marriage, noting that has wife had been mentally ill and had simply run off without leaving a note. He'd been able to obtain a divorce on the grounds of desertion.

After three months of dating seriously, he invited me for dinner one night to meet Chris. I was thrilled both to meet the boy and to realize that the invitation meant that Vic was truly serious about me, as I was about him.

On a Friday night, I went to Vic and Chris's house for dinner. Vic had wanted to order pizza, but I insisted on cooking. I'd made homemade spaghetti sauce and meatballs the evening before, so I brought it over, along with salad fixings, garlic bread, and uncooked pasta, to prepare at their house.

When I arrived, Vic greeted me with a kiss and a glass of wine. "Chris will be home in a few minutes," he said. "Excited?"

"Nervous!" I told him. "I just hope he likes me. He may resent having a woman in his father's life."

"He will love you," Vic replied confidently. "Chris's not the kind of kid to resent anyone or anything. He's a wonderful boy, always happy, always loving."

After another kiss, I begin preparing the meal, setting the sauce to simmer on the stove, boiling water for the pasta, and assembling the salad. Then I popped the garlic bread in the oven, and Vic and I sat on the sofa.

Just then, I heard a door open and slam, and in walked an adorable boy. When he saw us, he charged over to us.

"Hi, Dad!" he exclaimed. "Wow, something sure smells good!" He sniffed the air appreciatively. "Are you Sarah?" he asked me, smiling. "I've sure been wanting to meet you!"

Once I saw this happy, bubbly, energetic ten-year-old, my fears about him liking me immediately evaporated. He seemed to be a wonderful child, and something about him stirred my heart the moment I saw him.

"Yes, I'm Sarah, and I'm so happy to meet you," I told him. "I made my special spaghetti and meatballs just for you, so I hope you're hungry."

He grinned at me and turned to his dad. "Did you tell her that was my favorite?" he asked. He turned back to me: "It's my absolute favorite and it's so much better than sandwiches or hot dogs. Thank you, Sarah!"

Vic smiled apologetically. "We rely on easy-to-make foods more often that we should, I suppose," he said.

The evening was wonderful. Chris was chatty, affectionate, and gobbled up the meal like he hadn't eaten in years. Vic enjoyed it, also, and I was proud that they seemed to appreciate my cooking.

When I left, Vic and Chris both hugged me. When I held the boy in my arms, a strong feeling swept over me. It was a very familiar feeling; one of love and amazement. I realized I hadn't gotten that feeling since I'd held Alex and immediately chided myself.

He's not your son, I told myself. Don't be so silly.

All the same, I drove home on cloud nine that night, picturing Chris's beautiful face in my mind.

The following week, Vic and I took Chris out to a local pizza place for dinner. It was a favorite of Chris's because of the dozen or so video games lining the back wall.

After we ordered, Vic slapped the heel of his hand against his forehead. "I forgot to make an important call this afternoon at work," he said. "I know this is terribly rude, but do you mind if I run out to the car to make the call on my cell phone?"

Of course, neither of us minded, so Vic left the restaurant. Once he was gone, I looked at Chris. "Do you want to play some games?" I asked.

He was looking at me strangely, almost studying me. "Did you used to have long hair?" he asked. "Really, really long hair?"

Surprised, I touched my hair and replied, "Yes, but not for years. Why?"

He shook his head. "I don't know. I guess I just thought it would look nice on you. Yeah, let's play some games!"

He seemed to shrug it off, but I found his comment harder to forget. Like everything else lately, it stirred a strange feeling in me. The rest of the night went off without a hitch, and Chris and I had a great time playing video games. He won, of course!

When we returned to their house, Chris hugged me good night and went to bed, and Vic and I settled onto the couch to relax. As my eyes drifted around the cozy room, I suddenly saw something that made me gasp.

Perched on the mantel was a picture. A picture of Vic with a woman who was probably his ex-wife, and between them was a little boy. He looked to be around four-years-old, and he was gazing right into the camera with sparkling eyes. He was chubby, with baby-soft hair. An angel. It was my Alex.

I vaulted out of the sofa as though I had seen a ghost, grabbed the picture, and held it to me. "Alex," I cried. "Alex!" Crazy thoughts ran through my mind. Alex would be ten years old right now, Chris's age.

Alex would have floppy hair and sparkling eyes, just like Chris. Chris and Vic didn't look anything a like, either.

"Sarah? Sarah?" A puzzled Vic hurried toward me. "Are you okay?"

"My baby!" I whispered, whirling toward him in horror. "How could you steal my Alex?" And then the world went black as I fainted.

When I awoke, I was lying on the couch with a blanket over me. Vic was holding my hand. "Oh, honey," he said. "I don't know what's happened, but we need to get to the bottom of it. I've called the police and they're on their way. And I can assure you, I did not steal your baby. Unfortunately, I may know who did. Oh, honey, I'm so sorry." He told me to stay calm and helped me drink a bit of water, and continued to hold my hand reassuringly.

After the police officers had arrived, including Det. Marlin, who'd been in charge of Alex's kidnapping case, we began piecing the story together.

It turned out that when Vic met his ex-wife, Millie, she had a three-year-old boy—Chris—who she said was from a previous marriage. When Vic and Millie were married, Vic adopted Chris and grew to love him as his own son.

And after Millie deserted them, Vic considered Chris his true son in every sense of the word. In fact, he wasn't even sure whether Chris remembered that Vic wasn't his son by blood, and the two never discussed it. Vic was such a caring father that he never wanted Chris to feel any different from any other kids.

Det. Marlin, after looking at the picture, confirmed that Chris was indeed Alex, but just in case, he immediately ordered DNA testing. "I've never seen anything like this in all my years on the force," he told us. "The chance that you two would meet and discover that Chris was really Alex . . . well, that's a million to one." He beamed at us.

The following weeks were extremely busy, heart-wrenching but also incredibly happy. The DNA tests came back positive, so it was confirmed for sure that Chris was my son.

A warrant was issued for Millie's arrest. She was captured a week later and admitted to the crime. Seven years ago, she'd been a tortured, lonely soul. One day, she was driving past my house when she saw my little angel and decided to steal him.

Vic testified that Millie had shown signs of mental illness throughout their marriage and she was committed to a mental health facility. She has not yet shown any remorse for her terrible crime, but perhaps she doesn't understand what she's done. I do hope she gets better, and perhaps someday I can forgive her.

The first time I saw Chris after finding out the news, I could hardly contain my feelings. As I gazed at my newfound ten-year-old son, I saw in my mind a part of his life that nobody had been there for but me—Alex curled up in his crib, Alex splashing happily in his bath, Alex feeding the ducks at a nearby pond. I could almost smell his baby powder scent and feel his chubby arms around my neck. I couldn't believe my baby had been given back.

Vic and I have been married for a year and are now expecting a child of our own. I quit my job after our wedding so I could devote all my time to our family.

Chris is a very happy boy. He couldn't be more excited to meet his new little brother or sister and hasn't experienced any feelings of jealousy, perhaps because Vic and I try so hard to make him feel special. He called me "Mom" from the first day after I married his father and recently told me that I was the best mom ever. I feel blessed.

We have decided not to tell him about his kidnapping right now, and instead will tell him when he is a bit older and able to understand better. He has felt "different" enough from his classmates for years, because he only had a father and not a mother. We don't want to disrupt his life any further right now. Someday I will tell him that his name used to be Alex, and tell him about his first father, Sandy.

Occasionally I remember my three-year-old Alex saying, "Mommy, I'll never forget you," and then recall him in the pizza place wondering aloud whether I used to have long hair. I know my baby kept his promise and deep down never did forget me.

We spend lots of time with Jane, who is now married and also very happy. She and her new husband, Jimmy, know the secret of Alex and Chris being the same boy, and Jane is thrilled that Alex has, in a way, been returned to me. Our little family couldn't be happier, and every day I thank God for Alex's return and pray that other families be so fortunate.

THE END

## A Parental Tug-of-War That Pulls
## Every Mother's Heartstrings
# NOT WITHOUT MY SON!
## A woman's plight to rescue
## her captive baby

"Leah! I don't believe you're even thinking about going there alone!" my friend, Riley, yelled into my ear. I had to hold the phone away from my head so she wouldn't break my eardrum.

"I don't have a choice," I told her. "He's got Aidan. If I want him back—I have to go and get him myself."

"What about the police?"

"What about them? They haven't brought my baby back yet. I have to do something. Can't you see that, Riley?"

I heard her loud sigh of frustration on the other end. It had been two long weeks since my six-year-old son had gone missing from his schoolyard. Two long weeks of no sleep and imagining all the worst things that my ex-husband, Merle, could've done with him.

Merle suffered from depression off and on since Aidan was about two years old. Being young and with no experience of mental illness, I didn't recognize the symptoms. It didn't start overnight, just a few bad days at work here and there. But then the bad days gradually overtook the good ones and I found myself with a young son and a sick husband to care for—a husband who refused to see a doctor of any kind.

It's like a living death, living with someone who is so depressed. I can't imagine what it was like for Merle, but I was drowning in my own guilt, thinking that I did something wrong, thinking that I could change it if I only knew how. Aidan, as young as he was then, could sense something wrong between his parents.

Merle pushed me away whenever I tried to help. I learned that talking to him did nothing to bring him out of his gloom. He became more and more impatient with Aidan and me, like he didn't want us around anymore.

It was a long road from the day I met Merle to the moody man he became. I was eighteen and Merle was almost ten years older than me. At the time, he was playing in a country rock band and I was a serious fan. One night I managed to get his autograph at the end of a concert. I held the paper to my heart for a moment, and then I began to walk away reluctantly.

"Hey, you'd like to get a cup of coffee or something?" he asked.

I looked around just to make sure that he wasn't talking to someone else.

"Me? You want to have coffee with me?"

He smiled then, and it broke up that bad-boy image for a few moments. My heart did a somersault and a little dance.

"Come on," he said, reaching out his hand to me. "There's a great little all-night café just around the block."

So the romance of my life started that night. But what made me really fall in love with Merle was what happened the day my mother died.

We'd only been dating for a few months when I got the news that my mom had passed away unexpectedly from a stroke. Merle was on the road. I called his manager and left a message, then ran myself a hot bath. I sat in it for over an hour, just wanting to sink down under the water and not ever get up again.

Then the phone rang.

"Honey, it's me. They just told me. I came off the stage right away. I can be home in four hours."

And he was. By that time I'd dragged myself out of the bathroom and lay on the bed in a fog. Merle came home and knelt down beside the bed. He was still in his stage costume and I remember the long fringes of his fancy, leather jacket tickling my nose as I huddled close to him.

Merle stroked my hair, held me, and sang his favorite song softly—the one about wanting to die without the one you love. He never left my side for a moment.

I fell hopelessly, completely, in love with him that night.

And for about three years, my life was about as perfect as life could get.

"Heaven can't be better than this," I told Merle on the day our son was born. Merle just smiled and kissed me on the head as I held Aidan in my arms.

Merle wasn't one to scream and shout to the world that he was a father, but I could tell that he loved Aidan. It was in the way he held him, like he was so fragile that he might break, and in the way he kissed his head softly and rocked him to sleep in his arms. I loved watching them together. I could watch them forever.

But forever is something that isn't promised to any of us mortals, as I was quickly about to discover. I knew that Merle was moody. The truth was, in those early days of our marriage, he was still on the road a lot. I honestly didn't know what he was like until the band broke up and he was home all the time.

At first I put down his depression to the breakup of the band. It wasn't pretty and he lost a couple of good pals when the four of them decided to end their relationship. There were days when I could swear that there was a huge, black cloud over our house.

"It'll get better, honey," I would tell him, trying to draw him into my arms.

"It won't get better, Leah. Music is my life."

Merle eventually got a job as a manager in a music store, but I could tell that he hated every moment of it. It was even worse when someone came in and recognized him and then he'd have to answer a bunch of questions about the band breaking up. For Merle, the new job was a huge blow to his self-esteem. He was a true artist and his songs were the envy of his fellow musicians and all of that was taken away from him. Many nights he would go out drinking alone after work and then he wouldn't come home until I was in bed. He began living a separate life, even though we still lived in the same house.

Merle stopped playing with Aidan, who loved his daddy so much that it broke my heart every time Merle ignored his baby's arms reaching out to him. To compensate, I became Aidan's world. I gave him what I thought was enough attention for two parents, but it wasn't the same. Merle was his daddy.

"Merle, I want you to go to a doctor," I told him one day.

"A doctor? You think I'm nuts, don't you, Leah?"

"No, no, not at all. I just know that you've been depressed and maybe talking it out with someone would help."

"I'm not crazy. You're the one who's nuts," he said and pushed past me on his way out the door.

That's how the physical abuse started. It was never really directed at me, it was more like he became frustrated and I got in his way. That was the way I saw it at the time.

Merle went from pushing me away to throwing things—like his dinner plate. It narrowly missed Aidan where he sat in his high chair. Merle stared at him for a moment, and it was like the old Merle was back. He ran to Aidan, picked him up and kissed him, and then put him back in his chair. Aidan laughed wildly, desperate for any kind of attention from his dad.

But the moment didn't last long. It was like Merle slipped back into the twilight zone and just walked out the front door. I watched from the front window as he got into his truck and left. My world was coming apart and I didn't have the first idea how to fix it.

I kept thinking over and over, What am I doing wrong? How can I make this better? This is my responsibility, to make things better—especially for Aidan's sake. I tried not to make Merle angry, I made his favorite meals, and I mended his clothes. It was hard to believe that at one time I had a scholarship for one of the top colleges in the country. I'd turned it down when I met Merle and fell in love.

I was worried. I have my high school diploma, but nothing else. My husband was going to get fired from his job sooner or later—any fool could see that—and how was I supposed to support him and our son?

Things didn't get better. One day Merle just didn't go to work.

"Honey, isn't it time you should be leaving for work?"

He grunted something I couldn't understand.

I pulled back the covers slowly and tried to draw him out of bed.

"Get away from me!" he screamed. His eyes were pure hatred.

I recoiled, running from the room.

Merle had been impatient and angry with me before, but I never saw that side of him until that point. It was the loneliest feeling in the world to have the man you love look at you like he didn't even recognize you anymore. How I wished that my mom were alive so that I could talk to her.

Merle slept the whole day. I gathered up the courage to call his boss at the store.

"Leah, I hate to be the one to tell you this, but I had to fire him," Scott told me. "He was being very rude to a couple of customers and when they wouldn't get out of his way, he pushed over a CD display and ran out. I'm sorry for you and Aidan, but I just can't put up with that kind of behavior."

"I understand, Scott," I said very quietly, hanging up the phone.

I looked at our closed bedroom door. What am I going to do?

When Merle finally woke up, I told him that he'd have to seek some kind of counseling or I'd start divorce proceedings.

"What? What?" he asked, sitting on the edge of the bed. "You don't know what you're saying, Leah."

I saw the dark circles under his eyes. He'd lost weight, too. His once-muscular shoulders looked thin. He was the man I fell in love with. He was the man I love. It would've been so easy to just fall into this depression with him, to live like he did—a slow, painful death each day.

And I would've, if it weren't for Aidan.

I realized that my love wasn't enough to bring Merle back to life. Even Aidan's love wasn't enough to cure him. I reached out to touch him, comfort him, but I stopped myself.

"I'm saying that you need help. I'll go with you to any kind of counseling, but I can't live like this anymore. Aidan can't live like this anymore," I said, trying to keep myself from breaking down and crying.

He stared at me as though I'd been gone away for a year somewhere. He tried to hug me, but I pushed him back.

"It's too late for that. You need real help, Merle."

I braced myself for the anger. I was terrified of it even though he hadn't seriously hurt me yet. I was more afraid for Aidan, but that night I thought ahead and left him with Riley. I wasn't sure what Merle's reaction to my ultimatum was going to be.

As it turned out, he didn't even know that Aidan wasn't home. He walked around in circles for a while, then gathered some clothes together and stuffed them into a suitcase.

"Where are you going?" I dared to ask.

He just glared at me.

I didn't hear anything from Merle for three months. Finally he called me one night from some place in Texas, saying that he and one of his former band mates got a group together and they were on the road. I was very surprised, but I was happy for him. He asked to speak to Aidan and I let him.

Things went along like that for a couple of years. I had to get on with my life. I didn't think I'd get much financial support from Merle for his son, so I went to work at a small accounting office, starting out as a junior clerk helping people with their taxes. I liked the boss and my coworkers and I was surprised and delighted when my supervisors sent me on courses and seminars to improve my knowledge. They had faith in me and I began to have faith in myself.

Merle stopped in to see Aidan about twice a year. He seemed to be doing well and I didn't see the severe depression that plagued him while we were married. Maybe he just couldn't handle the responsibility of a wife and son. I knew that it wasn't my fault. Merle still had a big problem and there wasn't anything in the world I could've done to fix him.

I went ahead with the divorce. Bruce, my lawyer, drew up an agreement that would give me full custody. Since Merle didn't seem very interested in his son, I didn't think he'd fight it.

"If he does try to contest it, I recommend that we ask the judge for a psychiatric assessment based on his past erratic behavior. Then the most he'll likely get is supervised visitation."

Bruce said that Aidan was entitled to receive child support, but I had my doubts that we'd ever see a dime of it. Merle's work history was just too spotty. I had to get on with my own life and I had a son to raise.

Aidan. What I wouldn't have done for that little boy. The one thing I couldn't give him was his father. It would be a big hole in his little heart forever.

Then one cold, cloudy day in May, I got a call from Aidan's school.

"Mrs. Fox, when did you pick up Aidan today?"

"Pick up Aidan? I don't pick him up until three-thirty," I said.

"Well, he's not here. We thought—we were sure you'd picked him up early today."

"No! No, I didn't! I'll be right there!"

We searched the playground and the whole school. Finally, we spoke to Aidan's classmates.

"This is Kaylee," the principal said, her arm around a little blond girl. "Kaylee, do you remember when Aidan was picked up today?"

The little girl nodded solemnly, but she didn't say anything.

"Who picked him up, Kaylee?"

"A man," she said.

At first my thought was—child molester! Some stranger took my baby! Then I had an idea. I rummaged through my purse and found a picture.

"Kaylee, is this the man? Did he take Aidan?"

She looked at the picture for so long that I wanted to scream.

"But he was wearing green," she said in the perfect logic of a small child.

"But it was him, Kaylee? You're sure?" the principal asked.

She nodded.

I'd shown her a picture of Merle.

It took two agonizing weeks for Merle to call. I wanted to die during those two weeks. If I could die and just have Aidan be safe, I would've done it! But when Merle called in the middle of the night, I was so thankful I could have kissed him. Kissed my baby's kidnapper!

"He's safe, Leah," Merle said, sounding far away.

We didn't have a good connection and the line was scratchy with static. "Where is he? Where are you?" I pleaded, my voice drowning in tears.

"You tried to take him from me," Merle accused. "He's my son, too, and you tried to take him from me. I called your lawyer—all that talk about supervised visits. Who do you think you are, Leah? I'm his father."

"Merle, I'll do anything you want. I'll talk to the lawyer. I'll talk to the judge. Anything! Just let me see Aidan."

There was a long pause and the only thing I heard was the crackling of the bad connection. Where can he be? Is he even still in the country? My maternal instincts tried to picture where my baby was, tried to feel where he was, but I couldn't think of anything. I was just a big tangle of raw emotion.

"I won't bring him home, but you can come to see him," he said finally.

I couldn't believe my ears. I didn't trust him, but that was the first piece of real information he was offering me. I rushed around looking for paper and a pen to write down his directions.

"I'm not at that location yet, Leah, so if you're planning on a big police raid, think again."

"No! No, I wouldn't do that. I just want to see Aidan," I said, willing my legs not to give out. Is this real? Will he really let me see my boy?

I was about to find out. Am I wrong not to tell the police? Like I told Riley, they hadn't helped me find Aidan in two whole weeks. I trusted my instincts, but maybe my instincts were wrong. I was just so afraid that Merle would do something crazy if he saw the police. I was usually able to calm him down.

And part of me saw that address in my hand and only thought of how close I was to getting Aidan back. I wasn't thinking logically—as if any mother could think logically in a situation like that. I packed a small bag for Aidan, including his favorite teddy bear. I cried all the while, but I didn't stop. There was no time.

Merle might change his mind and not meet with me after all.

He took Aidan to a town on the East Coast. The final flight was a small commuter plane that battled the winds off the sea. When we landed my stomach was queasy, but I didn't stop—not for a moment. I fairly ran to the car rental desk and took out the first car available.

"Do you know where this address is?" I asked the clerk.

"That's down by the old wharf," she said. "Once you get out of town and toward the shore, you'll be able to ask for directions from some of the locals."

"Thank you!" I said, running for the car in the parking lot.

All around me was breathtaking beauty, but I hardly noticed a thing. My mind was on the road and getting to the house as fast as possible.

"The old Mill house? That's been abandoned for years," one old man with snow-white hair told me at a convenience store. He looked at me as if I was crazy to be going there and in a roundabout way he was trying to find out why I wanted to.

"If that's the right address, then that's the place I need. How do I get there?" I asked impatiently.

I'm sure that at any other time I'd find the casual conversational pace of the local people charming, but that's my baby out there in some abandoned house—with an unstable father! If only he'd talk faster!

"I go near there on my way home," the old man said. "Follow me in your car."

The old, dirt road looked like it wasn't used in decades. I followed the man's old station wagon for about five miles until he pulled over to the side and pointed to an overgrown driveway. He smiled and waved and then drove off on his way.

Once I was there, I didn't know what to do. I sat there, staring at the entrance to the driveway. I didn't have any way to protect myself out there. What if Merle had a gun? Even if he didn't, he was much stronger than me. I knew now how foolish I was by going on that journey with absolutely no plan.

But what do I do now? By the time I went back to town and explained all that to the local police, it might be too late for Aidan. His father might get frightened and leave with him again.

I might never see my son again.

I said a prayer and drove on down that long driveway. At one time it probably was quite a beautiful estate, but now the trees hung over the road, completely blocking my view of any house. Finally, there it was. At one time it had been painted white, a two-story Victorian mansion overlooking the sea.

I looked around and couldn't see any vehicle, or even any sign of tire tracks. Was this all a wild goose chase, a cruel joke by my ex-husband?

I got out of the car. It sure didn't look like anyone was there. The front porch was half caved in. When I got to the front door, it was open a crack.

The house was truly abandoned. Over the years the dirt and mice had settled in, leaving it a mess. It looked like local teens had made it a hideaway, too, since there was a giant peace sign painted on the dining room wall and discarded blankets strewn about.

Aidan can't be here. Merle wouldn't bring him to a place like this, would he?

Suddenly, I heard the sound of a car starting up. I rushed out of the house just in time to see someone drive my rented car away!

I ran after it. Whoever had stolen it wasn't in any hurry. They took it down a small side road and stopped in front of an old carriage house.

Merle got out of the car.

It was a shock, seeing him again. We stood there staring at each other like two people about to have a duel, but without pistols.

"Where is he? Where is he, Merle?" I demanded.

"He's—close," he said mysteriously. "And he's safe."

"Don't do this. Give him back to me and I'll never tell anyone where you are."

"God, I've missed you, Leah."

I can't believe my ears. Am I going crazy? This man who took my baby—he was talking to me as though we're still married!

He didn't look like he had a weapon on him, but I couldn't be sure. Merle used to carry a gun when he was on the road. Some of the fans could get nuts, and several of the guys in the band protected themselves with guns. I remembered, too, that they used to go to the shooting range to practice.

I looked behind him at the carriage house. I didn't think that Aidan would be there, but I called out to him just in case.

There was no answer. Merle looked at me with a smile on his face.

"What do you want, then?" I asked, my shoulders sagging in defeat. "I'll do anything."

"Yes, you will," he said confidently. "Come here."

I walked toward him and he hugged me. I stiffened in his arms.

"Give me this, Leah. Give me one last weekend with you, and I swear to God that you'll have Aidan. You won't have to worry about me for the rest of your life."

"You promise on your parents' graves?" I asked.

"I promise," he said.

I was shaking so badly that he had to hold me as we walked to the carriage house. I so desperately wanted Aidan to be there, but I knew it wasn't likely.

That place was in much better condition than the main house. It had two floors and Merle lead me up a narrow staircase.

When we got to the top of the stairs, I put my hand on his chest to stop him.

"Wait a minute. How do I know that he's safe?" I asked.

Merle took out his cell phone and made a call without taking his eyes off me for a minute. He spoke briefly to someone and then handed me the phone.

"Aidan? Baby, is that you?"

"Mommy!" said the angry, accusing voice. "I miss you!"

I laughed and caught my breath in the same moment. It's him!

"Baby, where are you?"

The phone was grabbed from me.

"I'll see you soon," Merle told his son, then tossed the phone on a bed.

He'll see our son soon, I thought. But will I?

Merle intended to keep me prisoner there. I had no idea if he would keep his promise and let me go to Aidan, but I had no choice.

I could argue with him and likely make him dangerously angry, or I could go along with his demands.

"I did what you said, Leah. I went to a doctor."

"You did? And—what did he say?"

"It was a she," Merle said, going to a small kitchenette and opening the fridge.

I didn't really want to hear that he had serious mental problems. I knew that already, but he didn't give me any explanation.

"You think I maybe brought you here for sex, don't you?"

I didn't know what to think when I took that long road down to the old house. Then I thought that he'd brought me there to kill me, and maybe himself. I thought of my six-year-old son being all alone in the world. Who will take care of him like I do? Who would know that when he slept and rubbed his eyes, that he's having a nightmare and has to be comforted? My God, no one can love him like I can.

"Whatever it is, please, just get it over with," I said.

I closed my eyes. I heard him walk toward me, and then he gathered me into his arms and held me. I could feel hot tears streaming down my face and dampening his soft shirt.

If I could imagine hard enough, I could almost believe that we were a couple again, just like in those first days when he was a sexy, experienced man who'd fallen in love with a teenager. I cried for those lost days and I wondered how we'd ever reached that point. Despite everything, I didn't believe that Merle was an evil man. A sick man, yes. But my confused heart would always cherish the good memories, no matter what, because those good days had produced the most precious thing in my life—Aidan.

"Sit down. I have your favorite wine," he said.

Merle pulled out the cork with a pop. I thought about how surreal my life had become. I might be living my last moments on Earth and my ex-husband is opening a bottle of wine like it's some macabre celebration.

I kept drinking glass after glass. I wanted to delay the moment when he made his next move. I could never handle wine very well and pretty soon I started to feel groggy. Nights of no sleep and the long trip there brought me to the point of exhaustion. Then when I'd heard Aidan's voice on the phone, I felt enormous relief. He's alive and safe somewhere. At least I knew that. I allowed myself to relax a little.

"Come to bed, Leah," Merle said, his voice almost gentle.

I slipped under the big, silk comforter with him. He drew me toward him and held me, breathing in my scent like he'd been longing for it. I wasn't thinking too clearly and every part of me needed sleep. I fought it.

I awoke once and it was night. I was alone in the bed. I struggled to get up.

"The bathroom's this way," Merle said, appearing from nowhere. I wondered if he'd been watching me sleep.

I went to the small bathroom and tried to wake myself up by throwing cold water on my face. There has to be a way to get out of here. But what then? How will I find my son?

Merle was waiting just outside the bathroom door.

"Come back to bed."

There would be no escape because I couldn't get past him.

148

"I want to make love to you, Leah," he said, drawing me back under the covers. "One more time."

"I—I can't," I told him.

I didn't know if that would send him into a rage, or maybe he'd even call the person who had Aidan and tell him to harm my baby. What was I thinking?

"I mean, I will, if you insist," I said, biting my lip.

"But you don't want to. You can't stand even touching me, can you, Leah?"

I didn't want to answer that. What would be the perfect answer to get my son back? I wanted to scream.

"Then just let me hold you. It's been so long since I've held you while you slept."

I settled down in the covers, letting his arms slip around my waist from behind me. I was tense, but he didn't seem to notice. After about half an hour I could feel him breathe deeply. He'd fallen asleep.

The cell phone was on the chair beside the bed. If I could just reach it, I could maybe make a call without waking him.

Merle, like me, was exhausted. I slowly pulled away from him, inch by inch, so slowly that I hardly noticed any progress myself.

When I finally got out of bed, I stood there for a moment looking down at him. There was a full moon that night and it cast a weird, white light on his face, like that was part of a bad dream. I'll wake up and the three of us will be together again. I'll make breakfast for us and we'll take our baby for a walk.

I shook my head. My son is still in danger somewhere. I have to get help.

I took the phone and walked toward the stairs, praying that one of the old floorboards wouldn't creak and wake Merle. One stair at a time, one cautious step at a time. I could hear Merle snoring lightly. Good. If he stopped snoring, that meant he was awake. When he awoke, he would find me.

I left my shoes upstairs, but I was still dressed in my sleeveless top and light pants. When I got outside the cold night air hit me like a frigid wave and I started to shiver uncontrollably. I reached the car.

The keys were gone. He must have them with him! There was no way I was going to go back up those stairs! I ran away some distance and hid in some trees. Then I dialed 911.

I whispered for help and the dispatcher sounded like an angel. She took down all the information I could give her.

"Please, he's got my son hidden away somewhere. You've got to find him."

"The best clue will be that cell phone you're holding," the dispatcher told me.

149

I could do nothing but wait for help to arrive. I resisted the urge to dial the number where Aidan was at. I knew in my heart that he was somewhere close by, and not just because Merle told me that he was.

It seemed to take forever until the police showed up. I heard a vehicle out on the road and came out from the trees to show them where I was.

"Leah?"

Merle was standing there by my rental car. He looked groggy, like he'd been sleepwalking.

"Leah, baby, what are you doing out here? You'll catch cold. Come back to bed."

His voice was the voice of the old Merle, the man that I'd fallen in love with. For one tense moment I held my breath. He was about to be arrested and our lives would change forever. His, mine, and Aidan's.

The unmarked police car was coming down the drive to the old house. Pretty soon they'd figure out the fork in the road that I told them about and they would be here.

Merle looked toward the sound.

Then he looked at me.

"Where is—where is my phone?" he asked, fully coming out of his sleep.

Suddenly, the car appeared through the trees. I would never forget the look in Merle's eyes.

"What have you done, Leah?" he asked.

Then he was gone, slamming the door of the carriage house. I could hear him fastening the bolt and dragging something in front of the door.

There were two police officers in the car. One ran toward the door while the other drew me back into the trees and safety. I couldn't see what was going on. There was shouting, and I guessed that Merle was arguing with the officer through the door.

Then I heard a shot.

The officer with me told me to stay put while she ran to the carriage house. Her partner managed to break down the rotting, old door and chased Merle down inside the house.

I waited, biting my hand to keep from screaming out.

At last, the female officer came back to the trees where I was hidden.

"It's over, ma'am. You're safe now."

"Safe? You've shot Merle?"

"He shot himself," she told me.

My heart almost stopped, but I didn't have time to think about it. I thrust Merle's cell phone at her.

"Please! Find out who has my baby!" I yelled.

It turned out that Aidan was hidden in plain sight. Merle had hired a local woman, a grandmother, to care for him. She had no idea that he was a kidnapped child.

"Aidan!" I called, running up to the house where he was staying.

"Mommy! I waited and waited. What took you so long?"

He was angry with all the fury of a six-year-old. I laughed and tossed him up into the air and hugged him over and over.

"Mommy, I can't breathe!" he complained.

It would take me a few weeks before I could get up the courage to tell Aidan that his daddy is in Heaven. The truth was, it took me that long to even come out of the fog of shock and sorrow. Except for my time with Aidan, those days were a blur.

I don't think Merle intended to kill me that night. I did think that he intended to kill himself. We later found out that Merle had a brain tumor. The doctor said his chances of survival after surgery were about thirty percent. Without surgery, it was hopeless.

I knew how Merle felt about doctors and hospitals. He would never have agreed to the surgery. He wanted to spend his last days with his son, and with me.

If only he'd told me the truth. If only he could've accepted help of any kind. I learned that his cancer was slow growing, and that those years of depression might've been caused by the tumor. I try not to think about how our lives might have changed if he'd been the kind of person to trust modern medicine and go for regular checkups.

They might have discovered the tumor years ago. He might have had the surgery to remove it, and it might have brought the old Merle back to us. Aidan might still have a father and I might still be married to the love of my life.

But I believe that we aren't meant to know all the answers. We just live our days, one at a time.

The older Aidan gets, the more he looks like his father. As his memory of Merle fades, I do my best to talk about all the wonderful things his daddy was.

Recently, Aidan brought home an A on his spelling test. It was Merle who taught him his ABCs. After Merle died, Aidan was having such trouble with his spelling, but not anymore.

I'll make him a special peanut butter–and-banana cake to celebrate.

We'll celebrate life.

THE END

# ARRESTED FOR
# HURTING MY BABY

I had just gotten off work and had gone to the baby-sitter's to pick up Tommy. "He doesn't look well," I said to my infant son's baby-sitter. He was usually such a happy baby, but he looked listless and tired.

I watched Priscilla, my son's baby-sitter, shrug before speaking. "He was fine all day. Just take him home and let him take a nap." She handed me his diaper bag. "See ya tomorrow."

She seemed anxious for us to leave, so I picked up my baby and left. He looked even worse when we got home. I lifted him out of his car seat. He seemed floppy, like he didn't have any muscles in his arms and legs. His eyes didn't appear to focus on me, even when I said his name. Something was terribly wrong with my child.

I called my mom to ask her if she had ever experienced anything like that. I was one of five children, so my mom had seen it all. She would know what to do. When I described Tommy's condition, my mother seemed very concerned.

"Nothing like that ever happened to you or your brothers or sisters. I would watch him closely through the night, and if he's not back to his old self by morning, take him to the doctor. I don't want to scare you, honey, but this could be serious. Keep an eye on him, and call me first thing in the morning."

I hung up the phone and was more worried than ever. My mom had seen her children through broken bones, stitches, a bout of scarlet fever, and even an emergency appendectomy. None of that seemed to worry her, but she seemed awfully concerned about Tommy. That gave me even more cause for alarm.

I had lain Tommy down on a blanket on the floor so I could use the phone. He was in exactly the same spot I had left him. Normally, he would have rolled over and scooted around. Now, he hadn't even moved his head. I picked him up and realized that he was burning up with a fever. And it was a high one.

"That's it," I told Tommy. "We're not waiting until morning to see the doctor. We're going to the emergency room right now." Tommy didn't even look at me as I spoke to him.

When we arrived at the hospital, I told the nurse at the admissions desk that something was very wrong with my son. She handed me a stack of forms to fill out with little sympathy. I began to argue, but I realized it was pointless. They wouldn't help Tommy until I completed their forms. I sighed, sat down, and got busy.

Two hours later, they finally called Tommy's name. A nurse took his temperature: 104.8 degrees! She tested his reflexes and looked into his eyes. She got almost no reaction from Tommy. She sighed and looked at me with sympathy. "The doctor will be with you in just a moment," she said before leaving the room.

The doctor came in and performed similar tests on Tommy with the same results. "Ms. Shepherd," he said somberly, "it appears that your son may have meningitis. We need to run some additional tests to be sure, but his condition is extremely serious. Is there someone who can come and sit with you?"

I burst into tears. I never dreamed that my tiny baby could be so sick! "No, there's nobody to call. My mother lives four hours away, and Tommy's father left me when I told him I was pregnant. There's no one." I shook my head sadly at the doctor.

"Then I would encourage you to go home. We will call you as soon as we have some information."

"Can't I stay and be with Tommy?" I pleaded.

"We will be running tests on him all night. You wouldn't be allowed near him, anyway. Go home and rest. We will call you in the morning."

Left with no alternatives, I drove home and went to bed. I cried for hours and finally dozed off at four o'clock. The phone woke me up at seven o'clock.

It was the hospital. "We need you to come as soon as possible."

"What happened?" I asked frantically. "Is Tommy all right?"

"We cannot give any details of your son's condition over the phone. You need to get here as soon as you can."

Oh, my God! Tommy died in the night, and I wasn't even there with him! Horrible thoughts ran through my mind as I threw my clothes on and sped to the hospital. I left my car in the tow-away zone and ran inside.

I went to the admissions desk and told them my name. They led me to an office and told me to sit down. A minute later, a man came in wearing a gray pinstriped suit. He was definitely not a doctor. In fact, his clothing and demeanor screamed "cop." I was frantic for news about Tommy, so I asked him if he knew how my son was doing.

He encouraged me to sit down and then said, "I'm Detective Peterson. I'm here to talk to you about your son. Tommy does not have meningitis as his doctors suspected last night. The evidence shows that he was shaken."

"What do you mean shaken? What is wrong with Tommy?"

"Someone has taken your child by the shoulders and shaken his tiny body. They shook him so hard that his skull was fractured. The doctors haven't determined the full extent of his injuries, but I can assure you that your child will never be the same again. To be honest, Ms. Shepherd, he may not live through this incident." He spoke these words without compassion. He simply stared at me as though he was telling me that it might rain the next day.

"Tommy might . . . die?" I began sobbing uncontrollably.

The detective continued, "Frankly, ma'am, in these types of cases, it is most often the parents who have shaken the child. Do you ever get angry when Tommy cries? Have you ever put your hands on your baby in anger?"

"No, my God, no! I would never hurt Tommy!" I shouted through my tears. "Please, can you take me to him? I just need to hold my baby."

"Ms. Shepherd, you will not go anywhere near that child until this investigation is complete. Shaking a baby is a criminal act, and you, Ms. Shepherd, are in a whole lot of trouble."

"I can't . . . I can't even see Tommy?" I whispered. "You honestly think I hurt him?"

"Ma'am, right now, we aren't sure what to think. But someone has hurt your child. If you didn't do it, you'll need to tell us who might have. Where is the baby's father?"

"He's gone. We had only been dating for a short time when I found out I was pregnant. He took off when I told him. He's never seen Tommy. I don't even know how to contact him. It wasn't him."

"Then who does that leave? Ms. Shepherd, if you cannot produce anyone who had contact with your child in the last few days, you will be our only suspect. You will go to jail for this."

"I didn't do it. Tommy has a baby-sitter who watches him while I work. He was there yesterday, but she would never hurt him."

"You will need to provide us with her name and address. If we can verify that your son was with her yesterday, she will become a suspect as well."

I provided him with the information and again insisted that Priscilla wouldn't hurt Tommy. The man raised his eyebrows before continuing. "Someone did this to your son. If it wasn't her, then we'll have no choice but to assume it was you. We will check her out and contact you soon. I'm going to have to ask you to leave the premises now. Until we clear you of these charges, you are not allowed to be on hospital grounds."

My jaw dropped open. "You're kidding me, right? You told me that my son might not live, and now I have to leave without seeing him? How can you do this to me? I'm his mother!"

"You are also the prime suspect in a very serious crime. Please leave now, and I'll call you soon."

Detective Peterson escorted me to my car and gave me strict instructions not to return without his permission. I sat in the car for nearly an hour. I was sobbing too hard to drive. My only child was seriously injured, I couldn't see him or hold him, and I was being accused of hurting him! The entire situation seemed unreal to me. Eventually, I gathered my strength and drove home.

I called my mother and my sister to give them the terrible news. Both of them offered to make the four-hour drive to come be with me, but I turned them down. "There's nothing any of us can do right now," I told them. "The police have to see that I didn't do it, and then I'll be allowed to see Tommy. It will all be okay when I can see Tommy."

Two days passed without any word from Detective Peterson. I was going crazy waiting and worrying about my baby. Finally, on the third day, the phone rang.

"Ms. Shepherd, it's Detective Peterson. I need you to come to the hospital. I have some news, but it isn't good."

"Oh, my God, is Tommy all right?" I only cared about my son and gave little thought to the idea that I was a suspect.

"Tommy's condition remains the same. The news is about the case the State is building against you. Please come down here, immediately."

I raced to the hospital, hoping they might let me see Tommy this time. As soon as I entered the hospital, Detective Peterson took my arm and led me to the office we had used a few days before. He encouraged me to sit down. Then, he began to speak.

"Ms. Shepherd, the baby-sitter you told us about is gone. Her house is empty, and we can only assume that she has skipped town."

"So that's means I'm your only suspect," I whispered. What would happen to my baby if I went to jail?

"That's not entirely true. I interviewed several of Priscilla's neighbors, and they reported seeing you drop off your son at her house. They said you had been taking him there for a few months. So even though she's gone, we have some evidence that she did exist. So she is still a suspect."

"The fact that she took off makes her look more guilty, right? Why would she leave if she had nothing to hide?"

"We are taking that into consideration, Ms. Shepherd. The fact that you have been very cooperative with the police helps your side of things, too."

"You don't think I did it, do you, Detective Peterson?"

"Honestly, no, I don't. You seem to be very concerned about your son. The perpetrators in these instances usually care more about what will happen to them if they are convicted. I don't think you hurt your child, but, unfortunately, you are still legally responsible for what happened to him."

"So I'm going to serve time for something I didn't do?"

"You probably won't go to jail. But it is going to be extremely difficult for you to regain custody of Tommy."

"What do you mean? I won't be able to take Tommy home with me? I'd rather go to jail than lose my son!"

"Ms. Shepherd, the State is considering charging you with child endangerment. You are his mother, and you left him in an unsafe environment. That is a criminal act. The prosecuting attorney will seek some jail time, probably only a few months, but you may be able to plea bargain to stay out of jail."

"Don't you see? My life is worth nothing without Tommy! I don't care what happens to me if it means losing my son!" I was verging on hysterical.

"Please calm down, Ms. Shepherd. I know it probably doesn't seem this way, but I am trying to help you. I don't think you'd hurt your child, and I have every intention of finding the person who did. I will also testify on your behalf. I have seen enough cases of child abuse to determine guilt, and I know you didn't shake your son."

"Then why are they going to take Tommy away from me?" I asked tearfully.

"Knowingly or unknowingly, you endangered the life of your five-month-old baby. At the very least, Tommy is going to spend some time in foster care. I'm sorry, Ms. Shepherd, but those are the facts."

I was going to lose my baby. I might even be convicted of a crime and go to jail. How could this be happening to me?

"Ms. Shepherd, did you hear me? I said I've received permission for you to see Tommy for a few minutes. I can't leave you alone with him, but you can see him."

My eyes flooded with tears of gratitude. "Thank-you, detective. Tommy matters more to me than anything. Thank-you."

"Please be prepared, though. Tommy is not the little boy you know. He's hooked up to many tubes and machines. He is barely conscious much of the time. He may not recognize you. I just don't want you to be shocked by his condition." Detective Peterson's eyes were filled with compassion as he spoke.

"It doesn't matter what he looks like. He's my baby, and I want to be with him."

The brave words I spoke crumbled the moment I saw Tommy. He looked worse than Detective Peterson had warned. He looked . . . broken. He didn't even look like my son. They had shaved his head, and he had dozens of tubes coming out of him. He looked so tiny with all of that equipment hooked up to him. Seeing him lying there, I knew that our lives had changed forever.

A nurse was sitting by the incubator. She said, "Tommy is too fragile to be picked up right now, but you can hold his hand and talk to him."

I nodded and slowly walked toward the tiny bed. I took Tommy's hand in mine. It felt cold. He didn't turn to look at me or act like he even knew I was there. He was like a newborn baby with no control over his body. I stroked his hand and whispered words of love to him while Detective Peterson and the nurse looked on. I was crying so hard that I could barely see through my tears. It didn't matter, though. I would not have recognized this child, as my own if weren't for the tiny band around his ankle that read: R. Shepherd.

After twenty minutes, the nurse came over and put her hands on my shoulders. "It's time to go now, Ms. Shepherd. I promise to take good care of your son."

I bent to kiss Tommy's hand. "I don't know when they'll let me see you again, but please know that I love you more than anything on earth. I will fight to get you back if it takes me the rest of my life. I love you, Tommy." I repeated those final words to my son until the nurse pulled me into the hallway.

As I attempted to pull myself together, Detective Peterson explained what would happen next. All I heard was that Tommy would be placed in foster care when he was released from the hospital. He told me what he expected would happen to me, but I didn't care enough to listen.

I drove home in a fog. I had finally been allowed to see my son, but I didn't feel any better. Tommy looked horrible. The nurse told me the reason they'd shaved his head was to put in a shunt, a device to drain fluid off his brain. They'd also had to put a feeding tube into his stomach since he couldn't take any food by mouth. My baby had been through two surgeries already, and it seemed there would be more medical procedures to come.

The next few weeks passed, and finally, I appeared in court. I told the judge my side of the story and everything I knew about Priscilla, Tommy's baby-sitter. I really had very little to tell. I was a single mother, and she was willing to watch Tommy for a price I could afford. I never asked her if she was CPR certified or had ever been convicted of a crime. The judge told me that I was partially to blame for what happened because I left Tommy with someone I knew so little about. I cried and begged to get my son back, but it was hopeless. The judge did not sentence me to any jail time, but I lost all rights to my son for a minimum time period of twelve months. Detective Peterson was there and he spoke on my behalf, just as he had promised. He looked at me with sympathy when the judge gave his ruling. I left the courtroom sobbing.

Months went by, and I considered suicide almost daily. The only thing that kept me going was a big red circle on the calendar. That was the day I would go back to court to fight for custody of Tommy. The possibility that I might someday see my son again was my only reason to live.

Detective Peterson called weekly to give me updates on Tommy's condition. He was released from the hospital four months after the shaking. He was now nine months old, but he had the abilities of a newborn. When most babies his age were learning to crawl, Tommy could not even roll over or sit up independently. The doctors were unsure if he would ever learn to walk or talk. The shaking had damaged his brain and they weren't sure if he would be able to overcome his problems. It was difficult beyond words to hear of my son's condition, and know that I could do nothing to change it. I couldn't even hold him or tell him that I loved him. I waited anxiously for word on Tommy's condition, but at the same time, those phone calls were always heart-wrenching.

One dreary afternoon, the phone rang and I considered not answering it. I had just talked to Richard, as Detective Peterson had now asked me to call him, so I assumed it was my mother calling to question me about Tommy's status. The reports were no longer changing, and it was depressing repeating Richard's words to my mom week after week. At the last minute, I picked up the phone and said hello.

"Yes, may I speak to Cindy Shepherd, please? This is Penelope Taylor, her son's foster mother."

"This is Cindy. Is Tommy okay? What's happened?"

"Tommy is fine. I was calling to see if you wanted to come visit him."

"Oh, my God! Are you serious? I can see him? Did the judge say it was all right?" I was nearly exploding with excitement. It had been over four months since I had seen my baby.

"Detective Peterson has been coming to visit Tommy every few days. I believe he talked to the judge and persuaded him that it would be good for Tommy's recovery if he was allowed to see his mother."

I was stunned. Richard had been going to see Tommy? I had always assumed he was calling the foster mother for updates on Tommy's condition. It never occurred to me that he was actually visiting. And now, I would be permitted to see my son! The very idea brought me to tears.

"Cindy, are you there? I asked when it would be convenient for you to see Tommy."

"Oh, my God! Can I come right now? This minute, I want to see my child this very minute!"

Penelope laughed and said that I could come as soon as I wanted to. I threw some clothes on, and drove to her house. I was so nervous as I knocked on the door. What would Tommy look like? I hoped he looked better than he had in the hospital.

Penelope opened the door. She was holding Tommy in her arms. He looked bigger, but at the same time, younger. I stared at him for a long minute, until Penelope pulled me inside.

She placed Tommy in my arms as she cautioned me, "Be very careful. The shaking has left him extremely fragile."

I could hardly believe it. After four long months, I was finally holding my child again. He looked more like himself, now. His hair was growing back, and the only machine hooked to him was a small tube of oxygen.

"Hi, Tommy, it's me, Mommy. I have missed you so much. Are you all right? You look really good. As handsome as ever." I whispered words of love to him as I cradled him to me. I could tell that Penelope was not exaggerating about his fragile state. His body seemed floppy as though he had little control over his muscles. I supported his head as I had when he was just a few weeks old. I looked at Penelope and silently mouthed the words "thank-you" to her.

She simply nodded and smiled at me.

I cuddled Tommy for hours, as though I'd die if I had to put him down. I rocked him, sang to him, and kissed his tiny fingers. It was a miracle even to be touching him after all those months.

Later, when Tommy was napping, Penelope made some coffee and we sat down to talk. "Tommy seems to recovering pretty well," I said optimistically.

"He is healthy right now, but developmentally, he has suffered a huge setback. It is difficult to determine the full extent of the brain damage right now because he's so young. But the doctors have not given him a good prognosis."

"What do you mean?"

"Tommy's eyes and brain were severely damaged. Cindy, the doctors think at least some of the damage is permanent. He may never fully recover from this incident."

"That's just what the doctors are saying right now." I waved my hand to dismiss their concerns.

"Cindy, they did a CAT scan. Tommy's brain activity is limited. I'm sorry, but I think you need to realize what you're up against. If you regain custody of Tommy, it won't be easy. He may never be able to do things like other children his age."

I shook my head. I couldn't believe that my child would not develop normally just because I left him with the wrong baby-sitter. "No, Tommy will just be a little slower than the other kids. But he'll be fine." The words rang false even to my own ears.

"Cindy, why don't you go on home now and think things over. You are welcome to come visit Tommy anytime you like." She patted me on the shoulder and left the room.

I got up and went to Tommy's room. He was sleeping on his back, the oxygen tube in his nose. I cried silently for the child I had lost, the child that would never be. I knew in my heart that Tommy would never again be the little boy whom I had given birth. I worried for his future. I wondered if I could handle caring for him the way he would be from now on. Maybe he would be better off if Penelope just adopted him. I touched my son's hand, telling him silently that I loved him, no matter what his problems were.

I left Penelope's house in tears. I didn't know if I would ever go back to see Tommy again. I was only twenty-two years old; what did I know about taking care of a kid with disabilities like Tommy had now? Penelope seemed to be doing a good job with him. It might be better for all of us if she kept him.

A few days went by, and I did not contact Penelope. I thought about Tommy constantly and missed him terribly, but I still didn't know if I wanted to try to regain custody of him. His problems seemed overwhelming, more than someone like me could handle. I just wanted to do what was best for my son.

The doorbell rang and broke into my thoughts. I was surprised to see Detective Peterson, I mean Richard, standing at my front door holding a pizza.

"Hi," he said when I answered. "I thought you might want some company. And some dinner," he added with a grin.

"Wow, that was really nice of you. Come on in," I invited. Neither of us spoke again until we were sitting at the table with the pizza box between us.

"Richard," I began, "Penelope called and asked if I wanted to see Tommy. She said you talked the judge into allowing it. I will never be able to repay you for that. It meant so much to me to see him again."

"Then why haven't you gone back, Cindy? He inquired."

"How did you know that? Oh, that's right. I didn't realize it was part of your job to visit Tommy."

"It's not," Richard answered quietly. "Neither is calling you or bringing you pizza. I did it because I care about you and Tommy. You have had a terrible thing happen to you, and I only want to help make things easier for you."

"Well, you have. Your phone calls were the only thing that kept me going for these last few months. I don't think I've ever really thanked you."

"Don't start now because I'm here to ask you for a favor. There is a special program at the hospital that teaches parents of children with special needs how to better care for them. It will look really good to the judge if you join the program. I'll go with you tomorrow if you want to sign up."

"Well, the thing is . . . I don't know if it matters what the judge thinks anymore." I was so ashamed of myself that I couldn't even look at Richard. Was I actually thinking of giving up my baby for good?

"What do you mean? You go back to court in six months. If you impress the judge with your commitment to this program, you may get custody of Tommy."

"Richard, I'm not sure that I can take care of a kid like Tommy. Not the way he is now. Do you know that he eats through a tube in his stomach?"

"Sure, I've fed him when Penelope was busy with something else. It's not that big of a deal."

"You've fed him? You've done more for my baby in the last six months than I have! I don't even deserve to get him back!" My confusion quickly turned to tears. How could I take care of Tommy now? But how could I let someone else do it?

"Cindy, none of this has been your fault. You made some bad choices, but it's not too late to change them. You can get Tommy back and learn to take care of him. I know how strong you are, and how much you love that little boy of yours. You can do it, Cindy. Please try."

I had never seen Richard look the way he did now. He was staring at me as though this was the most important thing in the world to him. He was practically begging me to try to get Tommy back.

I sighed. "You're right. I do love Tommy, no matter what. I just need someone to show me how to care for him. Let's sign up for that class."

Richard patted me on the back and said, "I know you're making the right decision. You and Tommy need each other."

I joined the parenting program and learned a lot about how to take care of a kid with special needs like Tommy's. After a while, it didn't seem nearly as overwhelming. I went to visit Tommy nearly every day. Gradually, he seemed to remember me. He smiled when he heard my voice and made little noises when he saw me. I felt like I was on top of the world.

Six months passed quickly and it was time to see the judge. Richard and Penelope were both by my side as I told the judge everything I had done in the last year to prove that I deserved to get my son back. Both of them spoke to the judge, saying that I was definitely a fit mother.

"I am impressed that you have worked so hard to regain custody of your son. I am granting you that custody. Remember that a social worker will be checking up on you, Ms. Shepherd," the judge said.

I thanked the judge and threw my arms around Richard and Penelope. I thanked them for all their help and support during the last year. A social worker brought Tommy to me. He was seventeen months old and still wasn't even crawling, but I felt like I had been given a million dollars. I hugged him tightly and promised him that we'd never be apart again. It was the best day I'd had in more than a year.

Tommy is now three years old. He is blind in his right eye, and he stutters when he speaks. He is able to walk, although he falls frequently. He is now able to eat regular foods, so we are hoping that his feeding tube can be removed sometime soon. It takes him longer to learn things than most children his age and the doctors think he may always have to be in special education classes when he goes to school. Right now, he receives therapy for his speech and motor skills. He is making progress every day, and he adores his therapists.

He is also crazy about his new daddy. Who else, but Richard? We got married last summer, and we are expecting a baby in the spring. I know that caring for Tommy is not always going to be easy, but I couldn't have done anything else. He's my child and I love him, no matter what.

Richard gave me the best present for my 25th birthday. He finally located Priscilla, the baby-sitter who shook Tommy. She is now serving a lengthy sentence for what she put us through. Of course, it's not enough; nothing can make up for what she did, but it is such a comfort knowing that justice was served. My name and my conscience are now clear, and I know that I am the best person to take care of Tommy. I am so proud of my son, and honestly, I'm proud of myself as well.

THE END

# MISSING BABY
## I found her, so she's mine!

$S$ince abandonment by my boyfriend and the miscarriage of my baby at five and a half months, life for me hasn't felt like much to cherish. I fight through my workday with pasted smiles and mock happiness.

Everyone around me seems relieved that I am doing so well. They have no idea that I cry nightly into the wee hours, waiting desperately for sleep to claim me, or that I wake each morning in a state of anger that the black velvet of night released me again to face another day. Weekends are always the worst—two whole days of my own company without my work routine to occupy me.

Sitting at my kitchen table crying another Friday night away like so many times in recent months, I thought I saw motion at the back window. Relieved for something to do besides sitting and feeling sorry for myself, I walked over to look out. There was nothing there that I could see, but it felt as if someone were watching me.

I had thought many times that I didn't know how I made it from one day to the next—unless a guardian angel was watching over me. Perhaps I did have a guardian angel, and she was trying to let me know she was there. I found myself wishing that such a thing were possible.

Seeing how late it had become, I decided to go to bed and at least lay still. Maybe tonight, I'd be lucky and fall asleep right away. As I turned out the lights in the kitchen and walked back past the window, I saw a flash of movement again. But just as quickly as it was there, it was gone again. No sign of anything or anyone—just the shadow of the trees that butted against the apartment complex.

The sight of those trees full of birds and squirrels and rabbits was one of the reasons I liked having a ground floor apartment. But the main reason was not having stairs. A shiver ran over me as I thought of my tumble down the stairs the night I fled from Jerome's apartment after he told me we were through.

I was glad to be rid of Jerome, but I was deeply depressed about the loss of my baby. The doctor said that fall was probably not what led to my miscarriage three weeks later, and that it would have happened whether I fell or not. But I felt certain the fall killed my baby. Tears threatened to take me over again. Turning from the view of the moonlit lawn, I ambled on back to bed.

Not long after I lay down, I was shaken from light slumber by some noise. I lay very still listening to see if I could hear it again. And then it came: a light rapping at the front door. As my heart pounded, I looked at the clock and saw that it was three in the morning. Who is at my door? It must be a mistake. Someone's at the wrong door, and they will realize it and go away, I thought. But the rapping came again. It was more persistent, but still light.

I didn't dare go to the door in just my gown, so I grabbed a robe and slipped on the flip-flops that I always wore around the house. Hurrying down the short hallway, I realized too late my poor choice of shoes when their telltale sound rang out as I scurried across the tile. My heart thundered, and I stopped and scanned the curtains on the far side of the living room to see if I could see any silhouette that would help me gauge the size and sex of the visitor. Nothing. I began to relax, thinking I must have been right about it being someone at the wrong door who'd gone away. But just as I got ready to return to bed, I heard a muffled sound. It wasn't a knocking sound that time, but it almost sounded like the mewling of a kitten.

Sliding my shoes off, I tiptoed across the room and positioned myself against the wall between the door and the window. Pulling the curtain back slightly, I peered out to my doorstep. To my surprise, there was only a laundry basket stuffed with a blanket and topped with what looked like a book. I couldn't be sure.

Various thoughts shot through my mind. Did someone set it down with the intent of coming back for it? Is it a lure to get me to come out so someone just out of sight can jump me when I open the door? Or perhaps burst in on me? Did someone leave it at the wrong apartment?

I told myself that I should just go back to bed and leave it alone. It would likely be gone by morning. But then, I heard the sound again. My heart lurched and before I could think it through, so I yanked my door open to inspect the basket.

What I had thought to be a book was actually a note. Lifting it, I saw the words, Please love me, written in a large scrawl. The blanket began to move. I had to smile then. Someone was ditching kittens. I wondered how many of them were in the basket. Never mind that pets were not allowed in these apartments.

Pitching the note back on top of the blanket, I scooped up the basket, and I pushed the door to with my feet. Then balancing the basket on my hip, I relocked the door and headed toward the kitchen table. It felt like maybe ten pounds. How many kittens does it take to make ten pounds? I wondered. Maybe, there was some food in with them, and that's why they weighed so much.

Pulling back the layers of the blanket, I was completely unprepared for what I found. Not kittens and not even puppies. It was a baby! It was a beautiful little baby with an angelic face, a tuft of hair and dressed in a pink gown. Her big eyes blinked open, and she began to squirm while greedily sucking at her fist. Nestled beside her were an extra diaper and a can of formula. That was all it took to spur me to action.

"Come here you beautiful little angel. Are you okay? Are you hungry?"

As soon as I touched her, maternal instinct overtook me. First, I checked her diaper to make certain she wasn't dirty. Then I searched every inch of her for bruises, cuts, scrapes, or any other sign of harm or neglect. She was in perfect shape, and she was clean from head to toe. By her navel, I could see she wasn't a newborn, but she was so tiny, she had to be just a few weeks old.

Holding her to me felt so natural as I crossed the kitchen to the pantry. In the very bottom of the pantry behind the trashcan, was a package of baby bottles I had bought a few months back when I was anticipating a baby of my own. Discarding the wrapping with one hand while hugging the baby to me with the other, I grabbed a pot from the cabinet and filled it with water. Depositing the two bottles and their companion ring and nipples, I set the pan on the stove and left it to boil.

At the kitchen table, I sat down and rocked on the edge of the dining chair, humming to the tiny bundle clasped in my arms. Just wanting to immerse myself in the joy of her, I pushed away all thoughts of what and why.

A gentle hissing let me know that the bottles were boiling. Carefully depositing the baby back into the basket on the table, I removed the pot from the stove and emptied its boiling contents into the sink.

As I ran cold water over the bottles, I found myself amazed that I knew how to do those things. When the bottles cooled enough to handle, I opened the can of formula. Following the directions, I fixed both bottles. One, I deposited in the refrigerator for later; and the other, I heated for the baby.

"Come here little April. There, there. Don't fuss. I've got a bottle for you." Scooping her once again into my arms, I settled back in the chair, and I watched her nurse. How can anyone leave a baby on someone's doorstep? I wondered. Suddenly, it occurred to me that someone must have been watching me earlier—just like I had thought. Are they watching me now to see if I'm taking care of the baby?

Cradling her in my arms and keeping the bottle level so that air bubbles didn't gather around the nipple, I crossed to the kitchen window where I'd seen movement earlier, and I peered out through the curtains. The night was completely still, and the only sound was that of a distant barking dog.

Someone would surely come back for the baby soon. I should probably call the police and tell them what has happened, I thought. But the social services agency would just take her away and someone undeserving would get her. I might as well be the one to keep her until her mother returns. And, if her mother never returns. . . ? I took a deep breath and decided to take this one step at a time. There was no point in disturbing the neighbors in the wee hours with cops and sirens. And there was no sense in cheating precious April out of a deep sleep.

Her tiny little fingers were now curled around my thumb that held the bottle. Swiping the tears from my face before they could rain down on her, I set the near empty bottle on the table, and I crept back to the bedroom. Settling on my side, I hugged her tiny form against my chest and curled my body around her.

The sun streaming through the bedroom curtains woke me. Stretching lazily, I couldn't remember the last time I had awakened so refreshed. Rolling toward the window to yank at the curtains to shut out the sun, my arm brushed the white blanket. Panic shot through me. The baby! I had forgotten the baby!

Frantic, I sat up and spread the blanket open, and there she was. Smiling and wiggling her hands and kicking her tiny legs and making the gurgle sound of excited babies.

"Oh, April. You little darling."

Though faint, I recognized the smell. She had soiled herself. Retrieving the extra diaper from the basket in the kitchen, I freshened her. As I fed her the second bottle, I realized I had nothing left to care for her. Part of me rationalized that it was time to call the police. Another part insisted I should give her mother more time to come back and claim her baby. The selfish part of me hoped she would never come. I'd give her the weekend to get the baby. That settled it. I would give the mother at least until Monday.

Meanwhile, I would need supplies to care for April. But I couldn't just openly carry her outside. Flustered, I tried to think of how I was going to get to the store. Of course! I'd carry her out the same way she had arrived: disguised as a basket of laundry!

I readied myself for the trip to town. With baby and basket in tow, I locked my apartment door and headed toward my car. My heart sank as the old lady next door popped out of her apartment.

"Taking your laundry to town? Laundry broke again?" she frowned.

"No, Mrs. Gerard. I'm just going to spend the day with a friend, so I'm going to wash my laundry at her house," I called as I scurried to the car, hoping the baby wouldn't make any sound before I could escape the old woman.

"Well, have a good day," she deadpanned.

Any other time, I would have welcomed the chance to chat—but not today. I gave a wiggle-fingered wave and a big smile to her as I backed my car from its space.

Hanging on to the basket, I wheeled out onto the street. It hit me that I couldn't go to the grocery store where I usually shopped. They would wonder about the baby. How would I explain her? I would have to go to a part of town where I wouldn't run into anyone I knew.

This is insane. I'm hiding a baby. What if she has been kidnapped? I could be arrested. My heart began to race as my mind flooded with all of the possibilities. I just needed to hurry up and get supplies and get back home.

When I was certain I was in a part of town that was far from where I lived and worked, I wheeled into a baby supply supermarket. Taking the baby from the basket, I carried her nestled in my arms while I wheeled my cart through the baby department. I tossed in diapers and baby formula. Then I realized she had just the one gown, so I found some little sleepers. Was she old enough for baby food? Or baby cereal? I had no idea. Probably not, or the mother would have given me some. And what about shampoo and baby soap? I grabbed that, too. And for good measure, I grabbed some baby blankets. I reminded myself that I would only have her until Monday at most—if the mother didn't come back for her before then, so I didn't need a lot.

Waiting in line to pay for my items seemed to take forever. I was extremely conscious of all the people around me. What if someone recognized the baby? It had never occurred to me that I might drive right out of my neighborhood straight into hers. I found myself nervously bouncing the baby and edging my cart forward.

The woman in front of me turned when the wheels of my cart bumped her heel.

"I'm sorry," I found myself stammering.

"That's all right. Cute baby you got there," she said as she stuck her finger into one tiny palm. The baby clamped her fingers around it. "A tight grip. What's her name?"

A wave of fear shot through me as I heard myself answer, "April. She was a gift. I thought I would never have a child of my own. And, well, here she is." I gave what I hoped was a convincing smile.

"God knows whom to bless," she responded as she bent and cooed into April's eyes. "How old is she?"

"Ummm, I think she's ten weeks old now." I prayed that sounded reasonable.

"Tiny thing for her age," she tittered. "How much did she weigh when she was born?"

Trying to stay calm, I shifted the baby and answered, "About six pounds."

"Really? Was she premature?"

I shook my head no.

"How much does she weigh now?" the lady continued, bouncing 'April's' tiny hand and cooing to her.

"I'm not really sure," I rambled. "We go back to the doctor next week." I couldn't believe I was telling all these lies.

"Did you have a long labor? Sometimes, the first one takes a while. She is your first one, right?" the woman continued.

"Yes, she is my first one. I lost a baby before her. So, yes, she's my first one." I couldn't believe I had said that, either.

"Oh, dear, I'm sorry. Well, we just have to trust that God knows what he's doing when He calls little ones home. It's hard though, but look at little April. Such a perfect name for her."

Seeing the cashier looking expectantly at us, I pointed so the lady would see it was her turn. "Oh, honey, here. You go ahead of me," she said as she stepped out of the way, "You probably need to get your little April home for a nap."

Anxious to be gone, I didn't wait for a second urging. Plunking all my things on the counter, I wrote a check and made ready to get away.

The cashier looked at the check, then smiled, and said, "You have a nice day, Mrs. Scott."

I froze. How could I have been so stupid as to pay with a check? Now they had my name, and they had seen me with the baby!

Fighting panic, I took the receipt and mumbled, "you too," and I left the store in as calm a manner as I could force myself. With a thundering heart, I transferred my purchases to the backseat, secured April in her basket, and made a beeline for home.

On the drive back to the apartment, I saw police cars everywhere. Anxiety was mounting as I worried they could be looking for April—and me. It felt so wrong to have this baby—even though I had done nothing wrong to get her. She was left on my doorstep. But I hadn't called the police. That was wrong. But I couldn't help myself. This precious baby needed me, and I needed her.

As I parked my car in front of my apartment, the mid-morning sun was beating down. I could hear the hum of the air-conditioning units of the complex running loudly. Only the throbbing pulse in my temples was louder. I decided it was best to get April back into the house, and then come back for the baby supplies. My heart squeezed tightly as I saw Mrs. Gerard throw her curtains open and peer out at me.

I barely got my door unlocked when I heard her opening her door. Hitting my hip on the door in my hurry to get in, I gave the door a rough shove. I guess it startled April, because for the first time, she began to cry—a pitiful bleating sound. I had to get her out of the living room, so there was no chance that Mrs. Gerard lounging outside my window would hear her. April's cries became more urgent, and I realized it had been quite a long time since she had eaten. While with me, she had eaten at three in the morning, and again at 7:00 a.m.

It was now 11:30 a.m. I was certain a feeding and change of diaper would do wonders for her.

Stepping back out onto the sidewalk, I aimed for my car to retrieve the baby supplies. Mrs. Gerard spied me, and she took the opportunity to strike up conversation.

"Didn't stay long at your friend's house. Figured you'd be gone all day. Woulda been good for ya to get out of your apartment and have some fun."

"Well, we were going to spend the day, but my friend got called into work this afternoon. Someone called in sick, and it was her turn to cover. She works at a restaurant," I lied. Lies were beginning to pop out of me without hesitation.

"Really? Where's your friend work?" Mrs. Gerard pursued.

"At a fast-food burger joint on the west side of town. I've never been there," I replied deceitfully.

Reaching to the backseat, I saw that the thin bags allowed the contents to be seen. Keeping my back blocking the doorway, I humped up in the backseat and redistributed the items so I could double the bags. Satisfied that their contents would be hidden, I hooked my arms through the bags and headed back toward the apartment.

Mrs. Gerard cocked her head and froze with one hand held out, "Shhhhh! You hear that?"

Indeed, I heard it. April was bleating in fury. Rustling the bags for cover, I claimed not to hear a thing.

"It's a cryin' sound. Like a cat wailin'! Ain't supposed' to be no pets here!" Mrs. Gerard harrumphed.

"Probably just somebody with the TV on too loud. I'm sure no one has a cat. Most people here can't afford pets—even if they were allowed," I replied, relieved that she didn't realize it was a baby's cries.

Rustling past her, I made way to my apartment so I could get back to April and quiet her. As I opened the door, her angry cries wafted out.

Mrs. Gerard's eyes opened wide, and then they narrowed as I shut the door on her, leaving her in silence. Dismissing thoughts of the old woman, I raced to April. A fresh diaper and another bottle were just the ticket. Weary and full of anxiety, I sat curled on the couch, holding her. Listening to her restful breathing, I dozed myself.

The rest of Saturday was spent fixing bottles, changing diapers, and napping. Shut in the safety of my apartment, my worries subsided some. The baby was healing to my broken soul. My child might have been just like this one. And my life would have been just like this—weekends of mothering, instead of miserable fits of crying. As ridiculous as it was to think I could keep this baby, I found myself running possibilities through my mind.

I could move away where no one would know she wasn't mine. No one ever asks to see a birth certificate. I could home school her. Then I wouldn't ever have to show a birth certificate. I don't think you have to show identification for medical treatment, April Scott. She should have a middle name. My name was Bianca Marlene Scott, so her name could be April Marlene Scott. That would sound natural. A daughter named somewhat after her mother. And I was named after my mother, and she after my grandmother. But this reminded me that I wouldn't be able to visit my mother. But she lived far away, anyway. I hadn't talked to her in months, so I figured that I should visit soon. Now, I guess I could hold off for a while, and then tell her I had a surprise for her—a granddaughter.

My mind kept whirling with one idea after another. And then it halted. What if her mother came back? Would she take care of her? She left her on my doorstep. How could she possibly be trusted with her again? She might just take her somewhere else and leave her.

I wouldn't let that happen because April was mine, now. I was going to have to move. Maybe I could make her mother think I had already gone. I could move my car to the store parking lot across the street. Then if I didn't come out or turn on lights or anything, the mother would think I was gone. She didn't deserve to have her baby back.

Just thinking of losing April made me protective and furious. I snuggled the little bundle more tightly. I knew I should call the police, but I also knew I wasn't going to because they would take away April. Instead, I got up and pulled all the curtains together and pinned them so there was no way anyone could see in. It didn't matter that I couldn't see out. Everything that mattered to me was here in my arms.

In bed that night, I found myself tense and straining with all my might for any sound. When April woke at midnight with demanding cries for a diaper change and bottle, I marveled at how much louder she was than when I first got her.

Was she getting stronger from being properly cared for? Had her mother fed her this regularly? But, I reminded myself, she was neat and clean with no injuries. And there was formula and diapers with her. Surely, she had been loved and cared for. So why was she left on my doorstep? Had April been kidnapped? Was there a new mother somewhere beside herself with grief over the loss of her child? Still grieving over the loss of my own unborn child, that last thought stung me deeply with guilt.

I stayed in Sunday and indulged myself in motherhood pampering April. She cried and fussed when wanting attention for diaper change or feeding, and she cooed contentedly in my arms as she drifted off to sleep after feedings.

Monday morning, I called in sick and went about the day caring for April—who cried all through the night with gas pains. Tuesday morning, I called in sick again and being exhausted, crawled back into bed after tending to April.

About nine o'clock that morning, a very persistent knocking came at the door. I bolted upright in bed and staged the pillows around April to keep her from falling off the bed while I went to see who was at the door. My heart was pounding as though it would fly out of my chest. Who would bang on the door so hard? It was probably the police. God, I should have called them. Now I was going to be accused of kidnapping and maybe go to jail.

I pulled the curtains back to peer out before opening the door. Mrs. Gerard stood with her back to me, and I could hear her grumbling to another person. At least it wasn't the police! Not yet, anyway. Opening the door, I pasted a smile and spoke.

"Good morning, Mrs. Gerard." And then my heart sank as I saw she had the apartment manager with her.

Mrs. Gerard's eyes narrowed as she spat, "Her! She's the one. I heard it. It's been here at least since Saturday. Cats are not allowed, missy! And I'm not about to be kept up all night while ya got one yowling away in your apartment! I keep to the rules, and you have to, too!"

The apartment manager stepped forward, "I'll take it from here, Mrs. Gerard."

Reluctantly, the old lady stepped aside and let the manager move forward. Almost apologetic, the young man, dressed in jeans, sandals, and a faded T-shirt full of holes, stepped forward.

"I'm Ronald Seaforth, the apartment manager. I was mowing the grass out front when she found me," he explained, motioning to his clothing.

Not knowing what to say, I just nodded my acknowledgment.

"Miss Scott, there is a policy against pets in these apartments."

"Yes, sir, I—I know," I stammered.

"She has a cat! I'm telling you, I've heard that thing yowl for the past three or four days. I'm not gonna put up with that. Make her get rid of it!" Mrs. Gerard demanded.

The young man turned to the old woman, "Mrs. Gerard, I'm taking care of it, okay? The problem will be resolved." Then he turned back to me, "Miss Scott—"

"Bianca. You can call me Bianca," I interrupted.

"Uh, Bianca, do you have a cat in your apartment?" the young man flustered.

I tilted my chin and looked him square in the eyes, "No sir, I do not have a cat in my apartment."

"She's lying! I heard it. She does too have one!" Mrs. Gerard insisted.

It was then that a young girl stepped around the end of a nearby parked car and strode toward us, waving cheerily. "Hi ya! Bianca, sorry I'm late. I got tied up. I hope my baby wasn't too much trouble for you."

Mrs. Gerard looked quite startled, "A baby?"

Without hesitation, the young woman replied, "Yes, Bianca has been watching my baby for me the past few days. I'm Nora."

Ronald stepped back and turned to leave, but Mrs. Gerard wasn't about to give up that easily.

"Check. Make sure it isn't a cat. If it is a baby, bring it out here." This time, the old lady tilted her chin and looked me straight in the eye.

I felt so trapped. I despised Mrs. Gerard at that moment, and I wondered what had made her such a crotchety, old complaining biddy that she would begrudge a kitten of a good home. If only it were a kitten. But here was the mother to claim April. What was I going to do?

The young woman nodded at me and said, "Let's go get her."

My heart thundered wildly, and my mind raced. Should I blurt out the truth to Mrs. Gerard and Ronald, the apartment manager? Or should I go along with this baby-sitting story and display April for them? What was this young woman going to do? Would she scoop up April and disappear? Would I get to know why this happened? Was April going to be ripped from my life? I had so many questions, but not one answer.

The young woman reached to open my apartment door. Quickly stepping in front of her, I opened the door myself, and I rushed across the living room to retrieve April from the bedroom. Clutching the baby tightly, I brushed back past the mother who was halfway into my living room.

Rushing back out on the porch, I showed the beautiful bundle to Mrs. Gerard and Ronald. I could barely control the quiver in my voice.

"Here she is. A pretty, sweet little baby." Then I looked at Mrs. Gerard, "I'm sorry if her crying disturbed you, Mrs. Gerard. She had some gas problems a couple of times."

Mrs. Gerard grumbled, "Pshaw! Well, you need to take better care of her. She kept me awake." And with that, the defeated old woman shuffled back into her own apartment.

Ronald smiled and touched April's chin. "She's beautiful. Well, sorry about the fuss. You ladies have a good day."

He disappeared down the sidewalk and back around the front

stand of apartments, presumably back to his mowing.

That left me standing outside my apartment, clutching the baby with the mother standing in my doorway watching me. One thing I knew was that I did not want to give up this baby.

The young woman motioned for me to come inside, "I suppose we should talk."

"Yes, I suppose we should," I replied with agitation and fear enveloping me.

I walked to my couch and sat down, still clutching April. I couldn't bring myself to let her go.

The mother seated herself in a chair across from me. "Bianca—Miss Scott. You probably think I'm awful because I left my baby on your porch."

She steepled her hands in her lap, staring long and hard at them as though choosing her words carefully. After a time, she continued with a choked voice. "The truth is, I picked you because I saw how happy you were when you were pregnant. How you used to sit on your back patio and hum and sew on that baby quilt. I've watched how miserable you've been since you lost your baby." She halted.

Rocking back and forth, clinging to the baby, I listened to her words while tears rolled down my cheeks. This girl had watched me.

"I knew you would be a good mother, and that's what my baby needs," she finished in a quiet tone.

She made it sound so simple. Burbling through my tears, I ranted, "And what? You leave your baby here in the middle of the night and then just waltz back in to take her away?"

"No, no. It isn't like that. I, uh. . . ." the young woman trailed off.

"Who are you? How do you know me?" I demanded. Now I was pacing in front of my couch, jostling the baby to keep her quiet.

"I'm Nora Ballenti. I live . . . I did live in an apartment across the way. I used to watch you. We were pregnant at the same time. Only I was heavy, and it didn't show, so people didn't notice. No one knew. Not even my dad.

My mom skipped out on us over a year ago because my dad drinks, and she couldn't stand it. They fought all the time. Anyway, she left. Then, four months ago, my dad got sent to jail for another DUI. So, I've been on my own ever since Jayne was born.

I quit school to take care of her, but the little bit of money my dad had for me ran out real fast so I couldn't pay for nothing. I had to leave the apartment on Friday, and I couldn't live in the street with the baby, so I gave her to you," she looked up at me with tears streaming down her face, "I knew you'd be a good mother for her like I can't."

She continued speaking. "I didn't have nowhere to go, so I've been sleeping in the back woods and looking through your window at night to make sure she was okay. I hope I didn't scare you."

Suddenly, I realized Nora was just a child herself. "How old are you, Nora?"

"I'm sixteen, but people say I look older. Probably because I'm kind of chunky," she tried to smile through her tears. Fidgeting with her hands, she raised her tearstained cheeks and asked, "Can I please hold her one more time before I go?"

I found myself drawn to this young girl, so I handed her the baby without hesitation. As she took the tiny baby into her arms, we both broke down and cried. Each of us sobbed loudly. There was no way I was going to turn this young woman back to the streets. Even though I didn't know very much about this girl, I knew that I wanted to help her, and I wanted to remain in April's life.

"Nora, you don't have to leave April behind. You're welcome to stay, too. You can go back to school, and I'll help out with April." Thoughts were coming like rapid fire. I knew what it was like to be abandoned and left on your own, and I knew what it was like to lose a baby.

As much as I wanted April, I couldn't bring myself to put this girl through the loss of her child. She wasn't the bad person I had wanted to imagine her to be. She was merely a girl in bad circumstances. I wasn't going to complicate them by calling the police on her. I truly wanted to help her.

"April?" the girl looked up from cuddling and kissing the baby in confusion.

"I mean Jayne. I didn't know her name, so I called her April," I smiled.

"You mean, you'd let me stay with you, too?" she asked bewildered.

"Of course," I replied.

"Do you hear that, Jayne? Mama gets to be with you!" she raised the baby high, and she gleefully spun in a circle and hugged the child to her again.

"Oh, Bianca, you are an angel. Thank-you! Thank-you!"

It was finally over. No more fearing and dreading police. No more wondering about when or if the mother would return. Nora was here now with her baby where she belonged and I was determined I would find a way to care for both of them. And I did.

With the help of an attorney, Nora's father signed papers naming me temporary guardian of Nora and baby Jayne while he was in jail. So far, our arrangement is working out pretty well. Nora joyously spends her days being a mother to little Jayne while I'm at work. Then, when I get home, I take over our little April's care, and Nora attends night classes to get her high school diploma.

Once she has her diploma, Nora planned to get a part-time evening or weekend job. I'm all for that. Caring for little Jayne has helped ease the painful loss of my own child, and I'm even learning to "mother" a sixteen-year-old. And I'm happy to say that sleep comes easily to me these nights. I am now able to see my life is, and always has been—something definitely worth cherishing!

THE END

www.ingramcontent.com/pod-product-compliance
Lightning Source LLC
Chambersburg PA
CBHW051515170626
46811CB00002B/840